Reckless Abandon

A novel by
Andrea Randall

For my parents, who have always loved each other with reckless abandon.

Chapter 1

"Stop! Stop!" My voice sounds like record player static as I race toward Bo.

"November!"

I stop in my tracks. Bo's lips aren't moving—the voice is coming from behind me. I turn to see Adrian charging my way with the force of a bull, his arms waving me out of the way. I turn back just in time for the buttons on Bo's shirt to introduce themselves to my face, and I land headfirst on the pavement.

Above me, they collide in a sonic boom of testosterone. Neither seems concerned with the blood pouring from my head. A shadow blackens my view of the fight, and suddenly a bear paw of a hand is in front of my face.

"Come with me." The smoky voice encircles my senses, making my blood run cold and scared.

"Get away from me! Bo, Adrian, help me!" I'm a foot to the side of them but they don't see me, *or him*. They're battling to the death; my voice sounds further and further away in my head each time I scream.

The paw snares my upper arm, yanking me with it. "Get up."

"Adrian! Bo!" I'm trying to shake free, but the snare tightens and drags me away.

By the time they admit there would be no winner of this fight, it's too late. My screams are going unheard as I'm pulled into the darkness.

"Ember, wake up!" a voice beckons from above.

Suddenly I am graced with the peace that this is a dream. I let his voice pull me back to reality. My eyes flip open and in one motion I'm seated, trying to regulate my breathing.

"Sorry, did I wake you up?" I say to prove I'm out of that hell in my subconscious.

"No, I haven't gone to bed yet. Another nightmare, huh?"

I glance at the clock; it reads 10:00 PM. I shake my head at the exhaustion I've been ignoring in favor of wallowing.

"Yeah, another nightmare. Thank you for staying with me the last couple nights."

"Of course." He runs his thumb across my chin and disappears to the kitchen, returning with a glass of water.

"Thanks, Adrian," I manage after half of the water is gone.

He just smiles and walks quietly back to the living room, giving me time to collect myself.

I gulp the water in fury, hoping to flush the nightmares of my last night in Concord from my body; but the S.S. Cavanaugh appears unsinkable in the turbulent waters of my soul.

After a few moments and another deep breath, I head to the living room. Adrian sits, flipping through the channels on the TV and settling on ESPN. After driving my soulless body back from Concord, he's stayed here the past two nights; and hasn't gone far during the day. My parents wanted to come stay with me, but I asked them for space. They reluctantly obliged. For some reason I felt I couldn't burden Monica with my mess, so Adrian stepped in and told her he'd stay with me until I felt safe and calm.

We haven't spoken much about what unfolded between McCarthy's and his hotel room, or between Bo and me. Frankly, we haven't spoken much at all. He's worked on his laptop in my living room most days, while I've traveled between my bed, bathroom, and kitchen. He's prepared at least two meals a day for me, and doesn't scold me like a child when they go largely uneaten.

"You OK?" He catches me staring and puts down the footrest on the recliner.

"Yeah."

I walk to him and stand for a moment, our knees touching. He sets the remote down and grips the arms of the chair, working me over with concerned eyes.

"Em ..." His eyes beg me for something, anything.

In one long blink I curl myself onto his lap. His hands hesitate for a moment before resting around my waist. He breathes in the scent of my shampoo as I settle my head on his shoulder. My breath falters against the words brewing in my throat. Adrian notices.

He nudges my shoulders, forcing me to sit up and look at him. "What's going on?"

"You called me Blue, Adrian."

"I know." He swallows hard; this is the first time I've brought it up.

"You're the only person who's ever called me that. That was *our* thing, and right there, on the beach, in front of Bo, you called me Blue like nothing had happened. Like no time had passed." I keep my voice quiet and calm, reliving the memory of his voice against the waves shortly after he and Bo told me about the blackmail. It's hard to believe it was less than two weeks ago.

"I know."

"I hadn't seen you in four years and we were standing in front of my boyfriend," I chuckle for the first time in a lifetime, "and, right there, you just blurt it out."

"Were you mad?" A grin tugs caution away from his face.

"Furious."

"Ha. You don't look furious." He tucks his bottom lip behind his teeth.

I shrug. "I was mad that it still made me feel the way it always made me feel." Heaviness pulls at my chest.

"How's that?"

I yawn and set my head back on his shoulder. "Special. Yours."

"You are," he whispers.

"Which one?" I ask as my eyelids close up shop.

If he has a response, I don't hear it before I drift off. There won't be any nightmares here.

* * *

"Good Morning, Ember. I'm glad you're back." My boss's smile is sweet as she settles into her desk, motioning me to sit.

"Thanks, Carrie, I really appreciated the week off ..." I trail off and briefly knot my hands before taking a cleansing breath.

"If you need more time -"

"No, it's really OK. It was just...a lot. But I do appreciate the week to collect myself." I tuck some hair behind my ear before I continue. "I suppose we should talk about the dissolution of the relationship between B- Mr. Cavanaugh and myself." I've practiced saying his name without crying nearly a hundred times over the last few days, but that doesn't stop the burn from hissing against my cheeks.

"It won't be necessary." Condolences rake Carrie's face. While she's my boss, she's also a woman—she gets it.

I pull my eyebrows in, rendered speechless.

Carrie takes a deep breath before continuing. "Mr. Cavanaugh sent me an email accepting full responsibility for everything that happened. He expressed his apologies and assured me that he would be handing the day-to-day operations of DROP over to David Bryson. He will remain a benefactor and handle behind-the-scenes duties. Further, he's asked that we still consider the collaboration."

Mini bombs titled "too much information at once" fire inside my brain.

"It's summer now," Carrie continues, "we have interns ready to go in whatever capacity I see fit. I can have one work with Monica on the DROP project—"

I stop her with my hand and a head shake. "No. Absolutely not. This collaboration is too important to leave to interns. DROP is a fantastic organization. Had I played by the very specific rules known to everyone on the planet— including myself—I wouldn't be in this position. I'm an adult and this is my job."

I think I just pulled off sounding composed.

"Who does DROP have in place for Grants and Community Ed?" I ask, trying to erase Bo's blackmailers from my memory.

"DROP's legal team will handle finances for a while, and David will work on the community piece with Rachel Cavanaugh. They'd like to get together ASAP to design a plan to move forward."

Rachel's name sounds like music to my years and feels like a kick to the head all at the same time. She's certainly aware of the details of the blackmail. Bill Holder and Tristan MacMillian had "compromising" photos of Rachel during the time of her life she was using drugs. I have no idea—and don't want to know—what the pictures entailed, but they were damaging enough that Bo didn't want them released. Bill and Tristan blackmailed him for enough money that Bo took his time paying them back. For reasons I don't understand, he employed them at DROP, and things seemed to unfold from there.

I'm not sure if Rae knows how much I know, or if she knows I know anything at all. I've ignored the few phone calls from a number Adrian tells me is hers. I haven't been ready to face her. It hadn't occurred to me that with school out for the summer, Rachel would be more active with DROP.

"Ember, are you OK?" Carrie reels me back to the present.

"Yes. Rachel's great. I met her in Concord. You're really going to like her." I allow my feelings for Rachel to show in a smile.

"Good. Well, go get settled back into your office and I'll get in touch with you later about meeting with Rachel and David."

I breeze past Monica's office and shut the door to mine before reorienting myself.

"Em?" Monica knocks and talks at the same time.

"Yeah, come in."

"How'd it go with Carrie?" She plunks in a chair and slides a latte in my direction.

"Fine. I told her I was still one hundred percent committed to the collaboration, and—"

"Pardon?" She cuts me off with judgmental eyebrows.

"Monica, it's my job. Period. Bo and I shouldn't have gotten involved with each other and neither organization should have to suffer because of it. Stop looking at me like that."

"OK, well, I need to show you something." Monica produces a sheet of paper and sets it on my desk.

"What is this?" I ask as I pick it up.

"It's the email ..." She freezes and waits for my reaction.

"Why the hell do you have it?"

"He sent it on Friday. Based on his tone, Carrie thought that you might not be coming back. Of course she wouldn't show it to me, even if I'd asked ..."

"But ..."

"But Tim owed me a favor after I hooked him up with

Callie, so ..."

I chuckle a little. "Nice. Taking advantage of our IT guy."

"Well...go on and read it."

I stare at her for about five seconds before scrolling my eyes down to the email.

From: Spencer Cavanaugh, Founder, DROP
To: Carrie Roberts, Director, The Hope Foundation
Subject: Collaboration

Mrs. Roberts:

I'd like to sincerely thank you for maintaining contact with David Bryson during this trying time for my family. I want to express to you my hope that our two organizations can continue working toward collaboration. David will be taking over day-to-day operations at DROP as I step back to sort through my personal issues. I assure you that William Holder and Tristan MacMillian are no longer employed by DROP and never will be in the future.

Further, I'm writing to accept full responsibility for the situation that occurred between Ms. Harris and me. It was a complete lack of judgment and ethics on my part. As the person in a position of authority, it was my job to uphold the moral conduct I expect out of my own employees; I failed in that regard.

If there is anything I can do to assist in retaining Ms. Harris with your organization, should she put in a leave request, please contact me. I'll give her a raise from my own funds, if necessary. She has a brilliant mind and would be an asset to any organization, but her heart is with Hope.

My sister, Rachel, and David will be in contact with you soon in regards to setting up a meeting to move forward with the collaboration, if you agree to continue.

Sincerely,
Spencer Cavanaugh
Founder, DROP

There it is. Everything that has to be said, with miles of subtext jammed between the lines. I'm not in the mood to translate subtext today. It's just been a week since everything went to hell in Concord, and *this* is the first piece of present Bo that I've seen since then. During the day it all feels like so long ago, but my nightmares play it in real-time. I relive seeing the fight at the garage near my house a week before I met Bo and finding out a couple of weeks later that Bo was involved in that fight. Not only that, but it was related to the blackmail with his sister, and...he knew it was me at the garage after we'd hung out a few times.

Hung out...

Today, however, I'm a damn "situation" that should have been handled differently. I don't know why that upsets me; I feel the same way about him—most of the time.

After staying at my place a few nights, and one half-sleepy conversation that we haven't discussed since, Adrian had to get back to Boston. I lied on the phone two nights ago and told him I didn't have a nightmare the night before. I repeated the same lie last night, telling Adrian I felt like my old self and that I'd see him after my first week back at work. I just need to be alone, and that's not something I can explain to Adrian. I don't speak Y-chromosome.

The truth is, the cuts on my face and body have mostly healed, but I'm beginning to wonder if the gashes to my heart will ever stop bleeding.

"Em?" Monica quietly leads me out of that dark place in my head.

I clear my throat. "Why didn't you call me after you saw this?"

"Would you have wanted me to?"

"No, I guess not. Why are you showing me now?" I try to keep my irritation to a minimum.

"I don't know, honestly. When he first sent it, I thought you might really want to leave if you knew the collaboration was still on the table. Now..." She struggles for the right words.

"It's OK, Mon. Thank you."

"So, what does all of that mean?" Monica motions toward the letter. Guess she can see the subtext, too.

I shrug. "Don't know. Looks like I was a situation."

"Have you heard from him at all?"

He fills my thoughts, my dreams, and my nightmares. The memory of him, and his touch, pound on the door to my soul with such force that cracks are forming in the wood. I do my best to act like no one is home by keeping the door locked and the lights off.

"Not for the first couple of days. Then he'd call and I'd ignore it. When he started calling three and four times a day, I deleted his number from my phone. I got tired of seeing his name, and I don't want to talk to him...I can't." My words throw Monica's eyes to the floor.

"Are you ever going to talk to him? I mean, besides work?"

I want to. I don't want to.

"I don't know." I take a deep breath and turn on my computer. Monica looks me over, seeming to study my body language.

"Are we done talking about this?" she asks.

"You got it."

"So," her voice brightens, "is Adrian in town this week?" The sound of his name steadies my heart. Funny, a week and a half ago it made me furious.

"He's in Boston right now." I allow a smile.

"That's an interesting smile."

"Monica," I caution.

"Are you telling me he's stayed at your house and *nothing* has happened?"

"Have we just met?" I chuckle sarcastically. "I just had my heart broken ..." I don't finish the sentence because I can't deny that Adrian does something to my insides. It's confusing navigating that *and* heartbreak at the same time. Like any other warm-blooded female, I want something, or someone, to heal my heart and make me forget.

"I still can't believe he called you 'Blue' again, in front of Bo no less!" She sort of changes the subject.

"Ha, I know. If I'd held my poker face a little better, Bo might not have noticed that it meant something...or used to...whatever." I chuckle.

"Have you talked to Adrian about that?"

"Once, but I fell asleep." I shrug and offer nothing more. "I'm sure he'll try to come down sometime this week, but I know he's got meetings in Concord, too."

"I guess we'll be heading there soon, huh?"

I tell Monica that I'm looking forward to seeing Rachel. Carrie pokes her head in to tell us that DROP would like us there by the end of the week. Looking pointedly at me, she informs us that the legal team, David Bryson, and Rachel Cavanaugh will be the only members present. *Message received.* Monica's eyes comfort me as she heads out of the office just behind Carrie.

I lean back in my chair and stare at the in-box on my computer screen. Thankful for Monica's suggestion that I have the IT guy delete all email conversations between Bo and me, I confidently sift through my messages and dive into work. I see an email from Adrian, discussing the intended Concord trip at the end of the week. He's been great, if slightly manic, about telling me anything and everything he thinks I might need to know. He saw my nerves shorten after being left in the dark about a lot of things, both with him and Bo. He wants to help heal that. Good luck.

By the end of the day I'm inordinately exhausted. I half-lie when I tell Monica I'm looking forward to quiet time when she suggests that she and Josh come over for dinner. I'm certainly looking forward to quiet, but only so I can fill it with the tears and screaming I've held in during the near-constant presence of Monica, Josh, and Adrian. Sometimes a girl just needs to cry and throw stuff.

Josh has been rather quiet with me. He looks painfully uncomfortable in my new, stone-like presence, as my mind replays everything about my time with Bo on a constant loop. Monica says it's difficult for Josh to see me so muted, and errantly mentioned to me one day that Josh wondered how Bo must be faring, since he was the one who was walked out on. I'm not mad at Josh's curiosity. I wonder, too. But only until tears threaten; then I scream...and throw stuff.

Chapter 2
Bo

I didn't know a look was something you'd never want to see again, until I saw that one. Fear, heartbreak, and anger shattered her beautiful eyes into a million pieces of despair and betrayal.

All hope drained from me as I dug my knees into the carpet of that hotel room, begging her understanding—her forgiveness. I don't blame her for pushing me across the room, or beating my chest until her fists couldn't take it anymore. In fact, I wish she'd done more. It's the only thing I deserved after denying she was the girl I'd seen in the parking lot a few days before singing with her on stage. The only thing I deserved after letting her fall in love with me when I never gave her the whole truth. The only thing I deserved after falling in love with her when my focus was supposed to be elsewhere.

While the pieces of that horrible puzzle were scattered around us the entire time, inching their way into place one day, one moment at a time, the whole thing was completed too late —we'd promised forever. Ha, I actually thought "forever" would be enough as I stared at her in that hotel room. She'd already left, even though her body stood at broken attention in front of me. The "no vacancy" sign blinked painfully through her eyes until it popped, hissed, and went dark. I wasn't welcome there any more.

My head presses against the pillow with the force of my regret behind it. I should have been honest with her from the beginning, but falling in love so quickly rendered me mute. Yes, in an instant I fell in love with her; the very instant I met her eyes when I was on stage for my first show at Finnegan's. When I called out "Monica and Ember" that night and saw she was one of them, I knew I was done for. My heart stopped at the sight of her, and started again when she sang her first note, leaving me no choice but to jump without a parachute into her emerald eyes.

I try to shake my thoughts free. When they don't cooperate, I drown them in one long conversation with Jack Daniels. With one more swig, I'm transported outside my personal hell and can see myself from the outside.

Pathetic, worthless, fuck-up.

"Bo?" Rae's voice drags me back into myself. I clear my throat and stash the bottle behind my pillow like a teenager.

"In my room, Rae." I try to sound composed. I'm failing.

She opens the door and immediately crinkles her nose while rolling her eyes.

She crosses her arms and tilts her head. "Christ, Bowan, are you drunk again?"

I know I should feel something. Remorse? Rae's spent the last few years cleaning up and playing by the rules. Yet, here I sit, a puddle of drunken regret. I can't think of anyone but November. Just thinking her name tears the scab off the place in my heart she vacated just a week ago.

"Get your ass up!"

"Dammit Rae, that's bright!" I have to shield my eyes as she opens the curtains.

"It's called the Sun. Get some. You've got to get to the office today because the group from Hope will be here Friday, and I'm sure you'll want to make yourself scarce." Her condescension claws at me.

"I fund the place. So do you. We don't have to be anywhere."

God, could I sound more petulant?

Without responding, she rips the covers from the bed and throws some clothes on top of me. As I swing my legs to the side of the bed, she focuses on something behind me. Rae reaches her hand behind my pillow, producing the nearly empty bottle of Jack.

"Nice." She stares through me and my heart bleeds through a Rachel-sized hole.

"You know, Bo," she continues, "*this* is why I'm not around a lot." The tawny liquid sloshes against the sides of the bottle as she gestures with her hands.

She's right. She's right and it kills me. I hardly feel bad, though—I'm not sober enough for that. I dig my elbows into my knees and tear my fingers over my scalp. When I lift my head, she's gone. I hear the shower running and a headache forms at the thought of having to be upright.

"Get a shower, get coffee, eat, and get your ass to the office. She's gone, Bo, and I assure you Jack Daniels won't campaign for you to get her back—if that's even what you want."

"What the hell do you mean if that's what I want? She's *all* I want." I stand too quickly, and Jack's fists force my eyelids closed.

"So she's ignoring your calls—what's stopped you from driving like a maniac to Barnstable and looking her in the eyes? You're just wallowing here in a sea of pity when she's the one who got hurt, Bowan. She's probably confused and scared." Rae sighs and throws her hands up in disgust. "You're so completely clueless, it's painful to watch. I liked her. I *like* her, and I haven't been able to talk to her because *you're* an asshole."

Rae's never spoken to me this way, and the shock is quickly tackled by my own anger. She sees the internal shift and heads for my bedroom door.

"What do you mean she'll be here Friday?" My heart races with panic and a dash of hope.

"She didn't run away from Hope on your account, she's finishing what she started. Now, I'll see her Friday. What am I supposed to tell her? 'Hey Ember, my brother is a dickless coward who plans on drinking his transgressions away, but wanna get lunch?'"

Rae must see a thousand thoughts cross my face, because she shakes her head and leans against my doorframe for a second. "Get in the shower" is all she says before dramatically gonging the inside of my head with a slam of the door.

I wipe off the mirror when I step out of the shower. *God I look like shit.* Something catches my eye on the floor. A bottle of lotion has fallen behind the toilet, but I don't recognize it until I smell it; then fresh wounds mar my insides. I stare at myself in the mirror, searching for some sort of resemblance to the man I thought I was and the man my parents raised me to be. Instead, a hung over, brokenhearted liar scoffs back.

"I couldn't have fucked that up more if I tried."

"You've got that right." Rachel unapologetically enters my bedroom again.

She's more pissed than hurt about the blackmail. We're working on a plea deal, and Rae demanded that our lawyer negotiate Max and Bill's mandatory presence at the meetings so she could tear them apart. She's mostly angry that I hid it from her.

My sigh fills the bathroom as I hang my head. "Rae …"

"Well Jesus, Bowan! Every single piece of this could have been avoided if you hadn't taken it upon yourself to try to teach those fuckers a lesson!" Tired tears crawl down her face as she continues, "I really do appreciate what you put yourself through to protect me. I do. But, quite frankly, I might have been less embarrassed if they'd just posted those pictures. Instead, my big brother thinks I'm a spineless child who needs protecting." Her accusations bounce off the frigid tile.

There's nothing I can say to her. She's right. Again.

She takes a breath and looks between the lotion and me twice before stepping over the threshold to the bathroom. She carefully removes it from my hands and studies the label.

"Hmm, lemongrass and cardamom," she inhales the scent, "this has November written all over it. Did you just find this, or did you get all psycho and buy her lotion for your own emotional cutting?"

"She left it here, I guess." I brush past her and head to my closet.

"You don't like it when I say her name, huh?"

"What's the point? It was a week and a half of my life and she's made it quite clear that it's over." My tone is short. My hangovers have started to dress themselves up in anger.

"You're a child." She leaves my room, but spares me by not slamming the door this time.

As I dress, I hear Rae open the main house door and speak in muffled tones with someone, and finally a car pulls away from the house. I do my best to get myself together. Khakis and a button down black short-sleeved shirt—no tie—is a vast improvement over my sweats and t-shirt wardrobe of the last week. I think absentmindedly that Rae's right, and I will need to get a ton of work done today in order to avoid having to go to the meeting Friday. Ember will be there. She's coming *back* here and isn't hiding from me—unless she's seen the email I sent to her boss, giving her reassurance of my absence. I shake my head, resolving to think more about it later.

When I get downstairs I head directly for the kitchen to take some Advil; it's the only way I'll make it through the morning. Rachel is standing by the sink, surveying my impending liver damage through X-rays of empty whiskey bottles that line the counter. Her eyes are empty, and her face is blank. This isn't good.

"Rae, just get out of here. I'll clean this up and meet you at the office. Did I hear you talking to someone down here?" I swallow the Advil and pray for the bricks in my head to crumble to dust.

Rae moves to the foyer and starts putting on her coat. "Yeah. Ainsley."

"Ainsley was here?" I ask, following her.

"She's been sniffing around since the night everything went down." Rachel stares crossly at me, her hand on her hip.

Ainsley sent several text messages when the story about the blackmail broke all over the news. When I ignored them, she came to the house. I told her none of it concerned her. She must have found out one way or another that November was involved, which explains her eagerness to reconnect, yet again. I learned quickly after my parents died that Ainsley Worthington is a force to be reckoned with as far as grief is concerned. She thinks her tight little ass will cure all that ails. Well, it won't for me. Not this time.

"I'll see you at the office in a few." I head upstairs to grab my laptop.

"Fine, just don't do anything stupid between here and there. Can you manage that?" She doesn't wait for my answer as her anger echoes in the squeal of tires down the driveway.

November will be here Friday. Shit. I have to talk to her. *We're in love. We promised forever ...*

* * *

"Great, Turner's here," I mumble to myself as I throw the Audi in park. He wasn't around at all last week, giving me a much-needed break from November's ex-boyfriend.

Maybe he was with her. I slam my door at the thought and head into the office, dodging sympathetic glances from the receptionist.

"Spencer." David nods his salutation as he walks into my office and shuts the door.

He's always called me Spencer, even when all my friends started calling me "Bo" in high school. He was my father's best friend, so I don't think he'll stop with the "Spencer" any time soon. He studies me with sad eyes. Eyes that look like my father's—grey pools that intensify the disappointment I already feel.

"Morning, David. Are we set for the legal briefing today in preparation for Hope's arrival on Friday?" I think I sound convincing enough, until I watch David's nostrils flare with a frustrated sigh.

"Son, what happened?" He sits. He's not leaving until he has an answer.

David's aware of the blackmail, but the details regarding Ember have been graciously absent from his questioning, until now. So I tell him. Everything. His eyebrows raise at all the right parts; his head shakes at the others. I've never been this open with David before about my personal life, apart from things about my parents. As a rule, I'm not open at all—music's always been my way of dealing. But, since taking over this organization, I've been doing a lot more talking. David's the closest thing to a father I have left, and right now I need guidance.

"What do you mean you stopped calling her?" This is the detail he's choosing to focus on. I remain still and scan the room for a respectable answer. His face tells me there isn't one.

I clear my throat. "Uh ..."

"Son, I saw you and Travis through some boneheaded things in high school, but this takes the cake." Travis is David's son, my best friend. He moved to Colorado after high school before enlisting in the Marines. He was in Iraq for a while, came home, and now he's in Afghanistan. He'd probably kick my ass for screwing things up with Ember.

"She's really pissed, David."

"Seems she has cause to be. All the more reason not to leave her stewing for a week—a state away, no less! Anyway, we've got to get to the meeting, but you better call her. Before Friday. Even if she doesn't answer and you have to leave her a

voicemail. She's a nice young lady and deserves at least that."
He doesn't await my confirmation of his orders before
sauntering out of my office and heading down the hall.

I follow him after the minute it takes to prepare myself to
see Adrian Turner for the first time since he dropped me off at
my house a week ago.

"Ah, there he is. Let's get to it, shall we?" David nods in
my direction, but my eyes immediately fall on Adrian, whose
face gives nothing away other than business.

Business it is, then. For the whole meeting we discuss how
well our public handling of the blackmail has gone. The legal
team breathes a collective sigh of relief at the news that The
Hope Foundation still wishes to continue with collaboration.
They're truly the only organization worth collaborating with,
and it would have been a mess if they'd backed out. At the end
of the meeting, everyone leaves in a flash, except Adrian, who
takes his time gathering his papers.

The room feels a lot more crowded than it did minutes
ago. I clear my throat, and he raises an eyebrow in my
direction before his eyes follow.

"I trust you'll be here on Friday to oversee the
collaboration contract?" This is what I open with—what other
option is there?

A smug smile changes his face. "Of course."

"Listen, Turner," *here we go,* "thank you for driving
November back to Barnstable..." I throw my sweaty palms into
my pockets, disbelieving I'm even having this conversation.

"No worries, Cavanaugh. Glad I could help her." He
inflects a little more on "her" than I care for, and I feel jealousy
reach for her box of matches.

"All right then, see you Friday, I guess." I turn for the door
before his voice stops me.

"Bo."

I turn on my heels to see him standing with fire in his
eyes, but the rest of his face is calm.

"Leave her alone."

Without a verbal response I shake my head, huff through
my nostrils, and return to my office.

Like hell I will.

Chapter 3
Ember

It turns out I only needed one night to scream and throw things. Two days later I'm heading to work, mentally preparing for the trip to Concord at the end of the week, when my phone rings. I don't make a habit of talking while driving, but a quick glance at the Caller ID tells me I don't know the number, so I absentmindedly answer. I never know where my parents might be, after all.

"Hello?"

After a second of silence, I have to repeat myself.

"Hello?" I try again.

"November."

Bo. Shit.

I never learned his number because he put it in my phone to begin with. My face flushes as my heart stumbles over itself. Thankfully, I'm pulling into the parking lot at work.

"November?" I haven't heard his voice since kicking him out of Adrian's hotel room. In a flash, I feel everything I've been pushing down for the last week.

"Bo...hi."

"Thanks for answering." The hope in his voice mainlines to my gut and sends a lump to my throat.

I realize I don't know if I would have answered had I known. "I didn't know it was you."

"Oh."

"So, what's up?"

He clears his throat. "I'd like to talk to you...before Friday."

Shit.

"I thought you weren't going to the meeting on Friday." If I keep my words to business, maybe I won't burst into tears as I walk into the office.

"Avoiding you won't help DROP, or us."

Us? Seriously?

Monica's talking to our receptionist as I walk in. She stops mid-word when she sees the look on my face.

"There isn't an 'us', Bo." With that, Monica follows me to my office.

"Ember, please, I need to talk to you." He takes a deep breath.

"Well, since you'll be there Friday, I guess I'll see you Friday." Behind me, Monica clicks her tongue and gasps.

I don't hear anything for a few seconds. I'm growing impatient with the pace and content of this conversation.

"Hello?"

"OK. See you Friday," he concedes easily, perhaps not wanting to push his luck.

"Bye."

Before I can even turn around, Monica starts in. "What. In. The. Hell?"

I arch a pissed-off eyebrow. "Bo says we should talk before the meeting on Friday."

"Ha! You've ignored his calls for days, he finally gets you on the phone some-damn-how, and he says you need to talk? If he wanted to talk so bad, he should have driven his ass down here after you." She crosses her arms in front of her as if something I've said offends her.

"Monica, he clearly respects me enough to *not* drive down here. Lord, can you imagine the shit-show he would have caused if he'd shown up at my place when Adrian was there?" I run both hands frantically through my hair in an effort to calm the inner storm.

"Respect or not, looks like you're band-aiding it now."

"What?"

"Ripping off the awkward conversation band-aid. We're working with *his* organization, Ember. It's not like he can hide in his dark castle forever. And, frankly, neither can you. If you're grown up enough to work together, then you're grown up enough to have a proper break-up and boundaries conversation. We'll leave early on Friday."

"Gee, Mom, *thanks*."

"I'm serious. No use pretending he never existed."

Shut up. "Yeah. Band-aid. All right, get the hell out of here so I can get some work done."

She leaves, and I briefly consider throwing something. Instead, I call Adrian. His absence over the last few days makes me miss him. Not just his company and his kind words, but *him*. Adrian Turner has a presence; a presence that heats you from the inside out, a presence that was once all mine. While I'm still sore in all the right places from my heartbreak, I'm human enough to acknowledge the steam coming from Adrian's gaze when we're in a room together.

"Hey Ember." I'm instantly calmed by his voice.

"Hey you."

"What's up, everything OK?"

How does he always sense what I'm feeling?

 "Bo called me this morning."

Adrian's tone tenses instantly. "At work?"

"Nope, on my cell. I deleted his number and didn't know it was him ..."

"What'd he say?" He sounds less than amused.

"He says we need to talk. Which, I suppose we do, since we're adults. He told me he'd be at the meeting on Friday, so I told him we'd talk then."

Adrian's sigh enters my ear and the pit of my stomach. "Are you OK?"

No. "Um...yeah. We really *do* need to talk. Monica says I should...work and all." I'm rambling.

"Maybe she's right. Hey, I've got the next two days off. I know you have prep-work to do, but do you want to get together for dinner today or tomorrow? I'll drive to you." Cool Adrian returns and, suddenly, fresh butterflies emerge from their chrysalises in my stomach.

"That'd be great. How about tomorrow night?" I hope he can hear my smile.

"Sounds good." I can hear his.

"Oh, and if you're around this weekend, Finnegan's is having a summer kick-off on Saturday. Josh wants me to sing. He's thinking of putting together a house band."

"I wouldn't miss it. See you tomorrow, Blu-" he stops

himself.

"It's OK, Adrian. I like it. See you tomorrow." I hang up. What the hell am I doing?

* * *

Thursday's here, and Adrian's on his way. A hopeful smile greets me in the mirror as I touch up my lipstick. I'm glad I decided not to dye my auburn hair black in a freak post-breakup impulsive moment. I feel good for the first time in a week. I feel almost normal. I'm looking forward to an agenda-free dinner with Adrian. Though, I'm beginning to think no dinner with Adrian will ever be completely agenda-free on either of our parts. There's history, and you can't erase history —no matter how hard you dig the eraser into the paper.

"Come in!" I shout from the kitchen when he knocks.

As soon as the door shuts, my apartment feels like it's suspended in air. His sweet cologne trails through the room and surges through my body. I've tried to ignore these biological responses to his presence since I saw him in Finnegan's for the first time in four years. It feels like a carnival ride to let myself feel them again.

He saunters toward me with a swagger that only he's allowed to use, pulling his hands out of his pockets. "You're gorgeous."

"So are you, as always." I grin. "Here's a beer, sit."

He grabs his beer and his hand connects with mine for the briefest of seconds, just long enough to weaken my knees.

"Thank you." He leans in and kisses my cheek before heading to the living room. I need to steady myself against the counter for a moment before following him.

I want your lips. I shake my head at the thought and try for normal conversation. "How was the rest of your week?" I sit next to him on the couch.

He seems a little tense as he stretches his arm on the back of the couch. "Good. Busy."

"You seem tense."

"I'm not supposed to say anything until the meeting tomorrow, but I have to tell you something."

In an instant, I'm left searching for the hole my stomach dropped into. "What?"

"Tomorrow is my last day with DROP." He sets his beer

down and watches me.

I'm relieved and confused. I was looking forward to working with Adrian, but a voice in the back of my head suggests that it was only because I wanted to spend more time with him— which I can do anyway. Sensing my confusion, he continues.

"I was signed on to consult for the collaboration. When the ink is dry, I'm out. I did my job and have no interest in working with DROP any further."

This is about Bo. "Don't make this about Bo." I swallow a gratuitous amount of wine.

"While I really like the organization, I feel uncomfortable working with Cavanaugh for a number of reasons."

There's only one reason.

"Thank you for telling me. I think tomorrow holds enough anxiety, and I'm glad I didn't have to hear this then." It's not lost on me that after tomorrow I could, guilt-free, run my hands over that chocolate washboard Adrian calls a stomach. My hormones are going to be the death of me.

"Let's get out of here and get some food." He brings our glasses to the kitchen and meets me at the door. My lower back catches fire as his hand guides me down the stairs.

We drive to the restaurant in silence, and are seated by a beautiful waitress that Adrian ignores. It begins to dawn on me that in a little over twelve hours I'll be face-to-face with Bo.

"I'm a little nervous about tomorrow," I offer before Adrian can analyze my face.

"I'm sure you are. I would be, too. Well, I kind of *am*." He sips his water and then folds his hands in front of him.

"What are you nervous about?"

"I don't want him to bug you with apologies. You will be there for business, and I don't want him screwing you up."

A twinge of annoyance takes over. "I can handle my shit, thanks."

"No, Blue, that's not what I meant. You know what, let's just enjoy tonight." His smile breaks down my anger, and our eyes rarely leave each other for the rest of our meal.

When Adrian drives me back to my apartment, he insists on walking me up the stairs. He's always walked me to my door, even in college, despite his friends who would drop their girlfriends at the curb.

"Tonight was nice, Adrian." I don't know why I'm

whispering.

He closes the space between our bodies with a hug.

His lips graze the top of my ear as he talks. "I had a great time too, November."

I take this opportunity to inhale the cologne from the dip above his collarbone. "You smell good."

Adrian pulls back slightly and lifts my chin with his thumb. Our eyes lock and I swallow hard. His lower lip twitches as his eyes flash with recognition. Heat surges through me in response. Out of nowhere a pang in my chest reminds me that my heart is still in emotional ICU somewhere between Concord and here. A sigh of resolve takes over, dousing my insides with cold water.

"See you tomorrow." Adrian smiles and softly presses his lips against my cheek before heading down the stairs and to his car.

* * *

"He wants in your pants, November."

I wonder if it's easier for her to say shit like that while she's driving so she doesn't have to look at me with a straight face.

"Monica, we've been over this. If he wanted in my pants that bad, I'm sure he would have figured out a way to get there when he was staying at *my apartment*."

"He's good. He's greasing the wheels." She chances a glance sideways, just to see me shake my head.

"What wheels, Monica? I'm not with anyone, neither is he. We're just spending time together ..." Those butterflies are making it hard to concentrate. Though, I can't be sure how many are stamped with *Adrian* and how many are stamped with *Band-Aid*.

"Do you have feelings for him again, or are you just using him as a distraction?"

I'm honest. "I don't know. Last night was the first time in five years we've had dinner without pretense. It was nice. It felt comfortable."

"He'll be there today, too, right?" She purses her lips.

"Yes. I can't believe you made me leave this early," I say in an attempt to shift the focus off of Adrian. I didn't tell her that today is his last day with DROP. If I tell her that, she'll know I care.

As Concord comes into view, my pulse quickens. I dry my now-sweaty palms on the hem of my skirt and look out the window.

"Are you OK, Em? You look pale."

"Can you pull over here for a second?" My cheeks are hot and my mouth is dry. I need air.

Monica pulls over on the quiet county road, and I open the door and throw up what little breakfast I managed to eat.

"Em ..." Monica's hands never leave the wheel. It's like she was expecting this.

I swish some water around my mouth and spit the rest of my nerves onto the side of the road and get back in the car. I take a cleansing breath and turn to Monica, who is still watching me with suspicion.

"Well, now that *that's* over with, let's get to it. I've got a band-aid that needs removing."

Chapter 4

"That's Rae's car." I tilt my chin to the lone blue Saab in the DROP parking lot.

Monica speaks through clenched teeth. "Should we wait here for Bo to show up—*if* he's going to show up?"

"First, he probably won't be here today -"

"No," Monica interrupts, "he said he wouldn't be at the meeting. He didn't say he'd ditch work all together. Is he ten years old?"

"Relax, Monica! I need to talk to Rachel anyway, regardless if Bo shows. I haven't talked to her, and she's tried to call me ..." I unbuckle my seatbelt and get out of the car.

"I'll wait here."

"Thanks." I shut the door harder than necessary and focus on my pace toward the building.

I reach the door and shakily grasp the handle, reminding myself that Rachel was the victim of Bill and Tristan's scheme—I just fell into the middle. As soon as the door shuts behind me, her voice sings from an office at the end of the hall.

"Hello?" I hear her chair move and her feet heading toward the door. "Is that you, Bowan? I thought you weren't—" She stops when she reaches the door and sees me, still standing by the entrance. I resist the urge to turn it into an exit.

"Hi."

"Ember ..." She takes a cautious step out of her office and two more down the hall.

"I just wanted to come a little early...to talk to you." This is only a half-lie. I break from her gaze and stare at the floor for a second. I look back up when I hear her running toward me. She has a smile on her face and tears in her eyes.

"I'm so happy you're here!" She throws her arms around my neck and squeezes the nerves from my body. Without consult, tears flee from my eyes as I hug her back.

"I'm sorry I haven't returned your calls. I just...needed some time. It was incredibly selfish of me." I pull back and run the tip of my index finger under my eyes to avoid a mascara disaster.

"Don't be silly. Come into my office, we can sit." She leads me by the hand to her office, not releasing her grip until I'm seated.

She seems as bubbly as ever, but there's a stress around her eyes that wasn't there a couple of weeks ago. She looks thinner, too, if that's even possible.

"How are you doing with everything that's gone on?" I cross my legs.

She brushes my question away with her hand. "Fuckers. They're such assholes to mess with me, *especially* through my brother, for God's sake! Bowan should have known better, too, than to keep it from me ..." I reflexively flinch a little at his name. She always calls him Bowan, and it reminds me that he's human, a real thing—not something that happened in my dreams. "I'm sorry. Listen, how are *you*? I can't believe Bill went after you like that. Ember ..."

"Yeah. No. It's fine. I mean, it wasn't, but now it is." My ramble is annoying me, so I shake my head and swallow to regroup. "Dude's clearly got some issues." I shrug and force out a chuckle.

"No shit. He likely won't spend any time in jail. And, really, that's fine with me—he'd never make it anyway. I'm just glad I never have to see him in these halls again." While her voice is firm, I don't miss the brief mist passing through her eyes.

She hasn't mentioned my knowing about the blackmail before she did. Maybe she doesn't know. I decide not to say anything.

"How is he?" I blurt out before I allow myself to think it

over.

Rae takes a deep breath, as she seems to carefully choose her words. "Well. He's been better. He's certainly been worse, but he's been better. He knows he fucked up, and I remind him of that daily. I thought it was him walking in when you did. He should be here ..."

I can feel my face flush as she finishes her sentence. *He'll be here.* It's what I wanted, but now that it's happening, I feel like I'm drowning again.

"Ember?"

"Oh. Sorry, yeah. You remind him that he fucked up? I've been trying not to think about it. I guess it wasn't that bad ..." I try in vain to protect his image for his little sister.

"Did you get drunk this morning? Of course it was that bad. He should have told you as soon as he knew it was you. I can't believe it was you that tried to help him when he got in that fight behind the garage, and then you two end up meeting a few days later? Damn." I've never seen Rae's face this shade of serious.

"We don't have to talk about it. I don't really want to get into it right now." The main door opens and closes. "That'll be Monica. Do you guys have a spare office we can use to prep for the meeting?"

"Of course, I'll show you."

I head for the door as she slides back from her desk. We step over the threshold and turn to greet Monica. Only, it's not Monica.

It's Bo.

I don't know if that gasp was audible as I take one step back. Rae turns left, looks between Bo and me, retreats to her office and shuts the door.

Traitor.

"November. Hi. You're early ..." A bright-eyed smile escapes him as his hand reaches up and grips my shoulder.

I'm frozen. My tongue is twice its size, and cement seeps down my throat. Seeming to sense his breach in boundaries, Bo lifts his suddenly sweaty palm from my shoulder and glides it into his pocket.

Say something.

"Hi. I was just checking in with Rachel." My eyes want to study the floor, but I don't let them. I swallow hard and continue, "I was hoping you'd be here a little earlier so we could talk before the meeting." I check my cell. "It looks like we're running out of time." My heart is racing so fast I feel like I have to run to keep up with it.

"No, we have time. Come with me." I think he's going to take me to his office; instead, he grabs my hand and heads to the back of the building. I tug my hand away before I can assess its sensation as he opens the far exit door. "Sorry," he mumbles.

Bo steps outside and holds the door for me as I step onto a grassy lawn facing a thick tree line. He walks around the corner and leans his shoulder against the brick building, crossing his arms in front of him. My heart searches for an escape. We're outside, so anywhere will do, but my pride roots her feet in place. I'm not going anywhere. I mimic his position as the foundation in my throat begins to crumble under threatening tears.

I allow myself a second to finally look into his eyes. They're tired. He looks pale, but put together. Too many feelings pulse through me at once, and I can't sort them out. The last time I saw his face, I was screaming at him. A few hours before that, I was kissing him. The thought of his kiss threatens to seal my throat again. I look over his shoulder when I start speaking.

"I don't want today to be weird," I start with a shaky cadence. "I mean, I know everyone knows everything, and whatever, but this project is really important to both organizations and I don't want to screw it up." I hug my torso and scan the grass.

"November ..." As soon as his voice hits my eardrums, my vision blurs with tears. If I blink, it's all over. I look to the sky and silently beg for a downpour. Bo takes one step forward and deliberately, but gently, places his hand back on my shoulder.

"Don't." I turn my back to him in time for the tears to stream wildly down my cheeks. I purse my lips tightly to prevent a sob from giving me away. In record time, my shoulders shake in response to the sheer amount of tears they're releasing.

"Ember, please don't cry. Damn it. Please, *please* don't cry." Bo doesn't raise his voice as he crosses in front of me and takes both of my shoulders in his hands. I tilt my head to the side and rest it on the cold brick, not meeting his eyes.

"Can I just...just have a minute?" My voice is reaching a

weird octave and I'm straining to form words. This is an ugly cry. The kind saved for the bathtub or a best friend's bedroom. This is not acceptable. I take a few deep breaths through my mouth and start dragging my fingers under my eyes.

"I'm so sorry, Ember. I was such an ass. I tried calling you. I stopped myself from showing up at your house, and I thought about not coming today. I'm sorry. I'm so, so sorry. You have to believe me when I tell you I never meant for you to get hurt …" He trails off as I shift and press my forehead against the building. He knows I'm about to bail, that's why he's speaking so fast. He wants to get it all out before I shut him down. I simply shake my head without turning around.

After a few seconds of silence, I hear the door shut and I look over my shoulder. He's gone. I sink to the soft ground and bury my head into my knees. I just need another minute of this and I should be good. After a few minutes, the door opens again, but I don't look up. A small hand brushes the hair away from my face and tucks it behind my ear.

Monica.

I look up and find her kneeling beside me, her eyes brimming with understanding and no judgment.

"I brought makeup," she states plainly.

Breaking into soft laughter, I let her lead me up from the ground. "Thanks. You're the best." She opens the door and I hesitate.

"He's gone. I stayed in my car until I saw him leave. Rachel's in the meeting room. I met her in the hallway and she pointed me out the back door. She's awesome. We've gotta hang on to her." Monica smiles as we head into the bathroom.

I take several deep breaths as I touch up my makeup, and pray the remaining red splotches leave my face by the time the meeting starts.

"Do we have a few minutes to get our shit together in a spare office?" I ask Monica as we head out of the bathroom.

"Yeah, I brought our stuff in there. Follow me."

We spend ten minutes preparing our notes before heading to the large meeting room. I see David Bryson, Carrie, Rachel, and what I assume is the legal team—including Adrian. Carrie and David carry on a quiet conversation, Rachel randomly shuffles papers, and Adrian watches my every movement until I meet his stare dead on. I give him a nod and a smile, but his smirk tells me he doesn't buy it. We'll be talking about this later.

The meeting goes smoothly. I don't have to say much, since Carrie and David do most of the talking; and David and I have already met, so he knows what I do. David directs our attention to the legal team, who formally present the contracts we've all already gone through. It's the first time I've seen Adrian on the job. I like it, he seems proud. He should be, he has an incredible game face that wouldn't lead anyone to believe he knows anything about the giant elephants flying through the room. It's decided that Monica, Carrie, and I will spend three days a week in Concord helping to develop and open the new DROP community center.

"This is the center Spencer plans to equip with a music studio ..." David's voice is drowned out by the memory of that very conversation Bo and I had when he first drove me around Concord. I like that David calls him Spencer. I catch Rae and Adrian staring at me, each seemingly unaware of the other, and I refocus my attention on David.

When all the contracts are signed, David speaks again. "I'd like to take this opportunity to thank Adrian Turner, a contracted member of our legal team, for aiding in the success of this collaboration. I wish we could pay you enough to stay on full time, Adrian. We're sorry to see you go. It's been a real pleasure working with you."

Adrian nods and starts a speech of thanks.

I'm trying to listen to him when Monica nudges my arm and slides me a note. It reads, "I'm going to kill you for not telling me." I stifle a laugh and shrug in response. She kicks me under the table.

As people file out of the meeting room, I'm overcome with a twinge of guilt for what happened between Bo and me outside. I really wanted to talk things out with him boundary wise, but seeing his face and *those eyes* made it impossible. He respected me enough in my moment of tears to leave me alone, but I can't leave Concord without another go at it. I thumb through my phone to the last time he called and text the number.

Me: Meeting's over. Can we talk somewhere private?
Bo: Yes. Meet me at Les's Diner. It's on Main.
Me: Be there in ten.

"I didn't know you were planning on leaving DROP, Adrian." Monica's voice pulls me away from my phone. It's seductively accusing.

He shakes his head and shoves papers into his leather messenger bag. "Get that grin off your face, Mon. Like I'd stay here after all that ..."

"Uh huh ..." Monica's grin elicits an eye roll from Adrian. "Ready, Em? We've gotta get back home so you can practice for the show tomorrow."

Adrian's brow furrows. "Won't all of that singing and playing stuff just remind you of Cavanaugh?"

While he has a decent point for a guy, it annoys me—especially since I already told him about the band and the show. "You know what, Adrian? Maybe. If I sing and play it will be because of him in some way; but if I stop it will be all because of him. I like it, so I'm going to keep doing it." I take a careful pause before turning to Monica. "We've got to head to Les's Diner on Main first. I'm giving my chat with Bo another try."

"What?" Adrian spits out as Monica's eyes widen.

"Mon, can you give us just a minute?" I ask, one peg below pleading.

"Yep." With raised eyebrows she leaves the room, but not before giving Adrian a careful once over.

Adrian paces toward me and then leans against the table a few inches from my body. "You talked to him already today?"

"We tried. I cried all over the brick wall ..." I sigh, and in an instant Adrian's hand is on top of mine.

"You don't *have* to do this, you know. You don't have to talk to him right now." He squeezes my hand.

"I do. I'll be spending half of every week up here from now until god-knows-when. Even if I'm not going to be working with him directly, I'm still in his friggen building. We need to set boundaries."

Wow. That sounded professional.

"I'll come with you." Adrian interlaces his fingers with mine as we walk to the door and I don't pull it away. My own reaction confuses me.

"Adrian, please." I roll my eyes. "It's fine. It's just a diner, and no matter what he was trying to talk to me about earlier—it can't happen." I recall the hope in Bo's eyes when he first saw me in the hall.

"You're right. Sorry. I'll be there tomorrow, OK?" His tone is brighter.

"Of course. See you then. Have a safe drive home." I squeeze his hand once before pulling mine away.

He heads down to the back offices as I turn for the door. Rachel is standing in the hall a short distance from where Adrian and I were talking. I briefly wonder if she saw anything, and then realize it doesn't really matter. I wave politely and head for Monica's car. We head to Les's Diner without a single word passing between us.

Chapter 5

Monica parks in front of Les's Diner and both of our heads turn to Bo's car, which sits empty. He's inside already.

"Why didn't you tell me about Adrian leaving DROP?" She asks as I unbuckle my seatbelt.

"Why do you assume I knew?"

"Because you didn't so much as bat an eyelash when they said goodbye to him."

I sigh. "Monica, he told me on Wednesday when we had dinner. He knows I'm not the 'surprise' kind of girl these days."

Understanding spreads across her face. "Just don't be into him because you're trying to get away from Bo."

"You're awfully bossy the last few days. Give it a rest. Are you coming inside or staying out here?" I change the subject as I exit the car.

Monica chuckles and shakes her head, giving me a mocking look as she kills the engine and crosses her arms. Given her fiery temper, she's been quiet about the 'Bo situation,' as she's come to call it. I'm sure it has more to do with the fact that she doesn't have all the details because, well, neither do I.

"Thanks," I mumble as I get out and shut the door.

Steam from greasy cheeseburgers assaults my nostrils as soon as I open the door. I pretend to scan the restaurant, but I spot him before the door closes. Bo Cavanaugh stands out in any room he's in. He nods as soon as I let my eyes meet his, and I head to the table. There's a glass of water with lime waiting for me and an internal smile allows me to acknowledge his thoughtfulness. He pushes back from the table and crosses to my chair, pulling it out for me as I reach the seat.

"Thank you." Sandalwood still trickles through his pores. I have to close my eyes for a second and breathe through my mouth to regain my equilibrium.

"How'd the meeting go?" he asks as he sits back in his chair. His smile is present, but his voice is distant.

"Fine, the ink's drying as we speak. We'll be up here three days a week until the project is complete." I chuckle. "Though, I suppose you knew that since your signature was already on all of the contracts...and it's your organization." I roll my straw between my thumb and index finger, watching the ice bob around the limes.

His heavy sigh pulls my eyes upward. "November—"

"I'm sorry about what happened this morning," I cut him off. "I just ..." I pause to breathe and slow myself down, preventing a ramble.

"No, it's OK. I was surprised to see you. Honestly, I hoped that I would but—"

"You hoped you would? You said you wouldn't even be at the meeting ..." *Oops. He wasn't supposed to know I saw the email.* "Carrie told us it would just be David and Rae," I add in quickly.

"I thought I should try to avoid you at first because I was scared of hurting you again. Then I made you cry anyway ..." As he trails off, he reaches across the table and grabs my hand. His heat travels to my heart and a million memories of his touch flash through my brain. I pull my hand away and anchor it on my lap before my resolve passes out.

"Bo. Stop. We can't do this. You hurt me. And, now, I'm kind of your employee. We can't go back. I just came here to tell you I'm fine. I'm ready to work with you, but only if you're ready to work with me. What happened two weeks ago was a fling and we both could have gotten into a lot of trouble for it. I hope sometime we can sit down and really go through everything that happened, but today's not the day." I push my chair back from the table.

I actually believe the words I'm saying, and that scares me. It scares him, too, judging by the white pallor that's overcome him.

"November, wait." He follows quickly behind me as I make my way through the diner. When I open the door, he reaches in front of me and pulls it shut; the loud jingle of the bells forces gazes in our direction. Bo leans forward until his mouth is an inch from my ear. "I'm not going to stop trying to make this right," is all he whispers before opening the door again and releasing me into the humid Concord air.

I turn back to look at him. I stare for a second too long; my memory feels his hands on pieces of my soul that no one else has touched. I part my lips to say something before realizing there is nothing I can say—sometimes when you fall head over heels in love you end up with a concussion. I force a well-meaning smile before turning back around and heading for Monica's car.

* * *

Once back on the road, Monica gives me about a minute and a half before launching in.

"Go ahead," she states, as if I've asked her permission to discuss what happened in the diner.

"That...did *not* go as planned, per se. He said he wasn't going to stop making "this" right ..."

"You two haven't talked about that night at all?" She takes her eyes away from the road to give me an accusing look.

"Not really. I'm not sure what it is that he could say. He admitted in the hotel that he knew it was me and basically panicked—didn't say anything until I was attacked and he was forced to." I try to force a strong tone through that line, but it doesn't work. I rest my head against the window in frustration.

"I'm sorry, Em. But we haven't really talked about it ..." Monica reaches across the car and puts her hand on my knee.

"I just don't know why in the hell he wouldn't say anything."

"What would you have done if he did?" She resumes a two-handed grip on the steering wheel.

I hadn't considered that. "I don't know...I mean how hard would it have been for him to share the revelation as soon as he had it? Like 'Oh holy shit, *that was you?* Listen—' and tell me the story."

"No, I get it. It's just bullshit. I really liked him for you. I'm sorry, November." Monica rarely calls me November.

"I know you are. I'm just glad Josh has this house band thing lined up to help me take my mind off of everything. Adrian's going to come to the show tomorrow." I don't really know why I'm smiling, but it feels good.

"Mmhmm ..."

"What?"

"Just watch your ass with him, OK? The end of that relationship did a number on you—"

"Give it a rest, Monica," I sigh.

Her sideways glance says more about her feelings than her silence does.

* * *

"Ember, I'm glad you came!" Josh jumps off the stage and greets me with a hug.

Things are better than normal between him and Monica. The two-day separation is never discussed, and their beautiful love story has resumed.

"Of course I'd come, this is a great idea!"

"Where's your guitar?" Josh asks as we head up on stage.

I give him a cautious smile. "Funny. Unless you were planning on having us play the single song I know, my guitar playing is out of the question without lessons. Do you want to teach me?"

He slaps my back. "Of course I'll teach you, November. What's taken you so long to ask?"

Josh and I go over the playlist for tomorrow with C.J., the drummer. C.J.'s our age and has lived in Barnstable since he was ten. When he holds a pair of sticks it's pure magic. With hands and abs like his, he could have any girl that graces this bar. I think he does, too—one night at a time, anyway.

"Josh, did you tell November about my cousin?" C.J. asks as he moves parts of his drum set around.

Josh turns to me with giddy hope in his eyes. "C.J.'s cousin, Regan, lives in Ireland. He's flying in tomorrow to spend the summer here. He plays the fiddle like nothing I've ever heard—we Skyped the other night."

My eyebrows shoot up excitedly. "Really? Is he interested in playing with us?"

"Yeah, Rapunzel, he is. That's why we're talking about it." C.J. shakes his head. He's called me 'Rapunzel' since we met last winter and I don't know why. I think it has something to do with my hair, but who knows? I hate it. He knows that. He's a bit of an ass—as any good drummer is, I suppose.

"Call me that again and I'll send you on a self-guided cavity search for your sticks." I throw his sticks at him.

"Guys, let's not have 'Behind the Music' drama on our first night, K? Let's play." Josh teases as he takes his seat on the stool and starts strumming his guitar.

It's the first time I've heard a guitar since the night Bo and I played together on stage. I feel my brow furrow for a second before I discard the memory. Music was in my bones long before Bo Cavanaugh, and I won't let one fracture ruin it for me.

We go through a few Sheryl Crow, The Script, and The Avett Brothers songs before calling it a night. C.J. and Josh have played together for years, and I know all the lyrics to the songs we sing. It seems like it's a good fit. When C.J. leaves, and Josh and I are alone in Finnegan's, the awkward silence takes its toll on me.

"It's OK to talk about it, Josh," I offer.

"I don't really know what to say. I'm sorry." Josh hands me a beer and we sit on the stage, our legs dangling over the edge.

"I just want you to know it's fine. Bo and I just went way too fast and ignored important things. We just got...wrapped up. He's my superior now, lines are clearly drawn, and we can each move on." Each time I say it, I'm reminded of its truth.

Josh puts his arm around my shoulders. "I think you're right, about it moving too fast. That was fucking intense with you two—" he cuts himself off as the main door opens. Just as he's about to launch into his "Hello, we're closed!" speech, in walks Adrian.

"Adrian?" I slide off the stage and walk toward him.

"Hey you." He smiles broadly and pulls me in for a hug. *Mmm* ...

"What are you doing here? I thought you were coming down tomorrow." My mile-wide grin doesn't shock me. Things feel so comfortable with him, so easy.

"I have some time and didn't want to wait till tomorrow to see you." As we pull away from our hug, he slides his hand down my arm and brushes my fingertips.

"I've got to finish cleaning up with Josh, I'll be out in a

minute." I turn and walk back to the stage, noting the question on Josh's face.

"I'll wait outside for you. Nice to see you, Josh," Adrian says as he exits the bar.

As soon as the door clicks, Josh's eyes nearly bug out of his head.

"Shut up, Josh. It's just Adrian."

Just Adrian ...

"What's with the hugging and hand holding and all of that?" Damn Josh, he's not afraid to just get right in there and ask what every other guy might be thinking.

"I don't know." I don't really know what I'm doing. I don't know why being around Adrian feels good. "Don't you *dare* say a thing to Monica about this." I never keep secrets from Monica, but I don't know yet if Adrian is a secret.

Josh puts his hands up in mock-defense. "Your secret is safe with me...*Rapunzel*." I punch him in the arm as he laughs.

"I'll see you tomorrow. What time should I be here?"

"Seven's good. We can get some last minute practice in before the masses descend." He winks and gives me another pat on the shoulder as he locks the door behind us and heads to his car.

I turn my attention to Adrian, who parked his BMW next to my Outback. He's leaning his side against his car, with his hands casually in his khaki shorts' pockets. How he always pulls off looking like a model is beyond me, but I'll take it.

"So, what do you want to do after driving all this way?" I try to make my grin match his as I lean against my driver's side door.

"I just want to hang out with you. We spent so much time together last week that it was weird not seeing you at all this week."

"I don't think I properly thanked you for last week." I step toward him, and he removes his hands from his pockets. "It was really comforting having you around. You didn't ask me any questions, didn't hound me about how I was feeling ..." I take another step toward him, wrap my arms around his neck, and set my chin on his shoulder.

He tightens his arms around my waist. "You don't need to thank me. I'd do it again in a heartbeat, Blue."

"Let's go hang out at my place for a while, I've got plenty to eat and drink." I pull back and suddenly find myself resisting the urge to kiss him. I visualize his tempting lips on mine and my breath yields. He presses his hands into my back and pulls me in tighter, kissing the top of my head.

His voice is deep and smooth. "Your place sounds great."

Taking a deep breath, I get into my car, begging my libido to get a grip as I click my seatbelt into place. I don't feel as off-balance as I think I should with all of the physical stuff happening between Adrian and me. Sure, it's only been a hand-hold here, and a peck there, but I want more. And there's been more before. We know each other, we've been there, but now we're older—we're adults. When everything went down with Bo in Concord, Adrian didn't get in his face or kick his ass; he was there for *me* and gave me what I needed.

When we pull up to my apartment, my libido buries itself at the sight of the station wagon parked in my space. Adrian shuts his door at the same time as me and cautiously approaches, as I stand with my hand on my hip.

"What's up?" he asks

I gesture to the relic. "My grace period is over. Raven and Ashby are here."

"What do you mean 'grace period'? You didn't talk to them this week?" Adrian knows I didn't speak to my parents the few days he was at my house.

"No...I've been busy." I shrug.

Adrian laughs. "Well, sweetheart, it's time to face the music." He takes my hand and leads me upstairs, where my parents are waiting inside my apartment.

Chapter 6

"See what happens when I give you people a key? You abuse the privilege," I start as I open the door.

"Well, baby girl," Ashby replies, "you can't go through something like that and expect us not to care. I was ho-- Adrian?" My dad's stern eyes soften as he looks over my shoulder.

"Hello, Mr. Harris, Mrs. Harris." Without missing a beat, Adrian crosses the living room to shake my father's hand before kissing my mother on the cheek."

Damn, he's smooth.

Raven blushes. "Adrian, it's great to see you. How have you been? Thank you so much for being here for November the last couple of weeks." When she finally stops rambling, she sits and pats her hand next to her for Adrian to join. My parents loved Adrian when we were together in college, which always struck me as odd since he's so different from me; but we seemed to make sense—even to the hippies.

Adrian sits and puts his forearms on his thighs. "You know I'd help her no matter what. I was in the right place at the right time." Seeming to sense my parents' questions on the tips of their tongues, Adrian continues, "Em, I'm gonna run to pick up our pizza, I'll be back in a few. Mr. and Mrs. Harris, in case you're not here when I get back, it was great seeing you. I hope to see you again soon." We didn't order pizza. He wants my parents and me to have time to talk in private.

"Please, Adrian, call us by our names." Ashby breaks his stunned silence and shakes Adrian's hand once more.

As soon as Adrian's car pulls away from the curb, I offer my defense.

"I'm sorry I haven't called you guys. This week I got back to work, and today we had our meeting in Concord."

"Your what?" Ashby asks.

"Ash, my organization is still collaborating with Bo's. I'm a grant writer; I've got a job to do." I plunk down next to my mom, who starts absentmindedly playing with the ends of my hair.

"Can you back up and tell us what happened?" Raven chimes in innocently.

I tell them about my time in Concord and how it ended. My dad starts wringing his hands when I tell them about Bill coming after me, and me falling flat on my face in front of Adrian on the sidewalk. I reference my conversation today with Monica, and am honest when I say I don't know how I would have handled it *had* Bo told me everything earlier on, but remind them that it's a moot point.

Ashby walks to the couch and sits next to me. "I'd hate to think what could have happened if Adrian wasn't there."

"Yeah, I know, Dad." I sigh as I rest my head on his shoulder. He doesn't correct me on calling him Dad. I need him to just be my dad right now.

"So have you and Adrian been spending a lot of time together since then?" Raven asks.

"He was here a lot last week, but we haven't seen much of each other this week. He's not contracted with DROP anymore, so we won't be seeing each other at work. I still want to spend time with him."

She sighs. "He's a good boy, November, always has been." Raven and Ashby share a look over my shoulder. They're being less colorful than usual.

"Guys, what's going on? You're being weird...normal." Raven's eyes mist over.

"Seriously, Mom, what is it?" I sit forward.

"I feel like some of this is my fault. I encouraged you ..."

"You encouraged me to listen to my gut. I did. I really feel like I loved Bo, but it was more of a firework than anything else. It was hot, heavy, and just too fast. I learned a lot about myself. It's OK, promise." I gulp when I realize that I now completely believe the things I'm saying about the end of our relationship. Maybe I'm right after all, it was just a fling.

"OK, Honey. You seem like you're doing fine. I just want to make sure you're not bottling it all up." Ashby knows my bottling tendencies.

"I really am OK. Where are you guys off to now?" I hope a change of topic brightens the heavy mood.

"Well," my dad's tone abides, "we'll be in town through the weekend, but then we're heading out to San Diego. Six wants to hit the studio again."

"Are you fucking serious?" I half-laugh at the thought of my parents and their friends in the studio once again.

"Watch your mouth," my mom teases, "and, yes, we're serious. We're all at a point in our lives when our kids are out of the house, and we have experienced a lot more life than the last time we recorded."

"Well, if you're going to be here tomorrow do you want to come to Finnegan's and hear me sing?"

My parents smile and hug me simultaneously. "We'd love to! Now, we'll get going so you can have some quiet time with Adrian. See you tomorrow, hun. Oh, Ember!" Raven interrupts her own exit. "Yoga tomorrow morning on the beach, just me and you." She smiles.

"Was that a question or an invitation?" I lean against the doorframe.

"Neither, see you then." She kisses my cheek and turns away.

Raven and Ashby walk hand-in-hand away from the apartment. I hear them say good-bye to Adrian, who is walking up the stairs. Suddenly my heart is racing, and I feel warm all over. I could use a yoga session right about now. When Adrian enters my apartment, he seems to study the look on my face—I'm sure I'm as red as I can be.

"Did they leave on my account?" he asks as he crosses the threshold.

"Sort of," I barely let out. My throat is suddenly scratchy. I take a step back and dig my hands into my back pockets.

Adrian's espresso-colored eyes steam into mine as he blindly closes the door behind him. I'm sure the lights are dimming; the charge between us is audible. Fireflies of memories illuminate my living room. Each flicker begs, "Go." My heart gallops me forward as a heavy sigh takes the reins.

Almost on command, he meets me halfway. Lightning's been striking around us for weeks, and until now I've been running for cover. I can't deny his pull any longer. Our mouths collide, his tongue tentatively tasting my lips before I open my mouth and let him all the way in.

"My God," he whispers as he pulls back for a brief second. His hand glides up the back of my neck and tightens through my hair as we resume our kiss.

Five years burns like wildfire between us as my hands run along his sharp jaw line and hold his face in place. This feels so good I don't want it to end. Our tongues dance, reacquainting themselves after their foolish separation.

"Mmm," is all I can manage as his hand finds the skin on my lower back.

We're all hands and tongues in the entryway of my apartment. I gently lower my heels to the floor, and Adrian bows toward me in response. My hands snake around his neck and my hand locks around my other wrist. I'm not letting him go. Adrian strokes his hands over my back pockets and nudges me up on my tiptoes once again. I pour all I have—all my gratitude, all my loneliness, all my longing—into this kiss.

He was there for me. He stood stoic and let me fight my own battle with Bo—he didn't try to dash in and save the day. He was there for the aftermath, sure, but he knows I'm no damsel. Adrian gets me. Just as our breathing turns to primal moans, he pulls away and rests his forehead on mine, placing his shaky hands on my shoulders.

"I've waited five years to do that again. I can't believe I almost lost you to someone else before I had a chance to get you back," he heaves through ragged breath.

He wants me back. He's always wanted me back. The speech he gave me on the beach two weeks ago about him loving me when we were together wasn't a lie. This is real. I press forward once more, attaching my swollen lips to his. I step back with intention, and he follows me to the couch without pulling away from my mouth.

As we sit, I'm suddenly unsure how to proceed. Adrian and I have slept together. *A lot.* But, it's been five years. We've had partners in the meantime...multiple partners. I'm fresh out of what could turn out to be the most heartbreaking experience of my life, and yet I can't seem to shake the feeling that my panties are searching for the emergency exit in my jeans. It's my turn to pull away. He doesn't fight it.

"Why didn't you tell me how you felt when we got together at Finnegan's, Adrian?" I know the answer.

"You were distant that night. I could tell you were keeping something from me, or at the very least, you were just on guard."

Yep, that's the answer.

We sit in silence for a few moments as our breathing finds even footing. Adrian grabs my hand. "Now what?" he asks.

I squeeze his in muted response. "This. This is a good start." I nuzzle my head between his neck and collarbone. Adrian releases my hand and runs his through my hair as I continue. "You weren't planning on driving back home tonight, were you?" I look into his eyes and watch them scan my face.

"I was going to."

"Don't. Stay here tonight."

"I don't know if that's a good idea ..." he trails off.

"I'm not asking you to *sleep* with me. I just want you to sleep next to me. I feel good with you, Adrian. There's no pretense, no nonsense."

He kisses the top of my head. "It *is* easy, isn't it?"

"Yeah, it's easy."

I'm not in the mood to set ground rules with Adrian, and he doesn't seem to need the discussion either. *See? Easy.* After a few minutes, we head to bed. He sleeps under the covers this time, with his bare chest against my back, and a tight arm hooked around my waist.

Chapter 7

My phone wakes me too early for a Saturday morning. Adrian groans something unintelligible as he releases his grip on my waist so I can blindly answer the phone.

"Hello?"

A husky voice startles me fully awake. "I'm sorry, did I wake you up?"

Bo. Facepalm.

"Yeah, you did. It's Saturday morning. What's going on?" I swing my legs over the side of the bed and make my way to the kitchen, where I fumble with the coffee—spilling half the bag on the floor. "Shit."

"What?"

"Spilled coffee all over my kitchen. What's going on, Bo? Do you need something?" I ask with irritation.

"Are you free tonight?"

What the hell?

"What the hell do you mean? Is something going on with DROP?"

"No, nothing like that. I wanted to know if you want to get together tonight."

"Wait, what? I'm sorry, did you not understand our conversation in the diner?" My volume has caused Adrian to walk into the hallway. I motion for him to be quiet.

"I did, and I also told you I wasn't going to stop trying to make this right, November." His voice has taken on a sharp edge.

"Look, we're working together, and I'm choosing to play by the rules. If that's going to be difficult for you then I can work with my boss to take me off the project." Adrian's eyebrows shoot up as I speak.

"Please don't do that. Damn it. I'm sorry, November. What can I do to show you that I'm sorry?"

"You can respect me enough to leave this alone. I'll see you next Wednesday." I end the call and toss my phone carelessly on the counter.

I'm angry. I'm frustrated. There are coffee grounds all over the place. I bend down to start sweeping them up, and Adrian squats into my eye line. I take a deep breath and sit cross-legged on the kitchen floor.

"Cavanaugh?" He joins me on the floor with bent knees.

"Yeah. He insists on making this right, whatever the hell that means."

"What do you want?"

"Are you kidding me? I want to do my job. I want to pretend that the last two weeks happened years ago, or not at all. I want to spend the day with you, and sing tonight ..." I trail off as I shake my head.

Hearing Bo's voice doesn't screw me up emotionally like it did a few days ago. It angers me. I haven't a clue as to why he's still pursuing something with me when we're working together. It doesn't make sense. It pisses me off that he's willing to put my career in jeopardy. *Once again.*

"Want me to have a talk with him?" Adrian extends his hand to me as he stands, I accept.

"Get over yourself," I joke. As I stand, my phone rings again. "Seriously?" I huff as I head toward the counter. "Hello?"

"Sweetie, it's Raven." *Good sweet lord.*

"Hey Mom, what's up?"

"You're becoming awfully flexible with the 'mom' term, don't you think?" she states flatly.

"Yeah, and you're becoming awfully flexible with calling me during hours when most people are sleeping." Adrian shakes his head and takes the broom from my hand and starts cleaning up the coffee grounds as I continue this back-and-forth with Raven.

"It's getting late, get your butt to the beach." *Yoga. Shit.*

"Crap, I forgot. I'm sorry. Now, when you say 'beach,' at what plot of sand in the nearly 560 miles of Cape Cod coastline am I supposed to find you?" I grin and Adrian smacks my butt with the dustpan.

"Don't be a smartass, November. Meet me at our usual spot." *Click.*

It's true. We have a usual spot for this sort of thing. And, unfortunately, it's the same spot I played my guitar at sunrise two weeks ago. I wish myself good luck as Adrian pretends to sweep me out the door. He's got his computer with him, as always, and will do work while I'm cleansing my aura with Raven. *Super.*

* * *

"Root your feet in the sand, Sweetie," Raven instructs as I slip off my Chacos.

"I'm familiar with the process," I grumble.

"Clearly you haven't been keeping up on your practice. Start in Tadasana," she scolds in a meditative tone. *She's already in the zone.*

Raven flows through the sequences, and I realize how long it's been since I've centered myself in any way. I'm off-balance and uncomfortable. I feel like a beginner. *In more ways than one.*

"You're struggling...just breathe, Honey. Adho Mukha Svanasana," Raven dips her head gracefully.

"I don't speak Sanskrit."

"Downward Facing Dog, Ember, just do it."

As soon as my heels find the sand and my hips find the sun, the tears come. Peppering the soft sand, they cloud my vision. She leaves us head-down for longer than necessary and, for that, I'm grateful. I feel the last two weeks wring from my body like a saturated washcloth and I want to leave it all in the sand. It's clear that Bo isn't forgiving himself for what happened between us. Two weeks ago I wanted him to see my bloody face every day in his mind. Suddenly, I don't want that for him. I've mulled over the entire situation for long enough.

I still have questions, but I don't care if they're ever answered. Some of them can't be answered. Regardless of what's happening with Adrian, I want peace for Bo. He's been through enough in his life and doesn't need a bitter ex-girlfriend spitting all over his efforts. We're in each other's lives for the foreseeable future, and I want that to be as pleasant as possible, while retaining solid emotional boundaries. I almost regret the tone I used with him on the phone this morning, but I still feel it was the only way for me to reassert that we can't be a "we" again. Raven hears me sniff.

"Now we're getting somewhere...Utkatasana ..." Her breath and her voice are one.

As I raise myself to Chair Pose, I let the sun illuminate, then dry, my tears. As we head into Warrior Pose, I feel my soul rip off her lingering bandages. We're forging ahead together this time, as one.

"All right Baby Blue, Balasana to Savasana."

As I mold myself from Child's Pose and sink into the sand for Corpse Pose, I feel grounded. I feel more like me than I have in a year. *Or Five.*

Suddenly, the flutter of my eyelids tells me I dozed off. Score. I prop myself on my elbows and see Raven sitting on the edge of the waves. I walk to her and sit down.

"I needed that," I start, "but you knew that."

She rocks her shoulder into mine. "Just because we're not around a lot doesn't mean I've lost touch, you know. You're still my soul sister, Baby Girl."

I lay my head on her shoulder and take a deep breath before standing and brushing the sand from myself.

"I can't believe how warm the Atlantic is sometimes," Raven says as she stands to join me.

"That's because this is Nantucket Sound." I try to hide my laughter but don't get very far.

Raven rolls her eyes and shakes her head. "It's good to know there are some things yoga *can't* erase—like your charming sarcasm."

* * *

Bo

"You're absolutely *not* going, Bowan!" Rae follows me through the house.

"Get over yourself, Rae. I'm a damn adult and will do whatever I want."

"I should have never told you she was playing this weekend ..." Rae shakes her head with her hands on her hips.

"No, I'm glad you heard that. I still don't understand why she needed to have a private chat with Turner after the meeting." Apparently, not being at the meeting had its disadvantages.

Rae's face blanches as she fills her chest with a contemplative sigh.

"What, Rae?" The hair on the back of my neck starts to rise. "Rae, you're not telling me something."

"It's nothing. They're friends, right? November and Adrian, I mean ..." She bites her lip.

I stand in solid silence, staring through her. My eyes narrow as she fidgets with her hands. Finally, she clicks her tongue in defeat.

"I think I saw them holding hands." Her mouth keeps moving, but fury heats my ears and I process nothing else.

"Bo!" Rae hollers as I fling my keys against the wall. "Listen to me. Ember saw me in the hallway after Adrian left. She smiled and said goodbye. She didn't look like she was hiding anything."

Great. I tear my hands through my hair and pace to the kitchen. Rae follows.

"No, Bo. What I mean is, it looked completely innocent. If it wasn't, wouldn't she have hidden it or told me not to say anything?"

She could be right. However, November is one of the most composed people I've ever met. If Rae saw something that November didn't intend for her to see, she wouldn't so much as bat an eyelash. That, and anything involving Adrian Turner is far from innocent.

"What the hell am I supposed to do now?" I beg of my little sister as I sit at the kitchen table. I've never asked this question of her before.

Rae smiles and sits next to me. "Leave her alone. You've made your intentions clear—you want to right your wrongs. Get out of her face for five seconds." She slaps her hand off my thigh. "Go to work Monday like a normal person, and don't talk to her again till you see her up here on Wednesday. Just. Relax. She loves you, she'll come around."

I know in my head that leaving it alone is the right and wise thing to do. My heart, however, is screaming, "Idiot!" It knows if I give her space, no matter how small, it could be too much.

"Yo, Bowan, you in there?" Rae jerks my thoughts away from November's hand in Adrian's.

"Yeah." I pull Rae's tiny body into a hug. "Thanks for talking me off the ledge." I kiss the top of her head before releasing her.

"Thank God! What the hell would you do without me, you basket case?" She giggles.

"Ha! I have no idea, Rae."

She leaves me alone to gather my emotional shit. I'll dial it down, but I refuse to turn it off. I love November, and I don't intend to let her forget it.

Chapter 8
Ember

"All right boys, what's our set look like tonight?" I hop on stage and take my seat on the stool. We don't play for another two hours, but my parents and Adrian will be here; I want to nail it.

"Just a couple of songs with me, then you and Josh will do your folksy shit alone." C.J. snickers. He wants to be in a rock band. I wish he'd go find one.

"Oh, C.J., you know you love my folksy shit." Josh slaps one of the cymbals as he walks past C.J.'s drum set.

We decide to start with some 70's and early 80's rock to appease C.J. before Josh and I take it away with our "folksy shit." By folksy, C.J. refers to Indigo Girls, Sheryl Crow, and artists like that. Josh is unbelievably talented at their guitar parts, and I can hold my own with vocals.

"That was great guys," Josh encourages as we finish our practice. "Keep that energy going later."

C.J. and I slip backstage. I don't want to see my parents before I go on, or I'll get too nervous. Josh is out front doing his manager stuff when Adrian sneaks through the backstage door.

"Hey you, what are you doing back here? Talent only." I smirk as I hug him.

"Your parents are out front, I told them I'd come find you."

Josh and Monica walk backstage, and Monica gives Adrian a top-to-bottom once over before casting her eyebrow skyward in my direction.

"C.J., this is Adrian. Monica and I went to college with him." I deflect Monica's impending judgment.

"Nice to meet you, man." C.J. shakes Adrian's hand. "So, Rapunzel, is that dude gonna be here tonight?" Four of us in the room seem to stop breathing as C.J. absentmindedly flips his sticks through his fingers.

"What *dude?*" I ask.

"You know, that one you sang with. That Bo guy—he wrote that song for you, or whatever."

Yeah. Or Whatever.

"No, he's not coming tonight." I shrug, Adrian stuffs his hands in his pockets, and Monica shifts uneasily. C.J. finally catches on.

"Ah, shit. Did a one night stand turn into an epic fail?" He chuckles while gesturing obscenely, like a teenager.

"Shut the fuck up, C.J." Josh growls through clenched teeth.

"No, Josh, he didn't know—" I start, but Josh cuts me off.

"It doesn't matter if he knows or not; he doesn't have to be such a dick to you all the time." The last time I saw Josh this angry, he was screaming in *my* face. Monica puts her arm around his waist.

"Babe, let's go outside for a few minutes," she whispers to him before leading him out of the room.

Turning to look at Adrian, I find him seemingly counting the floor tiles. "Um. So, tell my parents I'm not coming out till we play, but we'll have drinks after."

"K. You all right?" He places his hand on my shoulder and lassos my eyes.

"I am." I don't even have to fake a smile this time.

Inexplicably, C.J. follows Adrian out of the back room, and I'm left there alone with another Bo revelation splattered all over the floor. In a beat, C.J. returns with two beers. He unfolds two chairs, sits, and gestures to the empty one.

"Here." He hands me a beer without looking at me.

"Thanks." I accept the only apology C.J. is capable of before breaking the awkward silence. "I've gotta ask, is it the

Dave Matthews Band kind of 'Rapunzel' or 'and they lived happily ever after" kind?'" I figure it's worth a shot to decode his nickname for me.

C.J. spits some of his beer in laughter, but before he can answer, Josh returns sans Monica.

"You two OK?" Josh paces toward us slowly.

"Are *you?* You kinda freaked out there." I stand and hand Josh my half-full pint, he accepts with a smile and swallows the rest.

"All right guys, let's get on stage." C.J. leads us out front without further discussion.

As we start our set, I can't miss my parents waving wildly from a table directly in the middle of Finnegan's. I also can't miss that Adrian and Monica are sitting with them. Monica seems to be spending more time watching Adrian than our set. I'm sure she senses something's up between us, but since I barely know what that is I'm not going to offer anything.

When we finish our 80's mild-rock set, C.J. leaves Josh and me on stage alone, where we ready ourselves to start our "folksy shit."

"What do you want to start with?" Josh asks, as we readjust our mics. "We kind of practiced a lot of heartbreak-y stuff ..."

"Well, I'm kind of in a heartbreak-y place. Just pick something. We'll nail it." Josh's concern makes me smile, but it's a tad annoying. "I'm not a damsel in distress, Josh. Just play."

He shrugs and starts strumming.

Shit, me and my big mouth.

Mushy heartbreak songs are the easiest to learn in a short amount of time, and quite frankly, they're the most popular among this bar crowd. I have a brief flash of panic when he intros Sheryl Crow's "Strong Enough," but I take a breath, smile, and roll my eyes at Monica.

Actually, I really don't feel like hell tonight, as the song might suggest. It's amazing what a small amount of time and a large amount of space can do to bury things that need burying. Swaying with the melody, I smile through the lyrics...until we get to the chorus, which talks about believing lies in the name of love.

No shit ...

I realize this is the first time I've performed here since the night Bo worked my lullaby. I never told my parents about that night; and I don't think I can now. I almost lose track of the lyrics when all the feelings I had that night start to simmer in my gut. I kissed him on stage, I cried on stage. I did things that were miles outside of my comfort zone because I thought I was in love.

Just two nights after that I was sitting, battered, in the hotel room of my ex-boyfriend trying to sort out a two-week lie. My insides scream with anger and talk of revenge, but I'm better than that. Guess he wasn't strong enough to be my man after all.

A few songs later we end our set and head off stage. I meet my four fans at their table.

"November Blue that was *outstanding!*" Raven is nearly bursting out of her Zen shell as she squeezes the life out of me.

"Thanks." I pull myself away and hug Ashby.

"Gorgeous, Baby Girl, I knew you had it in you." They've never heard me sing in public before. This must have been heaven for them.

"Listen, hun, it's getting late and we hate to dash out of here, but our flight to San Diego actually leaves in a few hours. We've got to get to the airport." Raven puts her arm around me one more time.

"What are you heading to San Diego for?" Adrian asks.

My parents eye me with ancient understanding. We've been over this. No one, except Bo, knows about their band. I'd like to keep it that way for a while.

"Getting together with friends we haven't seen in ages. Adrian and Monica, it was lovely catching up with you two. Take care of our girl." Raven hugs them both before leading my dad out of the bar by his hand.

"*We* will!" Monica calls after them with a hint of sarcasm before turning to Adrian. "So, Adrian, how long are you in town?"

"Heading home now. Em, I'm glad I got to see you sing again. Beautiful. Shoot me a message next week." He gives me a quick hug, says goodbye to Monica and the guys, and heads out of Finnegan's.

Adrian is the epitome of cool; someone passing by might actually believe I'll wait till next week to "shoot him a message." He knows by Monica's tone that she's suspicious but doesn't know anything. I feel a little rejected by our staged goodbye, but I realize it was necessary.

"That was nice of him to come watch you." Monica's sarcastic smile loses the game of hide-and-seek with her face.

"Yeah, it was. I'll be right back—I left something in my car. Can you order me a drink?"

She nods and heads to the bar while I move to the parking lot. Once outside, I check over my shoulder and see Monica engrossed with Josh's lips over the bar.

Scanning the parking lot, I spot Adrian just as he turns on his headlights. He leaves his car running, but gets out as I wave my hands and run to his car.

He stands behind his open door. "What's wrong?"

"Thanks again for coming. Also, thanks for everything back there." I hitch my thumb toward the bar.

"Of course." He gives me a lopsided grin. "It was really beautiful watching you sing."

"Damn, and this whole time I thought you meant it was me who was beautiful." Grinning, I step around his door. He drops his hand from the door and takes mine.

"You are beautiful...I just ..."

"No, I get it. I was teasing. Thanks for not making things weird with my parents and Monica. Have a safe drive home." I lift myself onto my toes and kiss his cheek.

Without a moment's hesitation, his hand cradles the back of my neck and he pulls me into his mouth. This is a real-deal Adrian Turner kiss. I dig the pads of my fingers into his shoulders as my tongue is granted entry into his mouth. His hands work down my sides, igniting the goosebumps I thought may have gone away for good. Pressing my hips into his, I force his back against the door of his car. He can't hide his want with my body pressing into him like this; his throaty groan echoes his need. I suddenly love knowing I do this to him. *You've still got it.* I don't want to stop—he's a delicious escape—but I know we have to. As my hands beg access to his belt, I pull away.

"See you Friday?" My lips feel drunk as I speak.

Adrian squeezes my hips as he rests his forehead on mine. "See you Friday."

My wobbly legs carry me back into Finnegan's, where Monica flags me down at the bar. The place is still crowded and once my ears clear themselves of Adrian's lust-filled air, they tune into a fiddle on stage. She hands me my beer, and I try to keep the grin off my face as I evaluate the tall drink of water swaying on stage.

"What the hell? Is he playing "Smooth Criminal?" On his fiddle?" The well-over-six-foot beauty on stage has his brassy-red hair pulled back in a short, messy ponytail. Typically I hate when guys have long hair, but this dude is hot.

"Yeah, isn't he amazing? That's C.J.'s cousin," Monica whispers.

The crowd is completely mesmerized by the rock music floating from his strings. I've heard people play rock music on classical instruments before, but hearing it live is intense. His body moves slowly side-to-side as the bow races across the strings with passion.

"*That's* Regan? Holy shit."

"Right? He'll do in a pinch." Monica giggles, making her chocolate ponytail swing side to side. Josh elbows her.

"Take it easy, Mon," he teases.

When Regan finishes, the crowd hoots and hollers wildly, then filters out the various exits to enjoy the warm June night. C.J. and Regan approach the bar, and C.J. introduces us.

"November, this is my cousin, Regan Kane." C.J. steps aside and Regan shakes my hand with a sexy smile overtaking his face, promptly heating mine.

"Nice to meet you, November. I've heard great things about you."

"From who? C.J.? Don't believe a word of it." I laugh. "You don't really have an accent."

Regan smiles as he stretches his arms over his head. "I'm not *from* Ireland, I just live there. The accent is easy for me to turn on and off." He shrugs and thanks Josh, who hands him a beer. "You were great up there tonight."

My face ignites. "You were here?"

"Yeah, your voice is full, it has depth. You've been singing a long time." He says this with authority.

"I guess." I shrug. "Listen, I'm exhausted, and I have a long week of work coming up. Are we still playing here every other week?" I question Josh. I want to make sure I can hang out with Adrian this weekend.

"Yeah. Let's rehearse Tuesday, since you'll be in Concord Wednesday through Friday. Sound good, Regan?" Josh nods in Regan's direction, whose studious eyes never leave mine.

"See you Tuesday." Regan smiles through his words as I walk away.

Monica follows me to the parking lot, but I don't notice until I'm almost at my car.

"Ember."

I turn around to find her standing cross-armed. "Yeah?"

"What's going on with Adrian?"

"What do you mean?" I walk back toward her.

"Don't treat me like I'm dumb—I'm your best friend. I see what's going on, but I don't know why you're not telling me." Her face twists in hurt.

"Monica," I sigh, "I'm not intentionally *keeping* anything from you. I just don't know what's going on yet, so there's not really anything to talk about."

"Can we talk about the fact that his car was in front of your apartment this morning?"

Damn.

"We *can*, but nothing happened. I swear. Look, Mon. It's comfortable with him. There aren't any surprises and we've got history." I leave out the part about our hot make-out session in my living room.

"Fine. Now, I get that you're all guarded now because of what happened with Bo, but you can't keep stuff from me. That's not what best friends do."

She's right.

"You're right, Mon. I'm sorry. As soon as there's something to tell, I'll tell you."

Monica stares at me, picking through my brain with her eyes before releasing a frustrated sigh. "Just be careful, OK? Oh! Josh and I are going away Friday to my parents' house, so I have to drive separately to Concord on Wednesday."

"That's fine." I shrug nonchalantly while silently thanking whatever powers arranged that. Now I won't have to tell her about going to Adrian's on Friday.

"Night." Monica turns back to Finnegan's.

"Night."

Chapter 9

The first part of this week has been a total bitch. Carrie placed interns with Monica and me in our offices, and handed them the rest of our workloads so we can focus "one hundred percent" on the DROP collaboration. This means that yesterday and today I've had to put up with oh-so-many questions from college seniors that I know for a *fact* I wasn't annoying enough to ask when I was in their shoes.

"Don't friend potential contacts on Facebook. In fact, you need to make yourself as private as possible on that damn site," I huff as I walk over to the computer to adjust the intern's privacy settings.

"Or you could not have an account at all, like Ember," Monica chirps as she walks in.

The intern contorts her face in a mix of horror and disgust. "You don't have a Facebook account at *all?*"

Monica and I laugh and shake our heads as I try to offer an explanation.

"Believe it or not, when we were in college it was only available for college students. Period. Now that they let any old cat in, I've lost interest." I finish adjusting her settings before letting her go for the day. "Oh, Zoe? One more thing." I tap the screen at one of her photo albums. "Regardless of your privacy settings, just, please, never take pictures like these again. If you don't put them on the internet, someone else will, OK? If you wouldn't show your grandmother, don't show the world.

And, if you *would* show your grandmother...I need to meet her for drinks." I chuckle.

She turns white and crimson at the same time. "OK. Goodnight." She leaves quickly.

"*You* are such an asshole." Monica slaps the back of my head.

"Oh, am I? We need to see some girl using Zoe's belly button as a shot glass?"

We burst into a laughter that's eluded us over the last couple of weeks. Monica's seemed a little distant since I started back at work. Things with her and Josh are going well and I want her to talk about it, but she seems hesitant to brag about her bliss. Also, while she's not thrilled with Adrian's reappearance in my life, she's upset that I won't talk about him with her just the same. It's made things a little tense, and I don't really see the tension dying down any time soon since we're going to be in Concord for the rest of the week.

Within an hour after leaving work, I'm at Finnegan's for our weekly rehearsal. I'm the last one here since, apparently, I'm the only one with a day job.

"What took you so long?" C.J. grumbles behind his set.

"Some of us work, Ceej." I toss my backpack on the closest table and hop up on stage. "You'll have to forgive him," I turn to Regan while pointing to C.J., "he's an asshole. But I guess you knew that since you're his cousin and all." Regan hoots as C.J. flips me off and sticks out his tongue, exposing his tongue ring.

"C.J., it's not 1999, lose the barbell." He flips me off again.

Regan draws his bow slowly across his fiddle once before speaking. "OK, Ember, the guys and I were talking about bringing some Irish rock into the mix. Are you OK with that?" I lose myself in the movements of his lips with his muffled accent. "Hello?" He snaps me out of it.

"Hm? Sorry. That sounds great, I guess, but I don't really have a rock kind of voice ..."

"Oh, I think you'll do just fine." He ignores my concern and resumes stroking the strings with his bow.

"What's the difference between a fiddle and a violin?" I ask, studying the instrument that looks like a violin to me.

Regan stops and considers his fiddle, twisting it in the space between us. "Fiddle's just a nickname." He winks and places his chin back on his "nickname." He's intriguing. He's cool, confident, but seems safe. I need to figure him out.

As he vacillates between fast and slow rhythms, I find myself watching his hands and swaying along with him. I'm transported back to my childhood, once again watching my dad play for my mom while I peeked from my bedroom. Monica sneaks up behind me and hooks her arm through mine, swaying in time.

"He's a goddamn dream, isn't he?" Monica bats her eyelashes.

"I'll say. What are you doing here?"

"I wanted to watch this fiddle-playing god."

Regan chuckles but keeps playing, as Monica gushes.

"Jesus, Mon, Josh is right there!" I point to Josh, who sits and shakes his head.

"Not for me, smartass, for *you*."

What?

"What?" I unlink my arm from hers.

Monica places her hands on her hips. "Come on. You're a free woman. You've taken the dive back on stage here, you're having fun—you're over it. Let's move on."

Monica is clearly trying to divert my attention from Adrian, and that irritates me, but I don't want to get into it.

"I met Regan nine seconds ago. Plus, he might have a girlfriend ..."

"I don't." Regan stops playing and turns to face us with a crooked grin.

Whispering fail.

"All right, lovers, can we play now?" C.J. thumps the bass drum, and we fall into place as I kick Monica off stage.

Thankfully, I don't embarrass easily, or rehearsal would be a total waste of time. Regan's taste is even folksier than Josh's, and I fall into an easy rhythm with him. He plays songs that are familiar and beautiful, and Josh and C.J. are able to catch on quickly. When he's not playing, Regan sings with a tone that has me envisioning a gorgeous emerald mountain. I realize that while the stage at Finnegan's will always be backlit by Bo Cavanaugh, I'm more than capable of crafting new memories here. I want to.

Josh sets his guitar on its stand as we finish. "Great job, guys. Let's definitely do those last two songs next week."

"Sounds good. Who's playing here Saturday?" Thankful that Finnegan's closed on Tuesdays, I walk behind the bar and pour myself a beer.

Josh and C.J. share an uncomfortable glance before Josh shrugs. "It was supposed to be Bo ..."

Oh.

"What do you mean supposed to be? Did he cancel?" I walk back to Monica, who looks as confused as I do.

Josh hops off the stage and meets Monica and me at our table. C.J. and Regan talk in hushed tones by the drum set. "We kind of didn't know how to handle it. I texted him last week to see if he was still interested, and he said he didn't want to make you uncomfortable."

"Who's Bo?" Regan helps himself to a beer and joins us.

Everyone stares everywhere but at me.

"You guys can quit it with the awkward silence." I cast disapproving eyes to my friends, and then turn to Regan. "Bo's an ex-boyfriend. Well, boyfriend might be a loose term since we dated for less than two weeks, but we cared a lot ...you know what, he's an ex-boyfriend as of almost two weeks ago. That's all."

I feel my throat twitch slightly, but I remind it that those yoga tears were the last. Regan's eyes ask for more. One of his eyebrows pulls inward as he takes a breath, but he seems to decide against pressing for information. He's not getting it tonight, anyway.

"Well, Regan will be here, you should come watch Bo with him since Josh and I will be out of town." Monica toasts the air, and I mentally punch her in the face.

"Oh sure, why not?" I play along with Monica's version of revenge. Truth is, I'm not sure if I'll be in town Saturday or not. And, I don't know if any amount of intended revenge could make me feel comfortable enough to watch Bo play at Finnegan's. "I'll see you here Saturday, Regan."

Before things get any weirder, I head home to pack for Concord. And Boston.

* * *

The last two days in Concord have gone off without a hitch. As promised by his email weeks ago, Bo is largely office and meeting bound. Monica and I have been left to work with Rae and David for a majority of the day. Our conversation at the diner isn't choking the air between Bo and me. He's pleasant when we see each other—perfectly business.

Just like I wanted...

We've checked out the warehouse space Bo purchased to renovate for the community center, and I've spent today digging through Bill Holder's old files to try to organize his contacts and make new ones.

Monica's fallen as deeply in love with Rae as I have. She's so sweet, so good, and such a breath of fresh air. It's not awkward at all for me to be spending time with her, and I regularly check in with her to make sure she feels the same way. She asks Monica and me to lunch, and we accept.

"This week has been really great, Rae. DROP is really on top of things; you're thoroughly prepared for this center," I say as we settle into our table at lunch.

Rae starts to answer but stops mid-sentence with her eyes peering over my shoulder. "You've got to be kidding me," Rae sighs. I turn to see what she's looking at.

Ainsley Worthington. Of course.

"What?" Monica turns around.

"That," I whisper, "is *Ainsley*, Bo's ex-girlfriend." I ignore the glaring reality that I'm now a member of the same club.

"She's such a bitch." Rae rolls her eyes. "She knew we'd be here. I always come here, and she knows you guys are in town. She's trampy, but she's not dumb." Rae runs her finger over the silverware. "Perfect, she's coming this way." She throws her fork on her bread plate and sits back in her chair.

I can smell her bubble-gum-like perfume before I turn to meet her icy gaze.

"Rachel, hi! How've you been? God, I can't believe those assholes ..." Ainsley pesters Rae with her condolence speech regarding the blackmail. Rae nods and gives tight smiles throughout her rambling.

"Well, it's all fine now, but thanks for your concern." Rae turns her attention back to her empty bread plate as Ainsley turns hers to me.

"November, right? I'm sorry things didn't work out between you and Spencer." Her face is anything but sorry.

When the hell did she start calling him that? Rae looks at her like she's a complete idiot as soon as she says it.

"No, you're not." Well, that came right out. Both Monica and Rae throw their napkins to their faces to cover their grins.

"Excuse me?" Ainsley steps back, putting her hand on her

chest as if I just implied her baby was ugly or something.

Having lost my appetite, I push my chair back and stand. "I said you're not sorry. Why would you be sorry that I'm no longer with someone you've been pining after for years? The unfortunate part is—you burned that bridge with *Spencer* long before I came along." Out of the corner of my eye I can see Rae's eyes widen in excitement. "Now, if you'll excuse me, I have to get back to work. See you around."

Adrenaline pumps through me as I brush past the underweight ex-cheerleader and head outside. I pause, waiting for Rae and Monica. When they come out, sporting canyon-wide grins, Ainsley is a step behind them.

Oh for the love of ...

"You think you know me?" Ainsley starts in without invitation. "You don't know anything about me, except what you may have heard from baby sister over here." Rae simply rolls her eyes. She's gone a few rounds with Ainsley in the past, this appears to be nothing new to her ears. "The fact is you abandoned Spencer in his time of need. I would never do anything like that. Who's the tramp now?" As quickly as she can, Ainsley pushes past me and takes off in her car.

Holy shit. Is she right?

"It's Bo, Ainsley, *just Bo!*" Rae hollers after her.

"What the hell is up her ass?" Monica's first encounter with Ainsley was a doozy.

"Ember, don't listen to what she said. She's a bitch," Rae pipes in.

They continue to talk as we walk to the car, but their chants of reassurance and revenge are drowned out by a shrill voice condemning me of abandoning the man I thought held my future, when our short past was based on lies. I don't know what facts Ainsley has, but it barely matters. Her opinion is likely shared by those who don't know the story. We drive back to DROP in silence. I lock myself in the office and immerse myself in work for the afternoon.

Chapter 10

A soft knock on my office door pulls me out of my two-hour long mail-merge-a-thon.

"Ember?"

"Yeah, Bo, come in." I turn down Dave Matthews' voice and sit back from my computer, still trying to drain Ainsley's words from my brain. I motion for him to sit in the chair across from my desk.

He sits and rubs his hands down the front of his thighs before speaking. "Rae told me you guys saw Ainsley at lunch ..."

"It was a treat." I roll my eyes.

Bo leans in, placing his elbows on my desk, staring into my eyes. "Don't listen to a thing that comes out of her mouth. She doesn't know what happened between us. She's just bitter because I've been ignoring her calls."

"Don't ignore her calls on my account." I shrug, then instantly regret the words as I see him wince slightly.

The truth is, I don't know how I'll handle seeing Bo with someone else, because there *will* eventually be someone else. But, it can't be Ainsley.

Anyone but Ainsley.

"Sorry, that came out wrong," I backpedal, still not wanting to hurt his feelings or sound presumptuous. "I just mean ..." I don't know what I mean.

"I don't want *her*, November ..." His eyes beckon my heart, calling to me with their Siren's song of promises eternal.

I stand, hoping a change in elevation will help me refocus. Crossing my arms over my stomach, I pace around the desk, leaning against it in front of him. He sits back, crossing his arms in front of him as well.

"What she said...is that how you feel? Do you feel like I abandoned you?" I almost whisper.

Bo's eyes start at my knees, bare from my skirt, and swim up the length of my body before he stands, regarding me with tenderness. Our bodies are inches apart; the space between them filled with tension, anger, passion, and promises of forever. I relax my arms and place my hands on the desk behind me. My pulse drums a familiar beat, allegro in his gaze.

His voice is husky and serious as he opens his beautiful mouth. "What I did to you, November, is inexcusable. I abandoned *you* by not being honest with you. Ainsley assumed I'd come running to her, and I haven't. She feels threatened that you work here and will take every opportunity to try to mark what she thinks is her territory."

Bo and I ignore the boundaries I clearly set last week, as our bodies buzz inches from one another in silence. We're in a vacuum; ignoring the past and disregarding the future. I feel his hot breath against my mouth and I close my eyes for a second, reviewing my options for action, before turning my head to the side.

"Bo."

Without further instruction, he heads for the door while I wait for feeling to return to my legs.

I clear my throat. "You're still playing at Finnegan's tomorrow, right?" He stops and turns slowly toward me as I continue. "Josh said he'd text you. I appreciate your concern for me, but there's no need to tiptoe. They love you there."

He hesitates with an amused expression before he answers. "I'll play if you're going to be there."

Um.

"What?"

He shrugs and rests against the doorframe. "I heard Monica tell Rae that she and Josh are out of town this weekend. I don't want to drive all the way down there and not have any friends to hang out with."

He's kidding. Right? I tilt my head back and furrow my

brow.

He shrugs. "Friends, right?"

I don't like that word coming from his mouth, directed toward me. I loved him. I wanted to be his. Just his. But friends? No, I don't want to be *friends* with Bo Cavanaugh.

I force the smallest smile I can pass off as genuine. "Friends."

"So you'll be there." His sexy authority has returned, kicking the droopy-tailed puppy to the curb.

"Of course. See you Saturday." I turn back to my desk as he smiles and turns for the hallway. "Oh, Bo?" I call after him.

He leans his head back into my doorway. "Yeah?"

"I'm not singing with you."

He shakes his head, chuckles, and heads down the hall. I collapse into my chair; my head is tossing in a spin cycle of the lies and mistruths I've spewed in the name of this weekend. I could have easily lied my way out of Finnegan's for Saturday, *but...what the hell ...*

* * *

The W in Boston. This is where Adrian Turner lives, naturally. It's a world-class hotel that also plays house to over a hundred people who demand luxury full time. As a rule, I don't use the word swanky, but I make an exception as I stand in Boston's theater district staring up at Adrian's "home." He texted me to meet him at the private entrance. He's the kind of guy who would live in a place with a private entrance.

I text him when I'm downstairs. The valet has taken my car god-knows-where, but it's hard to care while looking up at this amazing building. I'm thoroughly grateful I had the good sense to pull over at the last available rest top to change into my green shift dress. Cinched with a black-patent belt and matching black heels, I feel like a knockout. I'm sure The W doesn't have an undergarment dress code, but I slid on my red lace thong, just in case.

"There you are, Gorgeous. You found the place OK?"

Texts don't do his cocoa butter voice justice. We've largely communicated through texts and email this week because I've been so busy at work. As he graces each square of the sidewalk toward me in his black pants and tight black t-shirt, I can't believe this is happening.

Adrian. Me. Here.

I smirk. "It's kind of hard to miss, hot shot."

Away from the watchful eyes of curious friends and family, his arm seizes my waist and I fall into his kiss. Its length is inversely proportional to its explosiveness—as soon as it begins, it's over—and I'm immediately left wanting more.

"I missed you this week." He kisses my hand and leads me through the private entrance, down the private hallway, and into the private elevator. He doesn't release his grip when the elevator doors close. "How was Concord?" He keeps his eyes on the floor numbers as he asks this question out of courtesy.

I shrug and squeeze his hand. "It was good; incredibly busy and exhausting."

"You make exhausting look good, Blue—even in those damn heels you insist on wearing." He chuckles as the elevator slows its race to the twentieth floor.

"These are different heels, smartass ..." I think back to the night I sat in Adrian's hotel room, barefoot and bleeding. He came back from the fight carrying my heels, and I could have kissed him in that moment for his thoughtfulness.

Ding.

Our hands have created their own humidity, but that doesn't disrupt Adrian; he tightens his grip and leads me down the hall. As he opens the door to his corner apartment, two different views of the city flood my senses. I drop my hand from his and wander to the window that showcases Boston Harbor—breathtaking from this height. Touching my fingertips to the warm glass, I smile.

I lean my shoulder into his as he joins me at the window. "You've done well for yourself, Counselor."

"Ha, I guess. That and Grandma Turner's trust fund." He shrugs and tucks his hands into his pockets.

"She passed away?" I pick up my head and study his face.

His gaze doesn't break from the harbor's white caps. "Two years ago."

"I'm so sorry, Adrian. She was always so nice to me." I cross my arms and lay my head on his shoulder as he pulls me in closer.

We stand in silence as daylight turns to sunset. Our history extends further than an Ivy League high-rise. After a few minutes of silently sifting through our past, Adrian ceremoniously claps his hands.

"Well, Blue, you want a tour of the place?" He's suddenly like a kid on Christmas morning.

"Of course. By the way, this kitchen is fabulous. Do you use it or just woo women with it?" I hurry over to the oversized island and try to spread my arms the length of it.

"Funny. What makes you think I try to "woo" women with my kitchen?" He leans against the exposed brick beam that separates the kitchen from the living room.

"Right, of course. You don't need a kitchen." I arch my eyebrow and grin as I slink toward him. Grabbing his hand, I lift up and whisper in his ear, "It's just a bonus, I guess."

He doesn't respond except with a shake of his head and a grin before showing me the bathroom, study, and guest room. As any good ladies' man, he saves his bedroom for last. The room bleeds Adrian—the whole place does, really. Strong lines adorned with leather and wood throw my senses into a tailspin and kick my body's output of estrogen to full-throttle. Adrian Turner is as man as they come, and I shift as my panties suddenly seem uncomfortable.

"This place is unbelievable. You really do seem happy." I bring up my inquisition from weeks ago on the beach.

"I am now." With his hands in his pockets, he swings out his elbow and I loop my arm through his. "Let's go eat."

* * *

Adrian and I reminisce through two glasses of Prosecco and the wild mushroom risotto before he asks the host to call us a cab. I don't see a check arrive at the table, but Adrian pulls out my chair and ushers us away from the restaurant to the main lobby.

"Do you dine and dash here often?" I look over my shoulder and notice no commotion over our exit.

"It's on my account." Without further discussion he opens the cab door for me, closes it, and enters on the other side.

"You're always such a gentleman." I sigh, and just might bat my eyelashes. He takes hold of my hand.

"You deserve a gentleman, Blue."

That seems to be an understatement. During dinner he remained guarded. Despite no one around that we knew, he didn't try to court my legs under the table, he didn't hold my hand while we were eating, and we haven't kissed since I arrived at his doorstep.

"Where are we going?" I attempt to shake the "insecure needy girl" thoughts from my head. It occurs to me I slid into this cab without question.

"To a club up here. I want to dance with you."

Insecure, needy girl banished. Enter, Hell. Yes.

"Oh. Are we overdressed?" My memory holds visions of jeans, bedazzled tanks, and platform flip-flops when I think of "club" and "dancing" with Adrian in the same sentence. I again have to remind myself we're in our late twenties in Boston, not teenagers in an underground bar that looks the other way at fake IDs.

"Even if we are, you look hot." Adrian's sentence is timed perfectly with the squealing breaks of our ride.

My heart has skipped every third beat since I got to his apartment. I'm staying the night with him, and making out will no longer do. The sound of the bass and the crowd humming from the door as we approach it has nothing on what's going on below the belt of my dress.

Adrian nods once at the bouncer, and we're granted unquestioned access to the foreplay inside the stone walls. He waves to some people I assume he knows, as he tears us through the crowd and onto the dance floor. He's been quiet since dinner, and I'm no longer sure what the hell it is I'm doing here if he can't even talk to me. I push the question aside, as his hands swallow my waist and move me in time with him.

After a half hour, Shakira and Pitbull's song "Rabiosa" comes on. Our smiles high-five one another as we take our positions. In college, the lacrosse team was invited to a formal party hosted by Monica's sorority. We were dating at the time and he took me, despite the hisses from some of the bitches of Delta Mu. He knew their game, and he wasn't playing. A dance competition closed that evening, and we took first place.

We'd each learned to dance at some point in our lives and pulled it off right there; stepping over the dropped jaws and bugged-out eyes who thought Adrian Turner was too good for the likes of a hippie nerd. The only problem was I was a hippie nerd that he happened to think was gorgeous, *and* that he loved—though I didn't know about the love part until a few weeks ago.

The reggaeton-merengue mix brings our past crashing

into our present once more, and we float through the crowd. My hips grind mercilessly into his as I pull his pockets to bring him in tighter. It's as if he has to force our bodies apart when he spins me, then they're right back together. I find myself staring intently at the beads of sweat on his neck.

"You still got it, Turner," I pant as Beyonce regains control of the speakers.

"Thanks for leading, Gorgeous." He smiles but doesn't lock eyes with me.

By the time Jay-Z's voice joins in the song, I've had enough of Adrian's distance. I grab his belt and yank him toward me, crashing his hipbones into mine.

"What was that about?" he grunts.

"What the hell is with you?" I'm forced to shout in his ear over the loud music.

He turns my back to him and I grind down his body. "What do you mean?"

"I mean, you're being aloof, that's what I mean. You kiss me when I show up, but you've said about twenty words since then. What gives?" I shout over my shoulder before he spins me back around.

Suddenly, he stops dead in the middle of the dance floor and presses his sweaty forehead into mine. "I'm trying really hard to respect your boundaries, Ember," he breathes onto my lips.

"I never set any with you." I tilt my chin until my lips make contact with his earlobe. "Take me home, Adrian."

He steps back, keeping me at forearms length. "Yeah?"

Seduction takes over my face. "Yeah."

Chapter 11

"Taxi!" Adrian wastes no time journeying back to his place.

As soon as he climbs in the cab next to me and slams the door shut, I'm pulled onto his lap and his tongue invades my mouth. The caged animal that claims Adrian's body is ravenous, desperate for me with every moan beckoning from the bottom of his throat.

"Adrian," I breathlessly pull away, "we're in a cab."

He grabs my hips and pushes me harder onto his lap. "I'm sure he's seen worse."

Adrian kisses me with hunger, while he runs one hand down the outside of my thigh and resumes its ascent under my dress. I circle my hips on his, and I can't believe I don't care about the cab driver a foot away from us, but I don't.

His hand reaches my hip and he runs his fingertip along the lace of my thong. My body remembers his next move, and I lift off him slightly as he tucks his finger underneath the fabric and slips it inside me.

"Damn." I exercise vocal control by breathing into his shoulder as he works his magic.

Just like that the cab stops, and in one motion Adrian slides me off him and hands the driver money. I sweep my hair over my burning cheeks, but the cabbie doesn't so much as look in the rearview mirror. I briefly wonder if he *has* seen worse, but don't give it too much thought as I shut the door behind me. Adrian takes my hand into his sweaty palm, and we walk hurriedly through the private entrance to the elevators.

When the doors ding closed behind us, I slam Adrian into the side of the elevator by my mouth. "Never do that to me in public again," I curse in the short time my tongue leaves his mouth.

I feel his grin against my lips. "Don't worry, Baby. Anything else I plan on doing to you has to be done in private."

We tear blindly through his door in a hurricane of need five years in the making. I glide backward with each step he takes forward, until my hips are backed up against the kitchen island. With the height of my heels, I'm able to lift up on my toes slightly and shift myself onto the marbled surface. Once anchored, I kick off my heels and wrap my legs around his waist.

"You have condoms, right?" I breathe onto his collarbone as I explore the peaks and valleys of his muscles with my lips.

As my tongue dances behind his ear, his breath takes any response away. He reaches into his pocket and produces the black foil between his index and middle fingers. My shaking legs can wait no longer. I open his belt and shove my hand down his pants, hungrily grabbing the last physical memory I have of him. He lets his pants fall to his ankles and tugs at the skirt of my dress. I lean forward, allowing the dress to settle on my hips and I drop my legs while I tear the wrapper open.

"I'll do it." He takes the condom from me and his eyes bore through mine as he rolls it on. We remain at-the-ready as our hungry bodies play catch-up.

"Adrian ..." I resume my leg-lock around his waist as he pulls back to look at me. "No, don't fucking stop."

I dig my fingertips into his shoulders and beg him forward. His lips meet mine at the same time he slams into me. I wince for a split second, before reminding my body to relax around him. He guides my hips to the edge of the island and picks up speed. Releasing my grip on his shoulders, I wrap my fingers around the edge of the island, tilting my chin to the sky while arching my back.

"Oh my god ..." Adrian groans.

My sentiments exactly. In our time apart we've clearly graduated from Little League and are starting for the pros.

His cadence is strong. He brushes my hair aside, exposing my neck. I rock my hips harder into him while he sucks on my collarbone, forcing his teeth to graze my skin. He pushes deeper and harder into me until my moans echo off the picture windows and sweat is pouring off of me. Adrian's breathing increases and a shaky moan accompanies a final pull of my hips.

Suddenly I'm in the air. Adrian kicks off his shoes and pants before walking me to the couch, still inside me. He sits, and I press my knees into the soft leather while gripping the back of his head. I push off my knees and stroke my body up and down his rock hard center.

"God, this is good. Faster, Blue," he commands, guiding my hips to the right speed. I concede and give him all I've got. I anchor my hands on the back of the couch and let him have it. I ride him with five years of angst, questions, and one hell of a breakup before he buries his face into my breasts and finishes inside me. I lean back and tighten my muscles around him.

"Holy shit, Ember." His voice sounds like he's speaking through a fan. I did that to him.

* * *

"Do you want a glass of wine?" Adrian kisses my temple. We've been lying naked on his couch for over an hour, watching Boston below.

"I do. And a shower, but I left my clothes in my car."

"They should be in my room by now, I asked the front desk to bring them up."

I shake my head. "This is unreal."

"What?" He laughs as I smack his shoulder and stroll to the master bedroom to shower.

A few minutes later, an oversized terrycloth robe hugs my clean skin while I walk back down the hall to the kitchen. Adrian is waiting with wine—in his boxers.

"Feel better?" He hands me my glass, and I walk over to the window.

"Much. This week was fucking weird."

"I bet. Anything you want to talk about?" Adrian doesn't want to say his name.

"No." Neither do I. "What's it like, living *here?*"

Adrian leans his back against the window and faces me. "It's nice. Private."

I find it funny how a monstrosity of elegance can be

classified as "private," but I choose not to call him on it.

"Tonight was fun, Adrian—and I don't just mean the last hour, either." I grin and he walks toward me.

When his lips take a break from mine, he responds. "I had fun too, Blue. I feel like I've waited forever to have you here."

"Why didn't you ever call?"

"You deleted your Facebook account, your interest—or disinterest—in me was clear. You didn't want to be found. At least not by me."

I force a guilty swallow. "I just didn't want to see you and all of your 'girlfriends.'" I include air quotes to denote their loose appearance.

"Ha. Ha. November, I've had one serious girlfriend since you. And, no, that doesn't mean I've had a revolving door installed in my bedroom." He's onto my suspicions. "Law school was a bitch; totally time-consuming. I wanted to be successful when I graduated, so goofing around was out of the question.

"Oh, all work and no play?" I turn back to the kitchen and pour myself another glass of wine.

"Whatever, like you've been locked away in an ivory tower somewhere?"

"Whatever to you. I'm clean, I've been checked." I quip, not wanting to divulge my entire sexual history.

"Me too."

"Good." I grin and cock my eyebrow.

"Good."

We laugh and spend the next few hours talking about what, exactly, a consultant of his kind does and how I like my job. I can't believe what a great time I've had tonight. I realize that the only negative feelings I had toward Adrian were cast in the shadow of Bo. Now that Bo's out of the picture, I take no issue with Adrian. He loved me. Maybe he still does, but we don't have time for that discussion tonight. He strokes his fingers through the length of my hair as I rest my head on his lap, my eyelids heavy despite my fight to keep them upright.

"Let's go to bed," he whispers just before I fall completely asleep.

When we reach his oversized bed, cloaked in what I'm sure are one-million-thread-count Egyptian cotton sheets, I let my robe fall to the floor and I meet him in the middle of the bed. My head finds its former home in the crevice of his shoulder, and we fall asleep wrapped up in each other.

* * *

The clock tells me it's 9:00 AM. My slight hangover feels like it could very well be 5:00 AM. The smell of bacon wafting through Adrian's apartment tells me he's made a huge mistake. I gather what I'm calling "my" robe from the floor and shuffle to the kitchen, wiping sleep from my eyes. Adrian hovers shirtless over the stove and bobs his head to the music from his laptop on the island. *The island.*

"Really? Bacon?" I tease.

He jumps at the sound of my voice. "Calm down," he laughs, "I've got your 'I-can't-believe-it's-not-meat' crap right over here." He slides a plate across the island that's piled with fruit and my fake bacon.

"Aw, you remembered," I exaggerate while batting my eyelashes. I don't eat this overly processed crap, either. But I'll make an exception for Adrian; he's trying.

"You're unforgettable. How'd you sleep?" He crosses over to me and kisses the back of my neck as I settle myself onto a stool.

When breakfast is over, he asks the question I was hoping to somehow avoid. "What are your plans for today and tonight?"

"Well, since Josh and Monica are away, I told them I'd hang out with Regan, a fiddle player for the house band, and watch some of the acts with him tonight."

One act. There's only one act. In an uncharacteristic mark of betrayal, I feel heat spread through my cheeks and ears.

Adrian takes our dishes to the sink. "Isn't Cavanaugh playing tonight?"

"Yeah. I told Josh and Bo it was fine because they were acting all weird about him still playing, but the crowd adores him. I said I'd be there, but I wouldn't sing with him. Boundaries." I shrug and smile into my coffee mug.

"Sing with him if you want." Adrian shrugs back and loads the dishwasher.

I'm instantly annoyed at his assumption that I said I wouldn't sing because of *him* and not because of my own comfort level. His "permission" has me fuming.

"I didn't tell him I wouldn't because of you; therefore, I

don't really need your permission to do it." I slide off the stool and head to the bedroom to dress.

"Ember," Adrian calls after me down the hall.

"Look, Adrian," I say as he enters the bedroom, "this past week was really hard. I was as professional as I could be while working fifty feet from someone who broke my heart. He says we can be friends, but I don't think he means it in the same way that I meant it when I agreed. I had an amazing time with you last night, and I don't need you fucking it up by trying to dictate my actions." I sit on the bed in a huff.

"November, I didn't mean that. I just meant do what you want. Don't worry about me, him—or Monica, for that matter. Just do you, Blue." He sits softly next to me.

"Oh. Sorry." The heat leaves my face.

"Want me to come tonight?"

Is he serious?

"No. I just...I haven't said anything to Monica about you, even though she suspects something's going on anyway, and she'll find out if we were there together. It's just...I kind of like having you to myself right now. I need to not have people in my business for a while." My ramble is honest, and Adrian's eyes show me he appreciates it.

"I get it. Here's the deal, you come see me as many Fridays as you can on your way home from Concord until we're comfortable with whatever's going on here, and I'll play by your rules."

Two men, two deals. God, if you exist, help me.

"Deal."

"You want to seal that with a kiss?" Adrian lays me back on the satin comforter and pushes my legs open with his knee.

"I want to seal that with a hell of a lot more than a kiss." I grab his face as we explore the beginnings of...whatever this is.

Chapter 12

Walking into Finnegan's, I'm relieved I beat Bo here. I need to find a place and settle into the scenery as I navigate our "friendship."

"Ember, over here!" Regan waves from a table directly in front of the stage.

Oh good …

"What's with the up close and personal seating?" I tease as I sit next to him.

"I've heard this guy's good, and I want to be able to hear him. How was your week?"

I lean back in my chair, trying my best to come up with a description of the week. I worked rather cordially with Bo, was verbally and emotionally assaulted by Ainsley, and was asked to be Bo's friend. However, I had an over-the-top amazing night and morning with Adrian, and now I'm sitting next to a hot ex-Pat waiting to watch Bo play.

"Interesting." I take a sip of my beer.

"November?" A familiar but out-of-place voice cuts through the bar chatter.

I turn around to find Rachel Cavanaugh walking toward me with a hopeful, but cautious smile. Relief bathes my nerves. I admit I was worried Bo would try to pull a stunt to try to stay the night, but seeing his sister here means he's playing it smart.

"Rae? I didn't know you were coming. Awesome!" I hug her and pull out a chair. "This is Regan Kane, he's a wicked fiddle player. Regan, this is Bo's sister, Rachel."

"Please, call me Rae." She morphs her lips into an endearing smile and shakes his hand.

"Rae, it's a pleasure. Can I get you a beer?"

Rae drops her hand and keeps smiling. "No, thank you, I don't drink. I'll take some water, though." Regan nods and heads to the bar.

"I'm happy you're here. Was this your idea or his? Where is he?" I scan the area behind her.

"Mine. I refuse to let him make an ass out of himself. He's on probation since that little maneuver on your first day at DROP. He went in the back entrance." She rolls her eyes at what I assume is his version of what happened in the diner. "Anyway," she continues, "where in the hell have you been hiding that hottie?" Rae nods her head toward Regan.

"Ha! I just met him last week. He's our drummer's cousin."

"Way to keep him for yourself." Rae stares at me in mock accusation, and it causes me to blush. It's clear she feels the same sisterly connection between us that I instantly felt upon my first meeting with her.

"Rae, to be honest, I assumed you had a boyfriend."

Regan returns in time to hear her response. "No, guys my age are idiots. Thanks for the water, Regan. How old are you?"

"You're welcome, and, twenty-five."

"Perfect." She grins and brings the straw to her lips.

My eyebrows shoot up. "Seriously? I thought you were, like, thirty."

Regan laughs into his beer. "What the hell is that supposed to mean?"

"You're just refreshingly mature."

Before he can respond, the bartender takes the stage and announces Bo. My fingers tingle, and I feel slightly dizzy. I notice that Rae is staring at me and I'm thankful that Regan isn't. I tilt my chin to the stage to somehow reassure her that everything's fine. Bo comes out wearing black jeans and a green t-shirt. The green t-shirt he told me reminded him of my eyes. I swallow hard as he sits on the stool, and, without saying a word, starts strumming.

Every feeling from the first night I heard him play flies

through me like a drunken seagull. I take several deep breaths as he makes his way through his original work, praying that what I'm feeling isn't regret. The strings, his fingers, the warm bourbon tone kissing the microphone—they're all lulling me into his presence, his being.

My phone vibrates against my thigh, startling me away from this apparent Bo-asis. I see that it's Monica, so I click "ignore" since she's probably just calling to see if I showed, and continue staring at Bo. I'm not even hearing what he's singing, my brain seems to not want to let me see and hear him sing at the same time. It's one hell of a defense mechanism. When my phone vibrates two more times, I decide to take the call outside.

"Mon, what's going on? Is everything OK?" The warm breeze resuscitates my logic.

"What the hell took you so long to answer?"

"I'm at Finnegan's with Regan and actually Ra—" I'm cut off by a squeal.

"Whatever, Josh proposed!" Her voice is pure bliss.

"*What?* Oh my God, Monica, that's amazing! Tell me you said yes!" The parking lot drowns under the happy tears rising past my irises.

"Of course I said yes!"

We meet each other sniff-for-sniff in tears of happiness and congratulations.

"Details, please!" I squeak through tears.

"Well, Josh helped my dad grill our food last night and asked his permission then."

"Asked his permission? Oh my God, how cute!"

"Right? Then the four of us went out on the boat this morning. Right in the middle of the ocean," her voice clips for a second, "Josh got down on one knee ..."

This is so Josh and Monica I could be sick, in the happiest way possible.

"OK," I prompt, "what'd he say? How'd he ask?"

"He said that the love he felt for me couldn't be measured, not even by all the water in the sea beneath us," she sniffs back more tears, "and he said he wanted to spend forever with me. Rocky seas and all."

"Oh, Monica." I'm openly sobbing in front of Finnegan's, but my smile prevents people from asking me if I'm OK. I'm perfect.

Ten minutes later, after talking dates and girly details, I nearly forget where I am when I hear applause coming from inside.

"Shit, Mon, Bo's set is done, and I've left Regan in there with Rae this whole time. I'm so freaking happy for you and can't wait to see you two. Will you be home tomorrow?" I quickly wipe under my eyes as people start filing out of the bar.

"Yes, we'll be home tomorrow. How was the set?"

That's not what she wants to know.

"Everything's fine, enjoy the rest of your weekend. I love you. Tell Josh I love him, too. Bye."

I lean my head back against the wall and take in what's just happened.

She said yes. They're getting married. Forever.

When the exodus slows and I realize my party is still inside, I turn and head back through the door where, of course, I find Regan and Bo chatting like old friends at our table. My fake smile is getting a workout these days, and I beg its appearance once more as I sit in the chair across from Bo.

"Sorry about that, Monica called."

"What happened? Your eyes are all red. Why were you crying?" Rae leans forward and puts her hand on my arm. Bo and Regan stop their quiet conversation and stare at me.

"Nothing." I smile. "Josh proposed to Monica today. They're getting married." I smile as salty tears roll off my lips and into my beer while I try to swallow.

"That's great, good for them," Bo chimes in, a genuine smile on his lips. His eyes, however, are steeped in sadness.

Yeah, maybe that could have been us.

Rachel clearing her throat is the only indication I have that my eyes have been locked with Bo's in a silent waltz of melancholy.

"It is great." I try to recover from my social fumble. "They're perfect for each other."

"Ember, Regan says you guys are going to try some Irish rock stuff? I agree with him that you can totally pull it off." Bo is talking to me like his friend. *Friends.* I look at Rae, who shrugs and smiles.

"Uh, yeah, thanks. We haven't really tried anything yet, but it'll be fun to learn something new."

This will go down in history as the most awkward conversation I've ever had. Ever.

"Hopefully you'll play up there, too," Bo says. His eyes carry hopefulness, familiarity, and pleads of a connection he clearly hopes still exists. He's my musical soul mate. He knows it, I know it, and he's trying to let Regan know it.

"What do you play?" Regan sounds surprised.

I shake my knee under the table nervously. Regan knows Bo's my ex-boyfriend, and that it's recent. I can't explain that everything I love about playing the guitar is wrapped up in Bo Cavanaugh. I can't explain why I don't want to play anymore, even though I thought I'd be able to—singing's hard enough knowing he's not the one backing me up.

"Nothing. I don't play anything." Sweat is popping up along my hairline and the dizziness has returned. I get up and rush to the bathroom.

And I throw up.

No way can I be friends with Bo. What I felt when he was singing was far from friendship. *It's not his fault,* I think between heaves on the cold floor. He seems to really be trying to maintain a pleasant atmosphere, since apparently, we're going to be seeing a lot of each other. I lean back against the stall door, contemplating making Lost Dog my new hang out, when the bathroom door opens.

"Ember?" Rachel speaks quietly as she knocks on my stall.

This is mortifying.

I wipe tears and saliva from my face as I stand to open the door.

"Sorry." I sneak past her and head for the sink in an attempt to clean up my streaked and splotchy face. "I just had a lot of emotions churn through me in the last half hour. They asked to be deposited there." I chuckle as I point to the toilet.

Rae doesn't smile. Instead, she comes up behind me and wraps an arm around my waist. "It's hard for him, too, you know. He was a mess the whole ride down. I'm surprised he didn't pull over to throw up himself." She takes a deep breath and meets my gaze through the mirror before she continues, "This is the only time I'm going to say this because I care about you too much as a friend to push it, but, he loves you, Ember. It's not going to stop anytime soon, no matter what I say to him, or how you act. I think you love him, too, though I'd never tell him that. He's willing to be your friend if that's what it takes to stay in your life. Let him be your friend."

"I really do love you, you know that, Rae? I can try, for

you and for *now*, to be his friend—a thoroughly embarrassed friend at the moment, but a friend. If it gets too weird, I'll need a new plan." I swish some water around my mouth, ignoring her assumption that I love her brother, and spit my anxiety into the sink.

We walk casually back to the table where I place my hand on Regan's.

"Sorry, Regan. What I meant to say is I don't *really* play anything. I know one song on the guitar and a few chords. Josh is going to help me learn." Out of the corner of my eye I see Bo's eyebrows twitch when I mention Josh.

You might be my friend, dude, but I can't let you teach me how to play the guitar. I still have boundaries.

"That's great. Hey, you guys should come down next week to see us play. I know it's a haul, but we've got something good brewing." Regan is all smiles as he brags us up.

For the rest of the evening, I'm able to smile and nod in the right places, maintaining appropriate eye contact, even with Bo. I don't know why it's so hard for me to wrap my mind and soul around being his friend. It seems truly absurd, on one hand. But, on the other, maybe being friends is what we should have been all along, before "I love you" and "a thousand lifetimes" and everything else pushed us into a box that we couldn't fit in. Something doesn't sit right with my insides about being his friend, even though it's the smart choice. I want Rachel in my life, period, and they're a packaged deal. I need to learn to play nice. And fair.

We all head out to the parking lot to say our goodbyes. I tell Rae I'll see her on Wednesday, smile and wave at Bo, and head to my car as Regan gives Rae his phone number.

"November?" I knew he was following me as soon as I walked away from Rae's car.

"Yeah?" I unlock my door, open it, and step behind it, begging the steel to barricade my hormones and emotions.

Bo tucks his hands into his pockets, leaning against the car behind him. "I'm sorry if I made things awkward tonight. This is your town, your bar...I don't want you to feel out of place because of me."

"It wasn't you. I didn't mean for you to feel that way. I just didn't realize how strange it would seem to try to slide back into a regular routine." I laugh. "Though, I guess we weren't really "routine" from the get go, were we?"

He laughs and crosses his arms in front of him. "No, we weren't. So, we're good?"

I nod. "We're good. I'll see you Wednesday. Oh, by the way, Regan seems like a good guy, so don't freak that he gave Rae his number, OK?"

"I'll try to keep that in mind. Night, Em." He walks casually back to his car, gets in, and drives away.

Em. Well, that's what your friends call you…

My car seems to drive itself home, and within a few minutes, I'm in my own bed for the first time in several days. I toss and turn over the last forty-eight hours. Last night with Adrian was incredible on a number of levels. I find myself excited for the next time I can see him, while my phone dings twice with text messages.

Adrian: Hope tonight went well. Call me in the AM. xo

Rae: I had a great time tonight. Thank you for trying. Regan's hot, so thanks for that. Xo

What a fucking mess…

Chapter 13

The splitting headache that accompanies sunrise has nothing to do with liquor. Last night was a disaster. Rae knows I'm having a hard time handling being Bo's friend. I don't think she'll say anything to him, but it's still disconcerting. The only bright light from last night came in the form of the phone call from Monica, telling me that she and Josh got engaged. I smile at the thought of their life together, and the headache slips slowly away. My phone rings, and my smile widens as Adrian's name graces the screen.

"Hey you, it's early." I yawn.

"Morning, Gorgeous. It felt weird not waking up next to you this morning. How'd last night go?"

I sigh loudly. "God, it was a mess. Rae was there, and we had a nice time. But, Bo wants to be friends."

"Yeah, you told me that before. What's the problem?"

"Ha! Adrian, come on. You and I didn't speak for five years and you're asking me what the problem is with being friends with Bo? He was perfectly nice and polite, but it felt so wrong. And, it feels even more wrong talking about it with you. What has my love life become?" I bury my face into my pillow and suppress a giggle.

"Ah ha! I'm in your love life now, am I?" Adrian teases.

"Yeah," I sigh again, "you absolutely are. Anyway, guess what? Monica and Josh got engaged last night."

"Awesome, good for them."

"I know. I can't wait to help her plan. I'm going to throw them an engagement party at the end of the summer—a clam bake, I think."

"Sounds great." Adrian's tone turns seductive, "When can I see your beautiful face again?"

"I can't really get away much since my time is basically spent between here and Concord. I can come to your place on Friday again; only, I'll have to address this situation with Monica. Hopefully, my schedule opens up more when the new DROP center opens by the end of the summer. Shit, Monica's calling. I'll call you later, K?"

"I can't wait until Friday. I'll look at my schedule and call you later about when I can come to town—Monday or Tuesday. Bye."

Grinning with satisfaction, I click over to Monica.

"Hey lady, it's early. Shouldn't you be busy making sweet engaged love or something?" I giggle.

"We've got that covered, don't you worry. I was calling to hear about last night, seeing Bo play. You sounded stressed right out when I called last night." Monica's tone is full of concern. She can't even bask in the wild love of her engagement without checking up on me.

"I threw up."

"You *threw up?*"

"Yes, I threw up. When I got off the phone with you, I was sitting with Bo, Rae, and Regan. Bo was playing *friends* perfectly. I got all sweaty, ran in the bathroom, and threw up." I shake my head at the recollection.

"Shit, that sucks. I'm really sorry."

"Oh, no, that's not the best part."

"I figured as much with you." I can almost hear Monica rolling her eyes.

"When I was done throwing up, Rae came in, hugged me, and told me to try to be Bo's friend. She said he fucking loves me, that she thinks I love him, and said Bo will take being my friend if that means I'm still in his life."

Crickets.

"Monica?"

"I ..."

"Whatever, it's fine. I'll figure it out. Look, I really need to talk to you about something, but I want to do it in person. So hurry your happy ass over here when you get home, OK?"

"Great. I'll be over this afternoon. Love you."

"Love you too, Mon."

It's time to come clean with her about Adrian. No one else needs to know anything but, frankly, I'm going to be in deep enough water as it is for withholding our "first kiss" from her, let alone Saturday night. I can't make up excuses as to why I need to travel alone to Concord. I like my new route home too much. I stare at the phone in my hand, clenching my jaw at what I'm about to do. When I push send, it's already a bad idea, and already too late. It needs to be done, however. He can't be the one tossing balls in my court all the time.

"Hello?" His voice sounds thoroughly confused.

"Hey Bo, it's November."

"Hi." The smile in his voice pricks tiny holes in my heart. Tiny, but holes, nonetheless.

"I just wanted to apologize for getting weird last night. Rae talked some sense into me. You're lucky to have her."

"Don't worry about it—it'll take some time for us to get used to being friends." The smile sounds like it's disappeared, and his use of the word "friends" sounds as smooth coming from his lips as every other word in that sentence. It sounds like he's already gotten used to it.

"OK, so, I'll see you Wednesday. We have a few potential donors checking out the site on Thursday."

"Excellent. See you Wednesday, Ember."

Click.

My phone stares back at me with an arched eyebrow. *You agreed to be friends, what's with the sinking feeling in your gut, missus?* I slide it onto my dresser and shower in preparation for my chat with Monica later. *That should be fun.*

Bo

"Rae?" I holler upstairs from the studio.

"In the living room. Get your ass up here if you want to talk to me."

Grinning, I take the stairs two at a time. Rae's matured a lot in the last couple of years, which also means she doesn't take my shit like she used to. I turn the corner and find her washing the windows.

"What'd you and November talk about last night in the bathroom?" Folding my arms, I lean against the doorframe. Rae pauses her circular motion against the glass, in thought, before resuming her task.

"Nothing, really. Why?" She shrugs but doesn't look over her shoulder to make eye contact with me.

"Well, she just called me, and—"

"Ember just called you?" Now she makes eye contact.

I nod. "She apologized for acting strange last night but said you set her straight."

A knowing smile waltzes across Rae's lips. "I just told her you truly were interested in being friends, and she seemed to understand. What? What's with that look on your face?"

"So she thinks I want to be friends with her?" The back of my neck screams with heat. I don't *want* to be friends with her.

"You do, don't you? You can't profess your love for her every day. If she loves you the way you love her, and the way you think she loves you, it'll happen. Be friends with her and leave it alone, Bo."

"You know I'm in love with her, Rae. It drives me mad when I'm away from her, but it's almost worse when I'm with her."

Rae's eyes assess my words in the distance somewhere.

"I know you do, Bo. It kills me that this is killing you. But, the fact is, she's great for DROP, I want to be her friend, and—oh, come on!" Rae's attention refocuses outside.

"What?"

"The girl's persistent. She's got that going for her." Rae throws the roll of paper towels down and runs up the stairs, slamming her door shut. I walk to the window and see Ainsley coming up the front walk. *Great.*

I ignore my irritation at Rae for promoting my friendship with November and hurry to the door, opening it before Ainsley has the chance to ring the bell.

"Spencer! You startled me!" She smiles playfully and whips her hair over her shoulder.

She called me Spencer when we were dating in high school, as a way to assert her position on the invisible top-rung of the high school social ladder. I'm not so sure it isn't different now.

"What's up, Ainsley?" Her smile fades slowly as she must read the irritation on my face.

"I tried calling you ..."

"Sorry, my phone was on silent—I was in the studio."

"Well, I wanted to know if you wanted to have lunch." She fidgets slightly on my front steps since I haven't invited her in.

"I don't know, Ainsley ..." I drag my hand through my hair and leave it perched on the back of my neck.

"Look, Spencer, we're friends. Can't friends have lunch?"

Her intentions are muddled inside that innocent smile of hers. I can never tell what her angle is. Either way, I give in. I'm hungry.

"Sure, let me just go get my phone downstairs. I'll be right back."

As I walk outside, my phone vibrates with a text message.

Rae: Big mistake.

Shaking my head, I climb into Ainsley's car, and head out for lunch.

Ember

My nerves increase with each minute I wait for Monica.

"Knock, knock!" She exaggerates as she bursts into my apartment.

Instantly, my place feels alive with happiness and excitement. Monica wastes no time before showing me the lovely ring Josh used to ask "forever." We make our way to the couch, where I have celebratory Brie and Riesling waiting.

"It's so perfect, so you." I run my thumb across the emerald-cut solitaire. "I'm throwing you two an engagement party on Fourth of July weekend, a clam bake."

Monica's smile is even bigger than before. "You're amazing! A perfect Maid of Honor."

"What?" I scream.

"Did you think I'd choose anyone else?" We scream in unison and hug, yet again.

"So," Monica continues after our second glass of wine, "what is this nonsense that you had to discuss with me in person?" She places her elbow on the back of my couch and rests her head on her hand.

"It's Adrian ..." I start with shaky cadence.

"I knew it." Her blue eyes grow wild, a million questions and assumptions swirling behind them.

"I told you when there was something to tell, I'd tell. Last weekend, when you saw his car in front of my house, we kissed the night before—hard. It was so good, Monica, I have no words. I didn't lie to you; we didn't have sex that night."

"*That* night?"

"No. That happened on Friday...in his apartment."

"*Ember!* A, what the hell? B, how could you not tell me?" She slaps my shoulder and crosses her arms.

"I know. I know. He asked if I wanted to come by his place on Friday on my way home from Concord. It worked out well that you had to drive separately anyway. I really didn't want to make a big deal if it turned out to be nothing." I feel my cheeks reach a temperature I haven't felt in a long time.

"So ..."

I can't help the grin. "It was perfect, Monica. We had dinner, went dancing, then...you know." I shrug. "I'm telling you because you're my best friend and now that I think this is turning into something, I need you to know about it. I'm going to his place again on Friday."

"Are you going to start spending all of your time in Boston, or is Big Shot going to grace the Cape with his presence?" Her tone is playful, but I know she's serious.

"Relax, he's coming here Monday or Tuesday for dinner. He's grown up, Monica. We both have. When we were together on Friday, it was like the best parts of our past and the best parts of our present collided. We got to skip over the "get to know you" stuff and just enjoy each other." I swirl the last sip of wine around in my glass.

"Judging by the glow you've had since I got here, I'd say you aced the "enjoying each other" portion of the evening." We break into laughter; mine is relieved.

"Thanks for not being pissed, Mon. Listen, don't tell anyone about me and Adrian. By anyone, I mean Rae or Bo."

"Don't get me wrong, I'm livid; I knew there was something going on that night we met Regan. I hardly talk to Bo at work, and I'd never say anything to Rae. Your secret is safe with me until you're ready. How is he, by the way? Regan, I mean." She can't stay mad for long. Who'd be able to with a gorgeous ring like that on their hand?

"He's great. I think he likes Rae. He gave her his number."

"I'll allow it, especially considering you seem to be tied up at the moment." She arches her eyebrow, letting me know this won't be the only in-depth discussion we'll be having about Adrian.

Chapter 14

"Hey Blue." Adrian is waiting for me at my apartment when I get home from rehearsal at Finnegan's. Rehearsal went great, but my Tuesday just got a hell of a lot better.

"Hi." I waste no more words. I wrap my arms around his neck and rise to meet his mouth. My lips are hot in an instant and my hips involuntarily press him back against my door. Adrian's sex appeal is an addiction, and I'm a happy junkie.

"It's good to see you, too." He grins against my lips as I reach past him to open the door.

When we get inside, I kick off my shoes and flick on the lights. I toss my bag to the floor and turn around. "So, what do you want for dinner? I can cook or we can go out."

A wicked grin takes over his face. Without response, he lifts me off my feet and spins me around; our mouths become the epicenter of desire. As I stroke my tongue through his mouth, I'm barely cognizant of the fact that he's walking toward my bedroom. Panic blazes through me, as memories of the last man in my bedroom flicker across the vision of my closed eyes. I pull away briefly to study Adrian's face, and all anxiety subsides. This is the face of pure desire—uninhibited need.

"Five years and now I can't go three days without seeing you. Take your clothes off." Adrian's voice turns to a low growl as he nudges me onto my bed.

My eyes widen to distract from my shocked grin as I surrender to his command. *Who wouldn't? Look at him.* Adrian's grey pants crumple at his feet as I toss my jeans and panties to the floor. I lean back onto my elbows and inch my way to the top of the bed as a naked and needy Adrian crawls after me.

"Your bra's still on." His hands shake as they work their way up my legs ahead of the rest of him.

"I thought you might want a challenge." In a second, his hand is around my back and my bra is unclasped. "Right," I tease, "I should have known." My smile disappears as all moisture leaves my mouth and travels south.

"What?" Adrian hums as he brushes my hair aside and has his way with my neck.

"Condoms are over there." I point to my bedside stand.

"Still against the pill, huh?" He chuckles.

"Some things *don't* change, you know."

"I know," he pulls a condom out of the drawer and rolls it on, "like how fucking hot you make me when you arch your eyebrow. It's like you're begging me to test you."

"Test me?" This is a rather ridiculous position to be having this conversation in.

"Yeah," he breathes onto my hard nipples before slowly circling his tongue around each one, "it's like you're waiting to see if I'll screw it up again, or what my angle is."

I bite my lip and shift underneath him. "Maybe ..." I admit, pushing on his shoulders while he kisses down my stomach.

"My angle is you, Blue. I just want you. My *God*, you're gorgeous."

It's hard for me to form a rebuttal while his tongue strokes me into oblivion.

"Adrian ..." My knees shake as my thighs tighten around his head.

Turning his head to the side, he kisses my thigh, releasing its vice around him. His eyes lock with mine. Rocking back slightly, he grabs my foot, and gently glides it up onto his shoulder as he leans over me.

"Go slow," I whisper as I anticipate the intensity of what's about to happen.

Thankfully, he indulges my request and leaves my leg resting on my shoulder while he places his hands on either side of my shoulders.

"Damn, I love how much you want me." He moans as he easily slides inside me.

He pulls out slowly and reenters just as gently, before picking up speed. Gripping my sheets and arching my back in response, I anchor myself on the one foot still on the bed. My neighbors slip into the periphery of my discretion as I groan each time he drives into me, louder and faster. I release my sheets and press my hands into my headboard behind me.

"I'm so close, Adrian...don't stop ..." Ragged breaths stutter my plea.

"Oh my God, November, you're so fucking hot."

His admiration is my undoing and my legs go limp as I wail his name into the ocean breeze blowing through my room. Adrian collapses on top of me in a sweaty thud a few seconds later, and my leg rolls drunkenly off his shoulder.

"November," he pants with his chin on my chest, eyes locked on mine, "that was the best fucking sex I've *ever* had."

Before I can answer, my phone rings. I grab Adrian's watch and laugh at the fact we've only been in my apartment for a half hour, though it's felt like a day.

"By the way, I love that you wear a watch," I tease as I answer the phone.

"What's up, Mon?" I yawn.

"Josh and the guys want to know if you can come back down here. They haven't left yet and got some idea for a song." She sounds bored.

"Yeah, I'll be there in a few." I click "End" and stretch out across my mattress.

"Where you going?" Adrian asks.

"The guys want me to go back down to Finnegan's to try something out for our set this weekend. This is our last time to practice till then. Wanna come?" I slide back into my clothes and pull my sex-hair into an overly messy bun.

"Sure. I love when you do that to your hair. What's that?" Adrian kisses me once before getting dressed, nodding to the composition notebook I've picked up.

"My music comp notebook for lyrics, notes, whatever." I shrug.

"Isn't that the one Cavanaugh gave you?"

"Yeah, it's my only one. Wait, does that bother you?" I watch a crease form between his eyebrows.

"No, but I figured it would bother *you*." I don't think I believe him as I watch his eyes search for anything else to focus on.

"I haven't had a chance to get to a good music store. I'll get one Saturday morning in Boston before I head back here." I throw the notebook in my messenger bag and head for the door, ignoring the screams from my heart to hold on. *Hold on? To what?*

We can't escape Monica's almost-glare as we walk into Finnegan's five minutes later.

"What's up, guys? Where's C.J.?" I ask as I head directly for the stage.

"We just wanted to try this fiddled-up version of "Foolish Games" by Jewel." There's no percussion in that song," Josh says as he hands me a sheet with lyrics on it. I stop him.

"I know the words, Josh." I chuckle. "All girls know the words to this song."

"All right," Regan chimes in, "here we go ..."

He slides the bow across his fiddle slowly, creating a chilling intro that sends goosebumps down my spine. Josh's fingers strum notes on the guitar where a piano is in the original version. Monica ignores Adrian as he sits next to her, and I ignore both of them as I perch on the stool—giving myself over to the song.

I open my throat as wide as possible to keep up with Regan's fiddling and Jewel's intentions for the song. It feels good, until we near the end. Josh, Regan, and I seem to intuitively slow down in time over these words and I close my eyes as tight as they'll go.

I sing the last three words of the second verse extra slow, and take a deep breath at the end; the guys do too. The silence feels longer in my head, I'm sure. I force my throat to reopen, and I finish the song with my eyes still closed.

"Jesus Christ, Ember, that was awesome." Josh stares at me slack-jawed as Regan nods.

"Yeah, November, you were meant to sing with a fiddle." Regan squeezes my shoulder and puts his fiddle in the case.

I can't bring myself to look up. I can't look at Monica. I'm sure she knows what I was thinking—what I was feeling.

"Ember, I gotta take this call outside, K?" Adrian holds up his phone and I nod, returning my gaze to the floor.

"You don't sing for him." Regan blurts out as Adrian leaves the bar.

"What? Who?" I ask, startled back to the present.

He lifts his chin to the door. "Your boyfriend."

"Adrian's not my boyfriend." I slide off the stool and square off to Regan.

"Whatever. Either way, you don't sing for him. If you did, your eyes wouldn't have been closed the entire time." He walks over to me and taps my forehead with his index finger. "Who you singing for, Beautiful?"

"Me." I shrug as I feel heat betray my face.

"Ha! OK. Whatever you say. Just don't stop singing for "you" then, OK? That was perfection." He walks his suddenly cocky self over to the bar and pours himself a beer.

I look to Josh. It's my turn to look shocked. "Did you hear that?" I ask incredulously.

Josh shrugs and puts his guitar in its case, seeming to have gone mute. I turn to Monica who holds up her hands in defense.

"I'm not getting into this with you, Harris. I heard what he said, and I agree with him." She tilts her head to the side, daring me to challenge her. Challenge accepted.

"You *agree* with him? About what, exactly?" I hop off the stage.

"The look on your face, that was all Bo. You forget, I've seen you with him more than anyone here, but Regan picked up on it after one song." Her face doesn't even get red. She's confident and unwavering.

"So you think I'm still singing for someone who broke my heart?" My volume increases, causing the guys to turn toward us.

"Oh for the love of *God*, Ember, would you listen to yourself? Bo was in a mess of shit, and all you can think about is how it made *you* feel." Here it is, the first time Monica and I are talking about what happened in Concord.

"Jesus, Mon, go ahead—tell me how you really feel." I put my hands on my hips, waiting for her response as Adrian reenters the bar.

"You want to know how I really feel? I'll tell you. I think you made a huge mistake when you walked out on him in Concord, and you're making a bigger mistake now." She points at Adrian without making eye contact with him.

My chest heaves under my anger. Adrian's eyes volley between us in silence. I stare through Monica as I address her and our friends.

"I'm done here. Let's go, Adrian."

Regan and Josh stand bug-eyed and silent as I brush past Monica and lead Adrian out of the bar.

"What was that all about?" Adrian asks as we get to my car.

"Monica's a bitch, that's what *that* was about," I huff.

"Is it because of me? Did you tell her?"

Before I can answer, Regan hollers after me.

"November, wait!" I roll my eyes as Adrian gets in the car. "What's up, Regan?"

"I'm sorry if I pissed you off back there, I—" I cut him off to spare him the torture creeping across his face.

"It wasn't you. It was Monica. She's engaged and suddenly becomes an expert on relationships. I've got a killer rest of the week ahead in Concord, so I've gotta get going. I'll be back Saturday, OK?"

His shoulders relax to their normal position and he smiles in relief. "OK. Hey, I've been texting Rae." His smile changes to one of endearment. "We want to hit up Coldplay's concert on Thursday in New Hampshire. You want in?"

"Hell yes! I've wanted to see them forever! And, any excuse to hang out with Rae is OK by me. Thanks Reagan, see you Thursday." I forget my anger at Monica for the moment as Regan and I say goodbye and I get in the car.

"You're in a better mood." Adrian's voice is tight as I start the engine.

"Regan has the hots for Rae," I giggle. "They're going to a Coldplay concert on Thursday, and he asked if I wanted to go. I'm psyched!"

"Who else is going?" His tone borders on accusatory, but I ignore it and shrug.

"I didn't even think to ask."

Chapter 15

Monica and I have made up by Thursday. She apologized for getting in my face in front of everyone, though she didn't apologize for what she said. A silent understanding has partitioned us at the moment. She disagrees about Adrian, how I handled Bo, and how I'm currently handling Bo. And I disagree with *her*. I've stepped into maid-of-honor duties and have planned their engagement party for Fourth of July weekend—just two weeks away. Despite our standoff about my love life, I can be fully supportive of hers.

"Was Adrian upset about the concert tonight?" Monica asks, as we enjoy lunch outside in the grass.

"Upset about what?" I scoff.

"Doesn't he know Bo's going?"

I didn't even know Bo was going until yesterday afternoon, when Rae was trying to find a "sixth" person to go. I'd asked if there was a ticket for Monica. She couldn't look me in the eyes when she told me Bo was the fifth.

"He didn't ask, I didn't tell, it doesn't matter. We're not in a relationship, Monica."

"For fuck's sake, Ember, when will you realize that you and Adrian Turner *cannot* do the "we're not really in a relationship" thing?"

In my head, I disagree. We're different people than we were when we first met seven years ago. Our needs are different. My needs are different. As we chew in silence, I catch Bo walking toward us out of the corner of my eye—with *that* smile.

"Hey Bo." I smile between sips of my Fiji water. It's not getting easier—saying his name or being around him—but I've become one hell of an actress.

"Hello, ladies." He sits down across from Monica and me, stretching his legs and messing a hand through his charcoal hair before leaning back.

Damn. Why. Why is he so hot? All. The. Time.

With her impeccable timing, Ainsley Worthington and her strawberry blonde hair interrupt what would have been a rather pleasant lunch. Her heels clack through the parking lot, and Bo rolls his eyes before she's close enough to see.

"Hey Spencer!" I swear she cheers just to piss me off. And, hearing her call him Spencer makes me want to throw up.

"Hi Ains." *Ains?* I see Monica's eyebrows lift as Bo uses a nickname for her. He barely turns his head toward her, but that makes her walk all the way over to us.

Shit.

"Well, I know how much you liked the steak salad when we went to lunch the other day, so I thought I'd bring one by for you." She holds out a brown paper bag and makes deliberate eye contact with me.

Time freezes in my head but seems to continue outside, as Bo and Ainsley engage in some sort of exchange. I turn to Monica in the slowest motion known to man. She just shakes her head and shrugs. *Because you're friends, remember?* The idea of Ainsley and Bo having lunch together overrides any rationale clinging to life in my brain. I stand up and brush myself off.

"If you guys will excuse me, I have to get back to work. Bo, stop by my office later so we can talk about when we're leaving for the concert." I turn for the building and catch Bo biting a smile away from his lower lip, as Ainsley's face goes flush. I can't deny that it felt good to make her jealous, but I'll try.

* * *

I've successfully avoided everyone for the rest of the afternoon by keeping myself busy with phone conferences. An hour before we're supposed to leave for the concert, Monica walks into my office.

"Good news, Josh got the night off, so he's our sixth. Can I borrow your red lipstick?" She pulls a mirror out of her purse and smacks her lips together.

"Sure. Are we getting ready here or at the hotel?" I ask, as I reach for my lipstick.

"Like hell! You guys are coming to my house!" Rachel bounces in with Regan right behind her.

Would it be weird if I just stayed here? I haven't been back to the Cavanaugh estate. The thought of crossing that threshold again makes me dizzy.

"Well then, let's get out of here so we can pretty ourselves up for Chris Martin. Josh will meet us at the concert." Monica slings her bag over her shoulder, says "hi" to Regan, and heads to the parking lot.

We follow her down the hallway and into the sweet release of fresh air.

"You feeling all right, Ember? You look a little pale." Regan breaks my reminiscent gaze into nowhere.

"What? Oh, sorry, yeah, I'm fine. Just tired—guess I should go get some coffee before we head to the concert." I chuckle as I stretch my hands over my head.

Although we've only known each other a short time, Regan has clearly tuned into me. Under ordinary circumstances, I'd like to think he'd be my best friend—I can feel that connection. He's dating my ex-boyfriend's sister, however, and seems to see my heart beating through my shirt whenever Bo's around. His head nods in understanding, while his eyes give away his doubt. Before Regan can call me out, Bo walks over from his car.

"Ready, Rae? Hey Regan, how's it goin', man?" Regan and Bo slap each other's hands.

"Yeah, Josh is meeting us there, and Regan can come with us. We're all heading to the house so the girls can get ready." Rae smiles and Bo's eyes immediately shoot to mine...as do Regan's.

"I'm ready." I force a smile while Bo and Rae head to his car, but Regan chooses to stick around and stare at me. "What?" I ask of Regan incredulously, bugging my eyes for effect.

He shakes his head and puts his arm around my shoulders with a chuckle. "Ah, Rapunzel," he teases, "I'm guessing this is going to be an interesting night."

"Oh, fuck entirely off, Regan." I laugh and slide into Monica's car.

When I close the door, I have to deal with Monica's face.

"What now? Why can't anyone leave me alone today?" I start in.

"You know *what now*. What the hell was that earlier today with Ainsley? You do realize you showed Bo that you still care about him by pointing out your plans tonight in front of her, right?"

I was so ticked off by Ainsley's presence, and her assertion in front of me that they'd had lunch together, that I didn't consider Bo's reaction to what I said.

"Whatever, just friggen drive." I motion to Bo's car that's pulled out ahead of us.

"You need to get your shit together, sister. You're skinny as hell, even Josh has noticed. Plus you're having sex all the live-long day with Adrian, oh, and you're in love with Bo."

I bite my lip in an attempt to fight the anger brewing inside. I fail.

"Here we go! Do you remember when we got loaded at Lost Dog? Before *that* was when you told me to "figure it out" with Adrian, or whatever you said. Well, I'm figuring it out, so leave it the hell alone, Monica."

"Oh, shut the hell up, like you do anything anyone tells you to do anyway. I could have told you to go after Bo that night, and you wouldn't have done it just to spite me. Don't use me as an excuse for your 'issues.'" She puts air quotes around 'issues' and I kind of want to punch her in the face.

"Shit," she continues, "I lost them."

"Turn left up here." I motion with my hand.

After I guide Monica to the private road, I watch her eyes widen to the same gauge mine must have the first time I came to this gate.

"Yeah, I know. He left it open. Just drive through, he'll close it from the house."

"You weren't kidding ..." Monica recalls the phone call we had when I was in Bo's bedroom after I met Rachel.

When the house comes into view, my wires and signals have become so crossed, they pack up and head home for the evening. I can no longer run on instinct or what I think I should be doing, I have to force myself through the motions and just get to the concert.

Chapter 16

When we're secured in the massive foyer, Rachel and Monica head upstairs, while Bo takes Regan to the studio.

I call after Rae and Monica, "I'll be up in a minute, guys. I want to see Regan's face when he sees the studio." Ignoring *their* faces, I follow the guys downstairs.

When I get to the studio, Bo has Regan in the control room. The last time I was in this room, Bo played the song he'd written for his parents. I glance at the piano, but there's no music there.

"Ember," Regan speaks through the mic, "why don't you show Bo that song Josh was helping you with. Bo, she can use your guitar, right?"

"That won't be necessary," I hold up my hands, "I haven't practiced it much—"

Regan cuts me off, "It's *good*, Ember."

"I'd like to hear it," Bo clears his throat. "Guitar's over there."

Come on!

Bo nods toward his guitar, and I nervously walk over and pick it up. Josh has helped me tinker with the lullaby that Bo worked on...for me. We're working on a second verse. I'm scared shitless to play it right now, but decide quickly that I need to. It's my song, damn it.

I look into Bo's eyes as I start strumming, and watch his lips part as he takes a seemingly shocked breath. The first part of the verse is a carry-over of something Bo had written, and a small grin pulls at the corners of his mouth as I nail it. I look to the floor as a tougher part approaches, and I stumble over it. Twice.

Great. Shit.

When I look up, I see Bo walking toward me. His brow is slightly furrowed but he still has the cautious grin on his face.

"That kind of chord transition is tricky. Good, but tricky. You're over thinking it— I can see it on your face. Try this." Bo moves to my side and places his left hand over mine. "See, normally you'd want to use this finger for the chord, but in order to accomplish that transition, it's OK to use this finger here." I go numb as he effortlessly moves my fingers around the strings.

My heartbeat pounds through my lips. I look at Regan, who is staring back at me with intensity. With my pulse increasing, I audibly inhale to try to slow it down.

Bo looks at me out of the corner of his eye and suddenly pulls his hands away. "Try that."

Despite the way he smells and how his hands felt against mine, I'm able to play. I flawlessly pull off the chord transition that's tripped me up for a week straight.

Regan hoots from behind the glass, "Yes! Perfect!"

"Thank you," I whisper as I slide the strap over my head. "I've gotta get up to the girls."

His hand slips over mine as he takes his guitar back. "Any time." The smile's gone.

I force a smile and race out of the studio and up two flights of stairs to reach Rae's room.

"Ember, I'm sorry," Rae says as if she didn't notice my eight-minute absence. "I didn't think about how this might be weird for you ...getting ready here." She stares into herself while she pumps mascara over her already impossibly long eyelashes.

"Oh, sure you did, Rae, don't protect her. She's being an ass." Monica glides gloss over her pouty lips, nearly cheek-to-cheek with Rae.

A bad taste infiltrates my mouth.

"What the fuck, Monica?" Between whatever the hell just happened in the studio, and her bad attitude, I've about had it with her shit.

Rae looks between Monica and me through the mirror.

"You're in love with him, Ember. The past few weeks have only made that more clear. Your face lights up whenever he walks in a room and falls when he's not in the room you thought he'd be. The reason why it was so hot and heavy at the beginning is because it is the *real* deal. Nothing you do with Adrian Turner is going to change that." Her betrayal is instantly evident to her as her cheeks redden deeper than the blush she started applying.

Rae swallows hard, forces the most uncomfortable smile I've ever seen, and heads into her room.

"Thanks a lot, Mon," I huff as I turn to follow Rae.

I find Rae shoving hangers from left to right in her closet, seemingly without purpose.

"Rae ...what Monica said about Adrian ..." I sit on the edge of her bed.

"No, Ember, it's fine. I saw you two holding hands after our first meeting, and I didn't think it was anything. I didn't think you'd move on—" She cuts herself off, shrugs and turns toward me with glistening eyes. My stomach slides away. "I've seen it too, you know. The past few weeks, the way your face changes when Bowan's around. It gave me hope, I guess."

I find myself scanning every conversation Bo and I have had with an audience. We've been professional, but that doesn't mean eyes and smiles cooperate.

"It's not about moving on, Rae." *Why am I defending myself here?* "Shit, you know, maybe I should just go home—I can pay you for my ticket."

"That's bullshit, November, don't do that. I know Bo hurt you. I was just hoping that by now he would have proven that he didn't mean to." She sniffs and slides a teal spaghetti-strapped dress over her tiny frame.

"I know he didn't *mean* to, Rae...and the stuff with Adrian —Monica doesn't even know what she's talking about. Please don't say anything." I rub my damp palms along the edge of her comforter.

Can this get any worse?

Rae sits next to me with her hands between her knees. "I won't say anything to Bo. Just...please don't lead him on, OK? He's in love with you, and if you give him even a sliver of hope that gets destroyed, he'll be crushed." She's not looking at me; she's talking to her closet.

Yes, this is much worse.

"I haven't meant to lead him—"

"I know you haven't. I'm not saying you have, but cut the bullshit banter with Ainsley, OK? It only fuels her fire, and gives Bo a reason to think ..." She shakes her head and looks at her hands.

"I'm sorry, Rae."

"I love you, November. You know that? For me, you're like a sister and that won't change. But you were the best thing that happened to Bo, and I don't care what anyone says about how fast, crazy, and reckless it was. It was you two. It was your story, no one else's."

I pull her into a tight hug, fighting tears for something I can't identify. I'm upset that Rae is hurting over me and Bo, my best friend isn't on my side, and a gorgeous fiddle player I barely know senses the screwed-up war raging inside me. I haven't let myself fully reassess my true feelings for Bo since I left Adrian's hotel room *that night,* and right now is not the time to start. I've been proud of how we've handled our working situation, but it seems like that isn't working for more than one person involved. Before I can give it any more thought, Monica comes in holding my ringing phone.

"It's Adrian," she says dismissively.

Caller ID, you traitorous bitch.

I grab my phone and answer, while I head down the stairs and outside.

"Hey you, what's up?"

"Not much, babe, haven't heard from you since Tuesday night." His voice tenses my insides.

"Adrian, I'm so sorry. This week I had like eight hundred teleconferences, and we've got the concert tonight—"

"Who's going?" I hear him swallow what I can only assume is beer, based on his cool tone.

I clear the shakes from my throat. "Um, me, Monica, Josh, Bo, Regan, and Rachel."

Silence.

"Adrian? Is that a problem? I can ditch and come see you."

Did I just say that?

"Nah, it's cool, Blue. Just do you, remember? I know who you're coming to tomorrow." The cocky smile is evident over the phone and makes me simultaneously roll my eyes and smile.

"I'll talk to you later. I miss you." *I really do.*

As soon as I hang up, I hear footsteps behind me on the porch.

"Ready? Who was that?" Bo asks as he snaps a leather cuff around his wrist.

"Just my parents. Oh my God, listen to this." I get closer and lower my voice, telling him about them going to San Diego to hit the studio again.

"That's awesome, November! I can't wait to hear their new stuff." He really can't.

I roll my eyes and chuckle. "We'll see ..."

"Oh stop, they're great and you know it." He playfully taps my shoulder, and for the first time since I walked blindly away from him, *I feel it.*

With closed eyes, I dip my ear to my shoulder and take a slow breath. In the span of a second, the front door opens and Bo shoves his hand into his pocket as our friends gather on the porch.

"All right, guys," Monica starts, "we can all fit into my car since Josh is meeting us there."

Bo rubs the back of his neck, leaving his hand in place. "Actually, I'm gonna take my car, too. Ember, will you ride with me?" Everyone turns to stare at me.

Oh for fuck's sake. Are we seventeen? Seriously? Breathe. Get your shit together, Harris.

"Sure, let's go." I head for Bo's car, pushed forward by the collective breath everyone was holding.

Chapter 17

When we exit the driveway, Bo turns the music down. *Please, not now.*

"I wanted to get you alone for a few minutes." He rubs his hand on the top of his thigh.

"Why?" Cursing the late summer sunset, I attempt to cover my red cheeks by looking out the window.

"You love Coldplay. I don't want tonight to be ruined for you. We don't have to sit next to each other." He glances my way as I mentally scan the group. *Crap.*

"Like that wouldn't be obvious." I chuckle. "Two couples book-ended by us."

"Are Regan and Rae a couple?" Bo turns to me in complete seriousness.

"Take it easy, you know what I mean." I wave my hand.

A few minutes later, I realize neither one of us has turned the music back up. Bo sees me eye the dials and reaches for the volume. I block him with my hand, and a zap of static electricity causes both of us to chuckle uneasily. I clear my throat.

"Listen. I need to tell you something." *Just say it.* "I know you didn't *mean* to hurt me." I take a deep breath, swallow a three-ton boulder, and continue, "I just, um, it was a lot all at once. You, me, the music, the perfection of it all. I felt like someone shot me from a catapult, and I was flying through the air with flailing arms and legs."

"Were you looking for an out?" Bo doesn't remove his eyes from the road. His jaw punches the skin on his cheek.

"What?"

"Were you looking for an out? Did what happened at McCarthy's give you the excuse to run from our intensity that you were looking for?"

I stare at Bo, waiting for him to exhale, to tell me he was kidding, that he understands why I ran. *Do you understand why you ran?* He doesn't say a word. We pull into the parking lot of the concert hall with the heavy, unanswered question leaving me to wonder if my fight-or-flight mechanism is faulty. Bo puts the car in park and gets out without a word, slamming the door behind him. When I walk up to the group, it seems Bo's face has spoken for both of us. No one says anything, except Monica; but she at least waits until she can pull me aside.

"What the hell happened in the car?" She whispers with all the concern she's been lacking over the past few weeks.

"I was honest. I told him I knew he didn't mean to hurt me; that everything with us moved really fast. He asked if I used Bill and Tristan as an excuse to bail." I hand my ticket to the person at the gate.

"Christ, what'd you tell him?"

"I didn't answer."

Monica stops in her tracks, shakes her head, and links arms with Josh. As promised, when we reach our seats, Bo and I take the last two. I opt for the very end, so I don't have to deal with people I know on *both* sides of me.

* * *

Coldplay has me completely hypnotized. My eyes haven't moved from the stage throughout the entire concert. My mind, body, and soul are more than thankful for the musical reprieve, prompting a momentary cease-fire between them. I peek at my cell phone and realize they probably only have two songs left in their set, when they start playing "Trouble."

I listened to this song on repeat, all girl-like, for a week after Bo and I broke up. I don't know if I pretended it was for me or him; either way, the notes lean me back in my seat and sink my shoulders. I cast my gaze to the floor as the opening line suggests I may have "lost my head." *Or was it Bo that lost his?* Bo shifts in his seat and his arm presses into my shoulder; he doesn't move it. Biting my lip, I glance up at him, only to find him staring at me with a furrowed brow.

"Come with me." He nods his head and crosses in front of me, exiting to the aisle.

Rae is sitting in the seat next to his and shrugs before mouthing *go*. I oblige. When I get into the mezzanine, Bo is a good distance ahead of me.

"Hey wait up!" I shout, slowing his pace. "What the hell?" I ask as I shoulder up next to him.

"I want to show you something. I know you're slammed with more meetings tomorrow and we won't have time . . ."

"You're taking me out of a Coldplay concert to *show me something?*" I stop and put my hands on my hips.

"Stop standing there and follow me." He rakes his hand through his hair, as he always does when he's nervous, and opens the door for me.

Silence mocks us on the walk to the car and on the drive to wherever we're going, despite the dings of incoming text messages sounding through both of our phones. Within a few minutes, we're parked in front of the DROP community center, still under construction for the studio they're putting in.

"I want you to be the first to see the studio. It'll be finished tomorrow." While he should be smiling, he's not. He exits the car and waits for me at the center's door.

Bo unlocks the door and flicks on the lights. My eyes widen in praise as I take in my surroundings.

"Oh my *God*, Bo, this is gorgeous!" My loud whisper bounces off the walls, and all the tension I've been holding onto melts into a smile.

The center has undergone a major upgrade in the wake of putting in the studio. It's modern: computers line one wall, large work tables are pressed up against another, and plenty of tables and couches are scattered around for reading and hanging out. I look back at Bo, who has clearly let go of his tension as well. His face is proud, as it should be.

"You like it?" He holds out his hands, showcasing his dream. I've missed the playful smile dancing across his face.

"Are you shitting me? This is amazing!" I head toward the studio addition, and he follows.

"Watch your step here—they've got to fix them

tomorrow." Bo holds out his hand and leads me down the narrow stairs.

I can feel his eyes measure each careful step I take without looking up. If I look at him in this studio—*his* studio, *his* dream...I don't think my heart could take it. I spot a gorgeous piano in the corner of the room with what looks to be a Shure Series chrome microphone hanging from the ceiling above it.

"Is that mic hooked up?" I ask without releasing his hand. *What's happening?*

"Yeah, why? You want to try it out?" I think he squeezes my hand, but I can't be sure—I lost all sense of rational feeling the second he grabbed it.

"Y- yeah." I have to swallow feeling back into my throat as I tug my hand away and head for the piano.

Bo walks to the control room and plays around with a few switches as I squirm on the hard lacquered bench.

"Don't stand in there the whole time. It makes me feel weird." I giggle. "Plus, I need you to hit a "C" for me before I try this out; I have no idea which keys are which."

His heavy sigh fills the two-way speaker from the control room. Bo walks almost robotically toward me and dings the middle "C" on the piano. I hum in an attempt to tune. He strikes the key one more time. My heart is racing, but I've wanted to sing into one of these mics forever—they're simply stunning and make me feel glamorous. I fly through the song Rolodex in my brain until I settle on the only option, the most beautiful song I've ever sung before—"San Diego" by The San Diego Six, my parents' band.

"The San Diego sun setting in your eyes
The taste of salt and sweet summertime"

Even though my parents only sang with Six until I was about eight, they sang this song to each other often. It's upbeat and sweet. It sounds like sunshine. My mom always started the song, and I'd blush through the second half of the first verse.

"Days were short, but the nights were long
Crashing through waves wrapped up in your arms"

I start to hum the musical interlude when I feel Bo sit next to me. In an instant, the piano sings the part my father wrote for guitar in this song. *Holy shit.* This song is on the album Bo has in his studio. My mouth runs dry, and for a second, I forget the words to the next verse as my heart takes over all noise in my head. I clear my throat to reach for my dad's part in the song, but Bo beats me to it,

"Oh sweet mama don't make me go
Take my hand, mmm don't say no
Dancin' through San Diego with you
That's where I want to go
Mmm I say dancin' through San Diego with you
That's where I want to go"

My cheeks burn as I turn to watch Bo sing the chorus of my parents' song without any help from me. I've been rendered speechless. His fingers skate across the keys, and his eyes are closed so tightly his lashes have disappeared. All levity has left me as I lean forward to stand and walk away from the piano. Bo stops playing when he feels me shift.

"Ember, stop." He grabs my wrist and pulls my arm toward him. I meet his eyes and see them catch fire as they look me over. Goosebumps form on my skin under his watchfulness.

Neither one of us says anything for what feels like a Thousand. Damn. Lifetimes. I wriggle my wrist out of his grip and slide off the piano bench. Bo drives his fist across the keys and the raucous clamor of notes makes me jump.

"Damn it, Ember, what the hell?" He leaps to face me and we're standing toe-to-toe, my chin lifted to meet his eyes.

"Me, what the hell? *You,* what the hell. You take me out of a concert to bring me to a studio, and then you play and sing along with me to *my parents'* song?" I'm yelling and I don't care.

"No, *you*, what the hell." He points his finger in my face. "You bait Ainsley at lunch, don't let go of my hand when we walk in here, and *then* you want to *sing* in here? We haven't spoken more than a few words at a time to each other in the last few weeks, and you start singing in my studio like nothing's wrong." He lowers his hand to his hip and takes a massive breath.

"What do you mean like nothing's wrong? What the fuck is wrong here?"

"Everything is *fucking* wrong here, November. I'm in *love* with you. I'm absolutely crazy about you, and you dance around my organization like walking away from us was the easiest thing you've ever done." His face darkens under his true thoughts about my actions.

"The easiest thing I've ever done? I did nothing but cry

and scream for a damn week after I left here. You didn't even try to call me, Bo! You didn't even try ..." My voice breaks into traitorous tears as I recall the heartbreak I felt when he didn't come after me. He left me alone. *Just like I asked.*

"Don't pull those tears on me now. You've got to be kidding me. I was on my damn knees in your *ex-boyfriend's* hotel room begging you to listen to me, and you expect me to chase you after he had to drive me home? How self-righteous do you intend to be, exactly?"

His words punch holes in my heart, and, I admit, my ego. I brush past him and head for the stairs, my vision blurred with angry, defeated tears. I make it one step past Bo before he grabs my arm, spinning me to face him.

"What?" I demand, trying to regain control of my arm.

"You love me, November. I know you do. I see it on your face and feel it from you whenever we're together. Why won't you let yourself be happy with me? What the hell is the problem?" His nostrils flare.

"I ..."

"I can't take this anymore," is all he says before grabbing my face and crushing his lips into mine.

Surprise jumps from my throat as I tighten my hands around his wrists, trying to pull his hands away from my face. He only pulls harder, burying his lips deep into mine—opening my mouth is my only relief from his pressure. His tongue feverishly searches mine, desperation seeping from each taste bud.

Fresh tears signal surrender as I relax into his body and snake my hands through his hair. A flip book of every passionate moment we experienced together flickers through my brain as his hands drag down my sides. His teeth tug on my lower lip before he dives back in, making my mouth his through pleading moans. Tightening my hands through his hair, I press my hipbones into his pockets. My heart beats through my lips, and I'm forced to pull away to catch my breath.

The previously silent studio records our erratic breathing. We stare into each other, holding each other, willing each other to say something. Bo's eyes are dark with an intensity I've never seen. He's still holding my face. I grab his wrists one more time, and he lowers his hands with mine. Adrenaline gushes through me, and I'm forced with a decision I don't take long to make. I step back and cock my head.

"*I'm* the self-righteous one?" I clench my teeth in an attempt to calm my quivering chin.

"Excuse me?" Bo cocks his head back and considers my half question.

"No one has *ever* spoken to me that way. You're an asshole." I turn and place my foot on the first stair to head out of the studio.

"I won't chase you forever, you know. I really can't do this to myself for much longer." He looks worn out and my chest tightens under the realization of what I've been putting him through, what we've been putting each other through.

"We can't be friends." I frown and head carefully up the stairs. When the studio door closes behind me, I hear him bang both fists on the piano. I reach for my cell and Monica picks up within the first ring.

"Look, we'll talk about it later. Can you pick me up at DROP?"

Chapter 18
Bo

"Dammit!" I growl as my front door slams behind me.

A few minutes after Ember left, I walked out of the center to an empty sidewalk. I called and texted to see if she was OK, but of course she didn't respond. I finally received a text from Monica saying, "Everything's fine."

No, it's not.

I know Monica's on my side, but I also know I'm missing something. Something is holding November back from me, and it's not just work.

Rae's not home, so I tear downstairs to the studio, grabbing my bottle of Jack as I pass through the dining room. Damn, her kiss tasted better than ever—I couldn't stop myself. I had to know her heart still belonged to me, and that kiss proved it still does. *Shit*. Whiskey burns my throat; straight from the bottle is best. I wasn't lying. I'm not going to chase after her forever. If she wants to act like a child, she can do it somewhere else.

After an hour of the Tennessee waltz with my liver, I hear my front door open.

"Rae?" I slur up the stairs.

"Spencer?"

Ainsley.

"In the studio, Ainsley." I set the glass bottle on the lid of my piano.

"I thought you had the concert tonight," she chirps as she walks through the studio.

"Then why are you here?" I watch her cheeks redden under my gruff reply.

Ainsley clears her throat and licks her cherry lips before speaking. "Well, I saw Rachel and some guy at Les's, and you weren't with them ..." She stalks toward me with panther-like eyes.

"Yeah?" I turn on the bench and face her. "You didn't answer my question—why are you here?" Cockiness takes over and turns up the corners of my mouth. I know exactly what she's doing here.

In a second, I regret my baiting tone. Ainsley pushes my knees apart with her knee, sliding her slender legs between mine. Her chest is inches from my face, those perfect breasts taunting my will. Another second passes and her bubblegum-like scent greets the whiskey that's overriding my system.

"Ainsley, stop." I swat her hand away from my shoulder, but she only presses forward.

"Oh, come on now, Spencer, you don't want me to stop—you never have." She picks up both of my hands and wraps them around her waist. A tan strip of skin on her stomach grins at me when she lifts her arms back to my shoulders.

I'm supposed to hate her. She took advantage of my grief after my parents died. It's hard to count her transgressions when her fingers tickle the back of my neck, chasing goosebumps across my chest.

"She's got you all twisted. You think you want her, that you love her." Ainsley throws her head back in mocking laughter. "She doesn't know you the way I know you. We were each other's first..." She lifts one leg at a time and squares herself on my hardening lap. Her delicate hands twist like thorny vines through my hair.

"Get off of me, Ainsley," I grunt into her ear as she leans forward to brush her lips across my neck.

"You hide from me any chance you get. I'm not taking no for an answer anymore. You can't hide how you feel about me. I see the way you look at me, the way your eyes sketch me from head to toe. Forget about her, she walked away from you—twice, judging by her absence after the concert."

She's good.

Gripping her tiny hips, I consider my options. Jack's betrayed me once again, and all I can feel is her ass rubbing against me. All I can smell is her want. My moment of indecision is a second too long, leaving an opening just big enough for her tiny body to slither through as her lips sear into mine. The force of her kiss sends my back into the piano keys. I ignore their warning; I'm tired of losing.

Chapter 19
Ember

"What the hell happened, November?" Monica volleys her attention between the road and me as my tears streak her car window. We've been sitting in the DROP parking lot for over half an hour in heavy silence.

"I just want to go." I sniff and look at her through swollen eyes.

"Where are you going? It's Thursday." Monica reminds me that I've still got work in the morning.

"I'm calling in tomorrow. I just have a zillion phone conferences—I can do that from home." I rub my eyes and tie my distressed hair away from my neck.

"What. Happened?" Monica begs, locking her car doors to prevent my exit.

I breathe out the sordid tale in one breath, my throat cinching around the details of Bo's anger—and his kiss. She shakes her head and rests it against the back of her seat.

"First of all...your *parents'* song?"

"Not now, Monica...I'll explain that later." I smirk at her attention to detail.

"I'm sorry, Ember. I'm sorry for the way I've been acting. I just...don't know why you don't want to be with him."

Her words pinch my heart. Bo's kiss felt exactly like it was supposed to, exactly *mine*. He sweeps me off my feet with every sideways glance and simple smile. His passion for DROP is awe-inspiring. He wants me. He loves me. *What the hell is my problem?*

"I think I still love him," I admit for the first time in weeks. "The worst decision I could have made to get over him was to work on this project." I thump the back of my head against the tear-stained window.

"Why do you *want* to get over him? If this is about work, have Carrie take you off the fucking project. Zoe is more than capable of taking over for you."

"It's Adrian, Monica ..."

"Oh, *fuck* Adrian." Monica rolls her eyes and presses her head against the steering wheel.

"I care about him, Monica—he's good to me."

"Yeah, whatever. Just go talk to Bo and clear up what happened tonight. You still have to work together. If there's any hope for you two, it starts with friendship. Deal with Adrian later. Will you take my advice, *for once?*" She gingerly slaps me upside the head.

"He didn't have to kiss me." I roll my eyes as my cheeks fill with fire.

"I think he did." Monica's long lashes sweep her cheeks as she takes a careful breath.

"How the hell am I supposed to clear anything up from tonight? I told him we couldn't be friends."

Monica shrugs and sweeps her hands toward the door, motioning for me to go. I shake my head.

"I'll go talk to him," I resign as I leave her car.

* * *

A twenty-minute self pep talk later, I finally pull out of the parking lot and head for Bo's house.

You just need to say you're sorry for bailing and that you still want to be friends...

I almost use the closed gate as an excuse to abort the mission, but I vividly remember the code he gave me. Shaky fingers tap out the four numbers, and the gate slowly swings open. I climb back in my car and head down the driveway, white-knuckled and dizzy.

Relief floods over me when I spot Rae's car next to one I

don't recognize, maybe Regan's, parked in the driveway. Their presence will make this easier. As I step out of the car, Regan walks onto the front porch. I hear yelling from inside the house. My feet catch up to my pulse, and I meet him on the porch.

"What's going on?" I ask as I head for the door.

"No," Regan huffs as he grips my upper arm and pulls me backward.

"What the hell, Regan?" I watch his face fall as he shakes his head.

Our heads turn to the voices getting closer to the front door.

"Get the *hell* out of *my* house, you tramp!" Rae's voice is full of rage as the acid in my stomach churns wildly. The yelling continues, but I can no longer focus on the words.

"Ainsley," I whisper, scanning the driveway. The car I didn't recognize, I realize several minutes too late, is hers—I've only seen it once before. Regan releases my arm, turning me toward him. His face is full of pity.

"We came back here after going to Les's Diner. Rae wanted to show me the place. As soon as she saw that car, she lost it. I chased in after her, and—"

"I'm good, Regan," I put my hands up, "I can put the rest together. I'm getting the hell out of here." As soon as my foot hits the top stair, the front door swings open, spilling three angry people onto the porch. If curling into the fetal position were socially acceptable, I'd be there in a heartbeat.

"He didn't invite you here," Rae seethes.

"He didn't ask me to leave, either, did you, Spencer?" I can hear Ainsley's snide smile tear through the back of my head.

"Stop calling him that!" Rae screams.

"Will both of you calm down? It's after midni -" Bo stops mid-sentence and I turn around to find his eyes wide in my direction.

My face feels like it takes on the color his loses in an instant. Rae's hand flies to cover her open mouth as Regan grabs her shoulders. *Swallow. Blink.* Ainsley's momentary shock is replaced by a wicked grin that turns her ice blue eyes black. *Don't bait her. Don't bait her. Smile. Shrug. Do something.*

"I had a nice time tonight, *Spencer*." Ainsley stretches up on her tiptoes to plant a kiss squarely on Bo's lips. His eyes don't leave mine before I look to the ground in nausea.

Breathe. You don't know what happened. Well, you know a little what happened.

As she brushes past me, Ainsley's bubblegum-like body spray makes my mouth water—the way it does right before one throws up. She snickers as she gets in her car; the sound thumps my eardrums. I watch her taillights until they disappear from sight before I turn around again. My jaw ripples beneath my skin, and I pray that my teeth won't break as I force my anger away with a deep inhale through flared nostrils.

Bo steps toward me. "November ..."

Yep, that's me.

"Jesus, November, what are you doing here?" Rae whispers. Apparently, we're all just catching up that I've been standing on the porch for several minutes.

My fingernails dig into my palms as I force myself to relax my jaw. I clear my throat before I speak.

"I, uh, just wanted to tell Bo "thank you" for showing me the studio tonight—it's lovely." *Swallow.* "So...thank you." I force a smile. "Also, I'm sorry about what I said about not being friends. *Clearly* that's all we'll be." I turn and dash to my car.

"Ember, wait!" Bo runs after me, beating me to my car and blocking my door with his body.

My arms cross in front of me, protecting me without having to ask my brain for permission.

"Are you about to tell me that wasn't what it looked like?" I bite the inside of my cheek until it hurts.

"No...I mean—" He kicks my tire with his heel before I cut him off.

"*Ainsley?* You warned me about her, Rae warned me about her, and all you did tonight was prove that you're no better. You *kiss me*, and come back here with *her?*"

"You kissed her?" Rae runs down the stairs toward us.

"It's none of your business, Rae!" Bo hollers through gritted teeth.

Rae looks like she's about to say something, but tears trickling down her pale cheek stop her. Regan reaches an arm around her shoulders and pulls her in, kissing the top of her head as she stares at us in defeat.

"I meant that kiss, November. *You* were the one who walked away." Bo grabs my shoulders, and I'm too tired to fight him.

"You called me self-righteous. Then, apparently, came here to fuck your ex-girlfriend." His head turns to the side and he winces against my accusation.

"It's *you*, November. You're the one I'm in love with. I'm insane over not having you." He's not making sense, and it becomes clearer that he's been drinking since he got home.

Suddenly, Bo's hands slide from my shoulders to my cheeks and he forces his mouth against mine. His tongue slides sloppily against my lips before I pull away and push him aside, opening my car door.

Three sets of eyes watch as I slide into my car and look at Bo.

"You taste like whiskey...and bubblegum." I slam the door, start the engine, and lock the door when Bo tries to enter the passenger side.

"God dammit, Ember, listen to me for once!" He screams as he pounds his fist into my car window.

Fearing for the glass, I leave the engine running but unlock the door. Seeming relieved, Bo slides inside. Before turning to face him, I lock eyes with Regan and Rae, giving them a slight nod to excuse them from the scene.

"What?" I ask, as I chew on my bottom lip.

"When you left, I came back here and went into my studio." Bo's words are quick and slightly slurred. The smell of liquor permeates my car.

"I don't want to know anything else, Bo. I don't. Please stop." I put up my hand to prove my point.

Bo fists his hair. "November, I'm not leaving this car until you hear me out."

"Well," I shrug, "it's going to be a long walk back from Boston for you."

Shit.

Bo's eyebrows knit together. "Boston?" Before he annunciates the n, realization sears his eyes. The rise and fall of his chest increases as he puts it together. "How long has it been going on?"

"What are you talking about?" I feign ignorance.

"Don't screw with me!" He punches my dash, causing me to jump. "How long have you been fucking Turner?" His teeth are clenched so tightly, I'm surprised words escape at all.

"Get out of my car. So help me God, Bo, get out of my car right now before I lay on this horn and have Regan force you out." I beg my chin to stop quivering as I force my eyes into his.

With a petulant shrug, Bo gets out. Hanging onto my doorframe, he ducks his head into my car.

"You're right. We can't be friends," he says before he slams the door.

I don't wait for him to step away from the car before I put it in reverse and tear out of his driveway like a bat out of hell.

Chapter 20

"Sorry to wake you."

"It's OK, Blue, you sounded upset." Adrian holds his door open well past midnight. I texted him after I left "Casa Cavanaugh" and flew here in record time.

I drop my backpack on the island and slump onto the couch. My body shifts to the left when he sits next to me.

"What happened?" Adrian's arm envelopes my shoulders and he kisses the top of my head.

I'll never listen to Coldplay again ...

"I can't be friends with him, Adrian." I rock my forehead side to side in my folded hands.

"Did he do something to you?" His body stiffens as he leans back.

So many things ...

I look up, forcing a smile before I shake my head. My face feels flush as I move to straddle his lap. Fighting the tears from the roller coaster bitch-of-a-night I've had, I take off my shirt and cast it to the floor. Adrian's eyes widen in praise as he cups my breasts in his hands. I lean forward, tracing my tongue up the side of his ear, eliciting a groan from his throat.

"God, I've missed you this week. Come with me, I want you in my bed."

I nod and take his hand, silently following the lion into his den.

Foreplay has no purpose here—need wants what it wants. Adrian's expert moves take me away from everything that's happened over the last few weeks. Thankful for the pitch-black room, I blink a few tears out of the corners of my eyes.

"Harder, Adrian," I whisper into his ear.

Make me forget ...

* * *

A gentle nudging of my shoulders pulls me from a deep, sex-induced sleep. I peel my eyes open and groan at the sunset peeking through the bedroom curtains.

"Hey, babe, your phone's ringing—it's Monica." Adrian places the phone in my hand and I blindly answer.

"Hello?" I yawn.

"Hello? *Hello?* Where the hell are you? Hello...God ..." she scoffs into the phone.

I pull the phone away from my ear to see it's just after eight, and Monica's just putting together that I didn't go back to the hotel last night.

"I'm in Boston—" I don't have time to finish before she launches in on her tirade.

"Boston? Ember what the christ are you doing?"

"What am I doing? I'm lying in Adrian's bed, pushing the image of Ainsley kissing Bo on his front porch out of my head—that's what I'm doing." I hiss into the phone so Adrian can't hear from the kitchen. I replay the scene, detail by gory detail, for Monica.

"So you're with Adrian for the specific purpose of getting over Bo?" She asks unapologetically.

"No, I'm not. But last night, it became clear that Bo and I are too toxic to even be friends, let alone anything else. So why not actually be happy with someone who lets me be me?" I pace into the kitchen wearing only my panties and one of Adrian's undershirts.

"Ha! Lets you be you? OK, we'll see how long that lasts. You forget—I was around last time Adrian was, Ember. You were the furthest thing from being you."

"What the hell is that supposed to mean?" I stop and Adrian lifts his head from his iPad with an arched brow.

"I mean you turned into a giant snob when you dated him in college, and I really don't want to put up with that again." Her tone is blunt and unforgiving.

This revelation is news to me. Further, it's irritating that she'd cast how we may have acted several years ago onto the people we are today. I spew a frustrated goodbye into the phone and begin pouring myself a cup of coffee.

"Not a pleasant call, I take it?" Adrian spoons cereal into his mouth and chews while waiting for my answer.

"Monica's had a rod up her ass for weeks now. She isn't keen on the idea of us being together." I perch on the stool across from Adrian and roll my eyes as I sip my coffee. Adrian swallows his cereal as a Cheshire grin swallows *him*.

"Together, huh?" He bites his bottom lip in the way that drives me wild.

"Looks that way, doesn't it?" I shrug and return the grin.

Adrian's gaze breaks from mine and his grin disappears. My stomach plummets.

"This doesn't have anything to do with what's been going on with Cavanaugh, does it?" Gut punch.

"Adrian..." I slide off the stool and pace toward him, while his eyes remain fixed on the floor. I slide hips between his knees and force him to look at me. "What are you talking about?"

"If we're going to do this, Ember, it's going to be the real deal. I want you—all of you. I screwed it up once before, and I'm not going to do it again. If you need more time—" He shakes his head slightly as he tucks my hair behind my ears.

In the refreshing light of a new day, last night seems so far away and even more ridiculous. Adrian doesn't deserve to be treated the way I treated him last night. I used him. He at least suspects that, which is why he's hesitant to move forward. Who can blame him? That was a shitty thing to do. Bo can do whatever he wants with whomever he wants, but I'll be damned if that will affect *my* actions. Studying Adrian's reserved expression, I realize I don't want to lose him. I care for him and everything we can have together. And, no matter what has happened or will happen between us, he would never pull what Bo pulled last night. Not in a million years.

Or a thousand lifetimes.

"Hey," I grab his wrists and bring his knuckles to my lips, "I don't need more time for anything. Things with Bo are going to be complicated until we're finished working on the collaboration. Then I can go back to my permanent office on the Cape and only deal with him a few times a year." In theory, seeing Bo a few times a year sounds like too much. The words, however, are somewhat difficult to say. "That's another thing," I continue, "you live here. I live on the Cape ..."

"Listen, you keep coming here on Fridays after you leave Concord—stay the full weekend when you don't sing at Finnegan's—and I'll stay at your place Sundays and Mondays. Sound good?"

The apartment brightens with the return of our smiles.

"You've given this some thought," I tease.

"You've been my only thought for quite some time, Ms. Harris." He seals his declaration with a kiss.

"I need to go for a run. Do you have a good route around here?" I pick up my backpack, which only holds my running gear.

"Sure, I'll go with you."

"All right, Turner," I tease, "but you'll probably have to slow down a bit."

"Ha. With you? You're probably right ..."

I playfully punch his shoulder before we dress and head out for a run.

* * *

"That was a great route, Adrian!" I feel exhilarated and refreshed for the first time in days.

"Yeah," he pants, "told you I'd have to keep up with you." He playfully smacks my butt as the elevator doors close.

"Good to see some things never change," I quip before kissing his cheek.

When I'm with Adrian, in the moment, thoughts of Bo are light years away. It's when I'm alone or too deep inside my head, that thoughts of what *could* have been seep in. Just stay in the moment, and no one will get hurt.

When we reach Adrian's door, I hear someone banging around in the kitchen and stop short.

"Is that housekeeping?" I ask.

"Nah, that's probably just Pace." Adrian unlocks his door with annoyance.

"Your brother's here? Why didn't you say anything?"

Adrian's older brother Pace was one of my favorite people at Princeton. He graduated the year Adrian and I got together, and I only saw him a few times after that. Adrian swings his door open, and I let out a childish squeal.

"Pace!"

Startled, he drops the spatula in his hand and whips around.

"November? What the hell?" He jogs toward me and pulls me into a hug, spinning me around twice for good measure before setting me down.

While it's clear Pace and Adrian are brothers, Pace is nearly six-foot-six, towering six inches over his younger brother. Built like a brick wall, and athletic to boot, he could have played nearly any sport at any college of his choosing. His family's tradition of Princeton, however, overruled any athletic aspirations he may have had.

"All right, you two," Adrian teases.

"Where the fuck have you been hiding her, Adrian?" Pace squeezes my shoulders, forcing all the air from my lungs.

"It's good to see you, too, Pace." I wriggle out of his hold and pour a glass of water. "I think the real question is what are *you* doing here?"

"I live here, smartass. Well, not here in this apartment," he continues when he sees my confused look, "but in this building. I'm one floor up."

"Of course you are." I roll my eyes at the brotherly competition that hasn't died down. "Guess medical school served you well?"

Adrian covers his mouth in laughter, and Pace punches him in the shoulder.

"What?" I ask.

"Pace dropped out of medical school two years in," Adrian says.

My eyes bulge out of my head. "You're kidding! Did your parents have joint coronaries?"

The brothers laugh and shake their heads. Pace tells me that his parents were understanding of his decision, being that he did try medical school for two years and promised to pay them back for their investment.

"Being a doctor just didn't turn out to be what I wanted to do long-term." Pace shrugs.

"What did you want to do long-term?" I ask.

"Make a shitload of money. I work for the company that owns this place." Pace grins. If there's one thing you can say about the foul-mouthed Turner brother, it's that he's one hundred percent honest. "Seriously though, November. Where'd you resurface from? It's been so long."

It's clear from the look on both of their faces that I haven't exactly been a topic of recent conversation.

"So, you live one floor apart and I've never come up?" I eye Adrian, who looks out to the harbor.

"Oh, you've come up all right." Pace crosses his arms in front of his chest, tucking his fingers under his armpits.

"Shut it, Pace," Adrian commands.

Silence befalls the previously light atmosphere. That's my cue.

"Well, I'm going to take a shower." I clear my throat and disappear into the bathroom.

When I'm dried and dressed, I find Pace alone in the living room, eating the omelet he was preparing when we walked in.

"Where's Adrian?" I ask as I slide onto the stool next to Pace. I've always been comfortable around him. The big brother role exudes from his core; it's nice to see that hasn't changed in the last few years.

Pace sips his orange juice and watches me from the corner of his eye. "He went around the corner to grab you guys some bagels."

"What gives, Pace? Tell me...before he comes back." I know he's holding something back, and it's irritating.

"Well, obviously when you two broke up in college," Pace launches in with little thought, "he was a mess for a while. After graduation, law school took up most of his time."

"And bimbos." I roll my eyes.

"Yeah, those too. Anyway, when he took the contract job with DROP, and saw that your organization was on the table, he became a nervous wreck. He thought about suggesting every organization *but* yours. I told him not to be such a fool, so he went for it. God," Pace pauses and shakes his head, "you should have seen the sorry sight that walked into this apartment the day after you guys all went out—when he figured out something was going on with that Bo dude."

My neck suddenly feels hot, and I look down.

"No, it's OK, Girl. Don't worry. I told him he should have just gone right for you, but, you know how he is all "respectful" and whatnot." Paces eye roll elicits a huge laugh from me.

"I take it you're still single?" Monogamy, and

relationships in general, were never Pace's strong suit.

"You got it, baby." He winks and brings his dishes to the sink. "I guess, given the fact that you're here...things didn't really ..."

"No, things with Bo didn't pan out—so to speak." I save Pace from his social fumble.

I spend the next several minutes telling Pace about everything that happened in Concord. Adrian walks in during the middle of it, but resigns himself to listening with his back turned, toasting our bagels. He slides my plate in front of me as my voice cracks around the details of the hotel room. I clear my throat several times in an attempt to sound composed, but the truth is, I'll never get used to telling the story. Someday I'll just have to stop. Adrian sweeps my hair away from the side of my neck, replacing it with his lips. Pace's eyes leave mine for a moment as he studies his brother; when they return to me they're different, softer. He believes in us—he always has.

"So, that's it. That's what the fuck I'm doing here." I shoot Pace a wry smile.

"Thanks for clearing that up, November." He chuckles and flashes a sexy, lopsided grin. It's really a shame he won't settle down. Well, I suppose it's no shame for the hordes of women vying for his attention constantly. He stands to leave.

"Hey, before you go—remember Monica? She and her boyfriend Josh got engaged a few weeks ago. I'm throwing an engagement party for them at Finnegan's in Barnstable—Fourth of July weekend. You should come."

"I thought she didn't like him," Adrian spits out.

"No, it's you she doesn't care for. She loves Pace," I tease. "You're coming with me anyway, so it's a non-issue. She's over it." I shrug.

Pace leaves, and Adrian and I finish our breakfast. I leave out the part about Pace telling me the emotional turmoil I inadvertently put Adrian through. Adrian heads to work, and I deal with my conference calls. Rae and Monica each call me once, but I ignore them both.

Chapter 21

"That was a great set, guys. Awesome work tonight." I chug water backstage at Finnegan's, grateful that I've made it all the way to Saturday night without having to talk to anyone about Ainsley and Bo. Judging by Rae's appearance in the crowd tonight, however, I know my grace period is over.

After a few minutes of anxiously winding my mic cord, I look up to find myself alone with Regan. Josh hasn't said much to me since the concert. I guess that's to be expected; Monica seems to be his barometer for interactions with me lately.

"Nice work yourself, Ember." Regan stares at me for an uncomfortable amount of time.

"Regan, I'm fine…really."

"That was intense, Ember. After you left …"

"Nope," I stop him. "I have *zero* interest in the rest of that sentence. I don't care what happened or didn't happen. I saw what I saw with Ainsley, he knows about Adrian, it's all settled." I nervously tie my hair into a disastrous bun.

Regan's shoulders sink with his long sigh.

"I see Rae's here. I should go talk to her," I cut in before he can tell me whatever was going to follow that sigh.

"Yeah, enough ignoring us—I gave you two days, I can't do any more." Monica busts through the door, Rae in tow.

Regan kisses Rae on the lips before excusing himself to the bar, leaving me alone with the firing squad.

"I'm sorry for ignoring you guys yesterday," I start.

"No, you're not. But you're lucky I only called once. This one forced me to leave you alone." Monica gestures to Rae.

"I don't want to talk about what happened at your house, OK, Rae? Bo and I both said things...look, I just don't want to talk about it. We've proven over the last several weeks that we can't be friends."

"Ember, stop," Rae ceases my rant, "I just wanted to tell you that I get it. It's all-or-nothing with you two, and nothing seems to be winning right now." Her face isn't as sad as the words she just let out. My brow crinkles for a second.

"OK, well, thank you. I don't want things to change between us, though ..." I walk toward her.

"You're not getting rid of me that easily." Rae smiles and gives me a hug.

"Anyway, let's talk engagement party. It's going to be here, the Friday of Fourth of July weekend. Rae, you've gotta come. Also, Mon, I told Pace to come."

"Pace Turner? How is that gorgeous asshole?" Monica laughs.

"He's good. Dropped out of medical school and is making, quote, a 'shitload' of money, working for the company that owns The W. He lives there too; one floor above Adrian, of course."

"Of course," Monica snorts.

With all of my fires currently contained, I'm able to enjoy the rest of the night with my girlfriends, thankful Rae's still on that list.

* * *

The next two weeks fly by with ease. Well, relative ease. I've been busy splitting my time between organizing Monica and Josh's engagement party and spending time with Adrian. Our arrangement has been seamless thus far. He spends Sunday and Monday nights with me, we enjoy a decadent goodbye on Tuesday morning, and we see each other again Friday evenings.

My time at DROP has been uncomfortable at best. While Rae, Monica, and I have worked well together, few words pass between Bo and me. And, when they do, it's typically in the form of email. I'll update him on grants I'm pursuing, and he'll send me info on ones he'd like me to investigate. That's. It. Except for the part that nearly every other day Ainsley Worthington and her clacky heels grace the halls of DROP when she brings Bo lunch. It's not lost on me that he rarely goes out to lunch with her; but that detail only makes me grin as far as naive Ainsley's concerned.

I, however, play a different game. It's no game at all, really—Adrian just never comes around here. There's no need for him to. If he did, it would be a clear sign that I'm trying to rub Bo's face in something that I'm not. I'm happy with Adrian. Just a few years older than we were when we first dated, things are much smoother. Each of us are more confident in who we are as people; physically and emotionally.

Today is the dedication for DROP's community center. I'm thrilled with how it's turned out. Rae took me on a final tour yesterday, and the place is beautiful. As we stand inside the office—me, Monica, Rae, Bo, Carrie, David, and other DROP employees—it dawns on me that this is the last day for a long time that I'll spend in Concord. I've been so busy, I haven't paid attention. I let out an audible sigh, and everyone except Bo turns briefly in my direction. He knows. Monica discreetly squeezes my fingertips. She knows, too.

"Thank you all for coming today," Bo speaks into the microphone, while the rest of us stand to either side of him. "The tireless hours put in by the people standing here with me have brought this center to life. A special thank you goes out to Carrie, November, and Monica from The Hope Foundation, who have uprooted their lives the last several weeks in order to get the center off the ground." His voice is proud but stern. It's all pomp, with loads of circumstance lingering in the background.

I notice his tight grip on the podium and cast my gaze to the crowd, where, naturally, I immediately spot Ainsley. Dripping in pearls and pretense, she beams at Bo through his speech.

"Choosing today for the dedication didn't come out of nowhere," Bo continues. "Today is the four-year anniversary of my parents' death. My sister, Rae, and I wanted to give the date a new and promising meaning. You've all helped make that happen."

Dizziness knocks me senseless as bile rises in my throat. I didn't know the date. We never talked about it, and Rae *never* talks about it. I turn my head to the right and see Rae lean her head on David's shoulder, dabbing her eyes with a tissue. Instantly, my vision clouds behind tears. I swallow hard and force a smile as the room erupts in applause.

Bo and Rae cut the ceremonial ribbon, and the crowd breaks into clutches of supporters wishing the Cavanaugh siblings well. I start toward Bo, intent on saying something congratulatory, but Ainsley beats me to him. This is the first time I've seen them in public together; and, judging by the way her arms fit perfectly around his neck—and his lips seem to fit perfectly on hers—they are together. Like, *together*. I don't like that it bothers me, and I curse myself for my own relationship double standard.

I clear my throat. "That was a great speech, Bo. I'm thrilled for you about this center. Your parents would be proud." My cheeks burn, as he seems to stare right through me.

"Isn't it great? I'm proud of him, too." Ainsley squeezes her twiggy arm around his waist and kisses his cheek. Bo pulls his head away from her lips almost as soon as they make contact.

"Thank you, Ember. And, thank you for all of your hard work." He smiles before his face greys a bit. "I know it's been challenging to live in so many different places over the last few weeks." Bo's face is blank, but his eyes scream *Boston*. I offer a tight smile and walk away.

Seeking out Rae, I find her talking with her friends. She nods in my direction, and they scatter through the crowd. Wordlessly, I embrace her with all the force I can muster, tears spilling down my cheeks.

"What's that for?" Rae pulls away, dabbing her eyes with her fingers.

"I had no idea that today was the anniversary, Rae. Bo and I never talked about it...I never asked."

"Hey, it's OK," Rae takes my shoulders and pulls back, "it's not something we harp on. It happened once, and we didn't want it to happen every year, if you know what I mean. Like he said, we wanted it to mean something new—something hopeful." Regan weaves through the crowd toward us and tenderly kisses Rae on the cheek.

"You two are so friggen cute, I can't even stand it," I change the subject, talking louder to drown the sound of

Ainsley's giggle from my ears. "Are you guys coming to the party tomorrow?" Monica and Josh's engagement party is finally upon us, and I couldn't be more grateful for the timing. I need a liquor release after the last few weeks.

"We are, but we won't stay too long. Usually I spend this weekend holed up in my room somewhere, but Regan's assured me it's healthy to get out of the house." Rae smiles up at Regan, who strokes her cheek and kisses the top of her head. He's probably eight inches taller than she is, but her larger-than-life personality fills the gap.

"All right, kids, I'm heading out of here." I rake a hand through my hair.

"Are you heading to Boston tonight?" Monica comes up behind me, linking her arm with mine.

"No, I've got lots to do to get ready for tomorrow." I kiss her on the cheek. "See you then, bride-to-be."

I return to the office to grab my bag and keys. The strap of my bag catches the arm of a chair, scattering the contents across the floor.

"Perfect," I mumble as I sink to my knees and gather my belongings. I ignore the shadow suddenly standing over me, pretending I don't know it's him.

"Need some help?" I allow a glance upward and find Bo leaning against the doorframe, arms crossed. His silver tie is loosened, hanging carelessly from his black shirt. This is the first time we've been alone since sitting in my car in his driveway.

"No. Thanks, though." I stand and brush myself off. "That was a great speech you gave today. I didn't know today was ..." I trail off.

"Yeah, we didn't really cover that, did we?" Bo bends over and picks up my lip gloss that landed next to his foot. He studies it between his thumb and forefinger before handing it back to me. Our hands touch for a moment, and we simultaneously clear our throats, forcing our hands apart.

"Thanks," I manage.

"So, I guess we won't be seeing each other for a while, huh? Now that the center's open and all." Inexplicably, he closes the door behind him. Out of the corner of my eye, I catch Monica's wide-eyed stare through the window. I can't break his gaze as he runs a hand through his hair. His eyes are more grey than blue today, taking on the emotion of the room.

"Guess not. Unless, of course, you're coming to Monica and Josh's engagement party tomorrow night."

Why in God's name did I just say that?

"Am I invited?"

"You're friends with Josh, aren't you? Come, it'll be fun."

You just can't stop yourself.

"I'll come." He shrugs.

"Please don't bring Ainsley," I spit out before I can stop myself. *Get. A. Grip.*

Bo laughs as he tucks his hands into his pockets. "Don't worry about Ainsley, Ember." His eyes gleam as he says my name.

What the hell is that supposed to mean?

"OK, then. See you tomorrow, I guess." I breeze past him and race to my car.

When I get to my apartment a couple hours later, I tear open my guitar case and play and write until my raw fingertips meet the sunrise.

Chapter 22

Waking on my couch late Saturday morning, I find my comp notebook splayed open on my chest, and my guitar on the coffee table. I sit and stretch my neck side to side before examining my fingers. I'm sure I'll have a blister or two before sundown. Placing the notebook on the table, I look at what I wrote last night.

I don't know where we're going, but can it be
somewhere good, baby, mmmhmm
The space between your heartbeat and mine
is filled with indecision, fear, and time
I just can't see past my own mistakes...

A knock on the door stops me from reading further. I toss the notebook on the table and open the door to find Adrian—looking rather tense.

"I called you all night, what the hell?" He brushes past me.

"Shit, I'm sorry, Adrian," I hurry to my coffee table, "I was playing last night and didn't want to be interrupted. I forgot to turn my phone back on when I was—"

"What the hell is this?" Adrian is aggravated as he picks up my notebook.

"My comp notebook—you've seen it before ..." I reach for it, pulse picking up pace, but he pulls it away.

"You also said you were going to get a new one." He throws it down and puts his hands on his hips.

I stare for a few seconds, confused from my lack of sleep,

conflicted feelings, and Adrian's aggressive stance. I mentally flip through the last few conversations we've had and nothing suggests why he'd come in so threatening this morning.

"What's going on, Adrian?" I place my guitar in the case and slide it under the couch.

"I hardly heard from you all week, Ember. Then I can't get ahold of you last night, and I come in here this morning and you've got Cavanaugh's present—" he stops himself and walks toward the door.

Now I'm pissed.

"Pardon me? Are you suggesting I've been cheating on you?" My actual voice is softer than the one in my head.

"What am I supposed to think?"

"What you're *supposed* to think," I walk toward him with clenched fists, "is that I'm honest, and I would *never* do something like that. Yesterday was the center's opening. We were busy as hell all week. Last night I was exhausted and stressed—you know what? I'm not going to explain myself to you. You're being ridiculous." Throwing my arms in the air, I walk into the kitchen to make coffee.

How dare he insinuate that my lack of attention had to do with Bo? I was busy with work, *and avoiding Bo,* and getting ready for Monica and Josh's engagement party, *and avoiding Bo.*

"Ember, I'm sorry. I just got nervous when I couldn't reach you. And this friggen guitar …" Adrian looks down and puts his hands in his pockets.

"This friggen guitar what?" I turn and rest my back against the counter.

"That's all you've been doing the last few weeks…you get up in the middle of the night and write or play." He leans his shoulder and head against the wall.

"I sing at Finnegan's every other week, Adrian. Last week Josh had me play a little with him. I've been practicing …" I look to the floor.

Truthfully, my increase in playing was an effort to help me work through my apparent "Bo" issues. Dealing with the kiss I've kept secret from Adrian, seeing Ainsley prance around under my nose, my flourishing relationship with Bo's sister—it's all become too much. I've been playing and writing as an outlet. The only problem is it's made things worse—a full-blown four-alarm fire is raging in my soul. I care so much for

Adrian, but I can't reconcile how much of that is reminiscence of our past together and how much is attributed to our present. I don't know, honestly, if my future holds Adrian. The present has been too fun to think of much else.

"You all right, Blue?" Adrian takes my hand and kisses my knuckles.

"I don't know." I shrug and force myself to meet his eyes.

"Look, baby, I'm sorry for freaking out. I love you, November. I want you. All day, everyday. Mine. I want to see you when I wake up in the morning and kiss you before I go to bed at night. I want to live with you—"

"Whoa, whoa, whoa...whoa." My adrenaline chooses "flight" as I put my hands up and walk back to the living room."

"Uh-uh, Ember, you're not walking away from me. We're going to talk about this." Adrian grasps my shoulders and spins me around.

"Who says they love you and they want to live with you all in the same breath?" I huff.

Someone who's scared...that's who.

"Don't you love me?" He drops his arms and takes a step back.

"Adrian ..." My eyes reach for the ceiling.

Then...he pulls the rug out ...

"I know something happened with Cavanaugh."

What?

"What?" Flames whip against my cheeks. If he was bluffing, I just gave it a way.

"The night of the concert ..." Adrian breaks his defensive stance and walks to my couch, taking a seat.

My eyes scan back and forth across the coffee table, as if it holds the answer to how he could possibly know about Bo kissing me. Monica would never out me—especially not to Adrian. The only possibility is Ainsley, but I don't think Adrian even knows who she is. Seeing the confusion on my face, Adrian continues.

"No one said anything to me...it was you." He bites his bottom lip and I sit next to him. He grabs my hand. "When you called to tell me you were coming, I knew something was wrong. When you came in and we had sex...you've never been like that before, Ember. It was crazy—it felt desperate."

I swallow, my mouth suddenly dry.

You have to say something.

When my voice returns, I recant the entire story to Adrian. I tell him about singing in the studio, my fight with Bo, and his kiss. Adrian listens patiently, never breaking eye contact, studying my expression. I don't lie; I tell Adrian I was furious when Bo kissed me. The conversation takes on a different tone when I tell him I went to the Cavanaugh residence to make nice.

"Why the hell did you go there after he treated you like that?" Adrian leans back, digging his fingertips into the tops of his thighs.

I try my best to explain that I needed to try for the sake of work, for the sake of Rae. I steady my inflection when I share details about finding Ainsley there, trying to deflect my emotion from that part of the story.

"It hurt you to see her there, didn't it?" Adrian rubs his eyes.

"It did. But not because of Bo. Ainsley's a whack-job. It was disappointing on a friend level." I sit back and reach for Adrian's hand, but he pulls it away and stands, heading for the door.

"I love you, November. I've loved you since we first met and I've loved you ever since—"

"Oh that's fucking bullshit, Adrian, and you know it. When you're that in love with someone, you don't disappear into scores of women for years before resurfacing." His attempt at a guilt trip is starting to piss me off.

"Isn't that what you're doing?" Adrian holds out his arms like he's in a courtroom. "Disappearing into me, despite being in love with him?"

"I'm not using you, Adrian. Man, you're on a roll. First, you walk into my apartment and accuse me of cheating on you, *now* you're accusing me of using you. Anything else you'd like to tear into me about today, or will you be on your merry way?" I defensively wrap my arms around my stomach.

Adrian takes his hand off the knob and walks toward me. "Look, Ember. I know that you were in love with him. I also know that he broke your trust. What I need from you is to know that you're with me, one hundred percent. Here. And Here." He points to my head and my chest, over my heart.

Instinctively I lunge forward and smash my lips into his, wrapping my arms around his neck and holding on tightly.

Adrian's hands press into my sides as he returns my kiss. I can't find the words to explain to Adrian that I care about him; those words still seem assigned to someone else. People are in love with more than one person all the time—right? This is just one of those times. I need to continue on with Adrian, while begging Bo to fade to black in the memory of my heart. When we pull apart, Adrian smiles foolishly.

"I've got some things I have to get done in town before the party tonight. I'll see you there, OK?"

"Absolutely." I kiss his neck once before backing away.

Adrian leaves, but stops the door from closing behind him and peeks his head back in.

"I do love you, Blue." He grins again and quickly shuts the door before I can respond, which I'm grateful for.

Chapter 23

"It looks great out here, Ember, you did an awesome job!" Marley, one of the summer bartenders, admires the twinkle lights and flowers adorning Finnegan's back deck.

I admit, the place looks amazing, a slice of heaven right on the beach. I can think of no two people who deserve this more than Monica and Josh—they're the real deal.

"Thanks for your help, Marley," I smile. "So where are you from?" I step down from the small ladder I'd been using to hang lights. Her black, bobbed hair nearly matches her eyes; her olive skin would lead me to believe she models full time.

"I'm from Framingham, but my family has a house here in Barnstable. I'm in law school, Columbia. When I graduated from BU, I immediately went to get my MBA without much thought—I hate it." She giggles and tucks some hair behind her ear. "I worked in the corporate world for a couple of years before deciding to go get my law degree. I want to help struggling companies survive attempts at large takeovers."

"That's impressive. Do you mind if I ask why the hell you waste your time here in the summer?" I fold the ladder and tuck it behind the fence.

"I've been coming here since I was a kid. Now that I'm saving for an apartment in the city, I need as much extra cash as I can get. Have fun tonight, Josh and Monica are lucky to have a friend like you." Marley walks back inside and easily picks up the slack at the bar, where I notice Adrian sitting.

I walk in and he turns to me with a smile.

"Hey you," I lean in and kiss his cheek as I spot Rae, Bo, and Regan out of the corner of my eye. Bo's back is to me and, admittedly, I'm thankful. "Where's Pace?"

"An ex-girlfriend is in town." Adrian's mischievous grin is the only answer I need. "Damn, I can't say this enough, you're gorgeous."

I playfully spin in the spaghetti-strapped, floor-length, flowing dress my mom bought me. Sometimes one must embrace their inner flower child. "Thank you. Finish your beer, I'm gonna go say "hi" to Rae and make sure Regan's all set to go tonight for the song we wrote." I give his shoulder a gentle squeeze. I hear him mumble, "Columbia, huh?" to Marley as I walk away.

I'm surprised Bo came, honestly. He said he would, but I thought he might bring Ainsley just for "fun." She doesn't seem to be anywhere around, so I smile and slide into the chair next to him.

"Hey guys, I'm glad you made it!"

"I told you I'd come." Bo doesn't turn in my direction, but I catch him swallowing hard when I turn in his. Rae and Regan stare anywhere else but between us.

"Well, I'm glad you did. Josh and Mon will be here soon, we should head out back." I stand and the rest of them do the same. I see Bo catch a glimpse of Adrian, in deep conversation with Marley, and he stiffens for a moment before falling in stride behind me.

I tug on Adrian's shirt as we walk by him. He shakes Marley's hand and joins us outside, directly by my side. I swear everyone can see the lines of fire between Adrian and Bo, but I guess that's just me—and Rae, who shoots me cautious gazes across the deck.

Josh and Monica arrive, along with more of our friends, and the party is a hit. Plenty of beer, liquor, and laughter flow through the crowd. Adrian rarely leaves my side; a point not unnoticed by Bo, who I catch staring at us more than once. I force a tight but polite smile every time our eyes meet. He doesn't return them.

After an hour, Regan suggests we move the party inside, so we can play our surprise for Josh and Monica. We've spent as much time as we can composing a song for fiddle and guitar that expresses their love for each other, and the love that others see when they're in a room with them. After each practice and performance, Regan and I would sneak to my place or his and work in it.

Everyone settles into their seats in front of the stage. Adrian always leans against the back wall when he watches me play, and I don't know why. Either way, he's standing back there, observing me and the crowd in one glance.

Regan seductively pulls his bow across the strings, and we begin the love song we've worked so hard on. My fingers are raw from playing all last night, but watching the looks of gratitude on my friends' faces, it doesn't matter. As hard as I try, I can't stop blinking quick looks over to Bo, whose eyes never leave my hands. The drink in his hand shifts from beer to liquor, and a dark look shades his face. We finish amidst a hearty applause. Rae hops up on stage and hugs Regan, and I notice a small smile pull on Bo's lips. Those two are really cute together.

"Great job," Regan whispers to me when he kisses my cheek.

"Thank you. Thanks for the extra lessons, too." I put my guitar in its case and lean it against the back wall.

"No problem. Take a break for a few days and let those babies heal, would ya?" He playfully grabs my fingers, making me wince.

"Rae and I are gonna get going, I'll catch up with you later."

"Have fun, guys. Thank you for coming." I pull Rae into a hug. "Do you have to go, too?" I ask Bo as he approaches us. I fidget with the fabric of my dress.

"We drove separately because I knew they'd be leaving early. Is it OK if I stick around a while?"

"Sure. I'm going to get a drink. Drive safe, you two."

Halfway to the bar, Adrian catches up with me.

"That was good, Blue. Real good." He pushes my hair aside with his nose and kisses my neck.

"Thanks. I've been practicing." I chuckle sarcastically in reference to our earlier argument.

"I'm sorry about earlier. I don't mean to push you."

"It's fine. Things have been stressful the past few weeks. Now that the center's open, I'll have less time on the road, and I won't be so crazy all the time."

Monica sneaks up behind me. "Like hell. Your crazy-ass

will find something to overwork yourself with." She smacks my butt and muscles her way between Adrian and me before hugging me. "You're skinny, what gives?" She pulls the strap of my dress and lets it smack against my shoulder blade."

I shrug. "Stress, I guess." I haven't been this thin since finals my junior year.

Her eyes slowly study my bone structure before she rolls them. "This party is gorgeous, you're an awesome friend. I can't believe you went ahead with it despite what a bitch I've been to you lately."

"Don't mention it. You're entitled to your opinion. I'm just gonna get a drink and head outside, meet me there." I shoo tipsy Monica away before she reveals her total displeasure about us right in front of him.

The regular Saturday night crowd pours into Finnegan's and, suddenly, cheers and hoots erupt as a gaggle of girls spot Bo sitting at a table near the bar. One of them, a regular, spots me and runs toward me.

"Is he playing tonight?" She squeals, pointing unabashedly at Bo.

I peer around Adrian's shoulder and study the three empty glasses in front of Bo. "I don't think so, he's just here for Josh and Monica's engagement party."

"I'll play," Bo shouts from the table. "Can I borrow your guitar, Ember?"

"Uh...sure." I can almost hear Adrian's jaw clenching as I leave the bar.

I walk on stage and pull out my guitar before heading to the mic and announcing a special performance by Bo. The moderately packed bar goes wild for him as he slides onto the stool next to me. Silently, I'm busy hoping that he, and the crowd, doesn't ask me to sing with him. I hurry back to the bar as he warms up for a few minutes.

"Let's go outside," Adrian whispers into my ear.

"Just a sec. I want to listen to him. Before you get all territorial, yesterday was the four-year anniversary of his parents' death. The least I can do is sit through one song."

"I'm gonna go get some air." Adrian whips off the stool and charges through the back door.

Despite barely making eye contact with me all night, the second Bo starts singing a song of his that must be new, he locks eyes with mine through the now-crowded bar. My pulse matches the speed at which goosebumps spread across the surface of my skin. Three songs later, his eyes haven't left mine, and I've lost track of time. He's singing to me, I know he is—my body knows he is. Adrian's fingers on my shoulder startle me.

"Shit, I didn't hear you come up behind me." I gulp my beer.

I engage Adrian in quiet conversation, my back turned to the stage. Suddenly, a familiar nineties tune echoes from the stage and pulls a lump to my throat.

"Pearl Jam...seriously?" I whisper as I turn around to find Bo looking directly at Adrian and me as he sings "Better Man."

My jaw drops as I stare at the stage while Bo sings about people convincing themselves they're in love with someone all wrong for them. I didn't notice Josh and Monica reenter the bar, but they hear the song too.

"Oh, holy shit." Monica shakes her head and tips back her beer with a mocking grin. Adrian's fists are clenched. I hop down from the stool, pulling him outside.

"Don't worry about him, Adrian. He's had a shitload to drink." I walk onto the beach, putting as much space between Adrian and the bar as possible.

"Fuck him, Ember. He sang that song deliberately to piss me off."

"Like you've never tried crazy shit over me before. Recall orchestrating a work merger?" I roll my eyes and walk down the beach.

After a few minutes of strained silence, I can tell Adrian's calming down. He's holding my hand, and his breathing has returned to normal. We turn and take a few minutes to walk back to Finnegan's. Once we get there, Josh, Monica, and a few of our other friends are outside drinking under the twinkle lights. Adrian heads inside for a beer and I pull Monica aside.

"Sorry for the almost-drama at your party."

"It's fine. That was some crazy shit." She giggles behind her beer.

"Yeah. Crazy is right. Where is he now?" I try to peer inside, but see no sign of him.

"He left after that last song. He threw his keys at Josh and walked down the road. He's probably headed for Lost Dog."

"Oh, that's just great. There's no fucking way he can go home tonight. He was drunk before leaving here and now he's headed *there?*"

I cut the rest of my thought off as Adrian returns with beers for both of us. I manage to push thoughts of Bo out of my mind for the next hour. We all enjoy the warm July breeze and tease Josh and Monica about perceived married life. None of us are married; they're heading out into uncharted waters.

Adrian's been distant since our argument this morning. I have, too. His accusations and assumptions hurt. I'd never cheat on anyone. That he questioned my character has weighed heavily on me all day. It's weighed on him, too, according to the amount of beer I've seen him put away tonight. I stop drinking since it looks like I'll be driving everyone home.

Two hours later, I've deposited Josh and Monica at her place and returned to get Adrian from Finnegan's, when I receive a text from C.J.

C.J.: Bo's here. Dude's in bad shape—he needs to get home.

I growl and punch my steering wheel. I knew this would happen, and I've used the entire night trying to plan how to deal with it. I text Regan.

Me: Hey, are you guys in town or in Concord or what?
Regan: Concord, why? Everything OK?
Me: Not really...don't say anything to Rae but Bo's drunk and can't drive home. I'll figure it out. Seriously, don't say anything to Rae.

Instantly, my phone rings. It's Regan.

"Ember, what's going on?" I can tell he's gone outside by his breathlessness.

"Bo drank a lot tonight. I don't know if he's planning on driving home to Concord, but C.J. texted me and said Bo's in rare form at Lost Dog right now. Adrian's gonna be pissed." I mumble the last part under my breath.

"Listen, I'll tell you where my spare key is. Take Bo there, if you'd like. I actually just left Rae's." Regan dictates where I'll find his spare key before we hang up, and I prepare to deal with Adrian by resting my head on the steering wheel.

After a few minutes I return to Finnegan's, resolved that I have to take Bo back to my place. I can't leave him alone in a stranger's apartment—not in the state he's in. Adrian is once again chatting up Marley at the bar. Ordinarily, his attention to her might irritate me, but right now I have other issues stalking my nerves.

"Hey, we gotta talk a sec." I reach around him and give his waist a squeeze.

"What's up, Blue?" His slur tells me he's drunk, too. Great.

"C.J. just texted me. Bo's at Lost Dog and he's too drunk to drive—" Marley's eyes widen just before Adrian cuts me off.

"Hell no, Ember." Adrian hastily pushes his chair back, crashing it to the ground as he walks outside.

Mouthing a *sorry* to Marley as I right the stool, I follow behind Adrian. I catch up with him outside in time to see him kick over a trashcan.

"What the hell, Adrian!"

"God dammit, Ember, how deep is his hold on you?" Heads turn in our direction as he yells.

"So because yesterday was the anniversary of his parents' death, and I don't want him to drive drunk all the way back to New Hampshire, that means he has a hold on me?"

"He's not staying with us tonight."

"And where do you suggest he stay?" I place my hands on my hips, bored with Adrian's insistence that this is a pissing contest.

"How about his car—he's no stranger to that, if I remember correctly." Adrian accurately recalls Lost Dog's last involvement in our lives.

With an annoyed sigh, I turn for the parking lot. Adrian doesn't follow. Turning back around, I see him walking the opposite direction toward the beach.

"Where the hell are you going?" My head is spinning with anxiety.

He doesn't turn around. "Going for a walk."

A frustrated growl punches its way out of my throat. "Adrian!" I call as I jog toward him. "You're too drunk to drive, and your car is at my place. Just come with me and we'll figure everything out. I can take Bo to Regan's apartment," I concede.

"Blue," he sighs, "just go pick him up, and I'll catch up with you later." Adrian continues his walk without another word.

Before getting in my car I leave Marley my number, instructing her to call me if Adrian comes back in. She agrees, tucking the paper in her pocket as she pours shots. I remember to grab my guitar from the stage before driving to Lost Dog with giant knots strangling my stomach.

Chapter 24

"Rapunzel, over here!" C.J. shouts from the corner of the bar as my eyes squint to adjust to the dungeon-like lighting of Lost Dog.

C.J. is sitting with a few guys I don't know, but I easily spot Bo's broad-shouldered torso hunched over the bar. I've never seen Bo drunk before; it's sad. His forehead rests on a clenched fist, while he grips a short glass with the other.

"Thanks for texting me, Ceej," I mumble.

"No problem. His pissing and moaning over you was a major buzz kill." C.J. and his friends laugh at his joke.

I roll my eyes and cautiously place my hand on the small of Bo's back. The gesture startles him, as if I've woken him up from a deep sleep. He whips around to face me. Hollowness has filled his eyes and his paleness makes me worried that he'll throw up—there's no way I can leave him alone at Regan's.

"The hell are you doing here?" He slurs as he cocks his head back.

"Saving your ass." C.J. snickers behind his beer, as I reach for Bo's arm to throw around my shoulders.

"Need help, Rapunzel?" C.J. half-heartedly asks.

Of course I need help, dickweed, look at the size of him.

"No thanks, Ceej. This princess doesn't need rescuing."

I'm relieved at Bo's lack of protest at my guiding him out of the bar; a struggle would have tossed me to the floor for sure. I fold him into the passenger seat of my Outback and put down the window. I beg him to ask me to stop the car if he has to throw up, but stop my speech when I hear him snoring. I pray, for the first time in my life, that I can get him safely into my apartment and that he doesn't have alcohol poisoning.

When we pull in front of my apartment, I throw the car in park and slam my head against the headrest. He didn't throw up on the drive, but I glance at my second floor window and wonder how I'll get him to my apartment with the same success. I exit and walk over to his door; his head is resting on the window. As soon as I pull the handle, the door flies open under his weight, and I have to steady him from falling to the road.

"Ugh. Ember?" He struggles to find his footing as I, once again, wrap his arm around my shoulders.

"Yeah, just take it easy so we can get up the stairs, OK?"

"Isn't this your apartment?" He squints despite the post-midnight darkness.

"It is." I grit my teeth as I try to take a step forward but trip a little. He's probably got 70 pounds on me, and I begin to wonder if we're going to spend the night on the sidewalk, when I hear someone run up from my left.

"Ember!" Regan dashes behind me, scoops up Bo's other arm, and leads us forward.

"Where'd you come from?" I breathe a sigh of relief as we start up the stairs.

"Yeah, where's my sister?" Bo asks, eyes barely open.

Regan answers Bo, looking at me, "She's at home asleep. I don't stay there." He gives a proud smile and I understand. He's falling for her.

"You didn't have to come to get me, Ember," Bo mumbles as we trudge up the narrow staircase.

I'm slightly out of breath. "Don't worry about it."

"No, no, I mean it ..." He stops and tries to turn and address me, but it throws me off balance."

"Shit!" I yell, afraid I'm about to fall down the stairs. I catch myself on the railing, but Bo doesn't even notice I was falling. "Just...shut up until we get you up the stairs."

Regan gives me a concerned look. I shake my head and tilt my chin toward the apartment, where I'd like to get going.

As we reach the top of my stairs, Bo seems to gather a second wind and is able to stand without much assistance. He leans against the wall opposite my door— just in case, I suppose.

"Where's Adrian?" Bo asks as he stuffs his hands in his pockets.

I shrug. "Out."

"But, you're all *with* him." He knocks his head back into the wall.

"Yeah, and you're all *with* Ainsley. What's your point?" I say with my back to him as I unlock the door.

Regan and I flank Bo and guide him into the apartment, onto my couch.

"Yeah," he slurs, "but I don't love her the way you love him." Regan winces a little at Bo's words. My sigh carries me to the kitchen, and I return with water for Bo.

I sit on the coffee table across from Bo and hand him the water. "You shouldn't drink so much. A lot of people depend on you."

We lock eyes, staring into each other as Regan shifts uncomfortably to my side. Bo's eyes toss like waves back and forth across my face, drowning me in their darkness.

With a deep breath I continue, "Judging by your closing song this evening, I'd say you don't really believe I love Adrian." I'm human, I can't help it.

Bo chuckles gruffly and runs his hand through his hair. "I don't know why you believe you are."

"Who the hell said I believed that?" Absentmindedly, I take off his shoes and put them by the door.

"So you don't love him?" Bo asks, sounding almost sober. Regan's eyebrows shoot up in apparent amusement at my banter with a drunken fool.

I shake my head and ask Regan to help me get Bo to my bed. It's closer to the bathroom, and he's too big to pass out on my couch. Bo's able to get there without much physical assistance, and lays face-down on my bed.

"At least take your shirt off, for god's sake. If you puke, I'd rather you didn't have to drive home half-naked tomorrow." I lift the bottom of his shirt. He sits back up and wraps his hand around my wrist.

"Why do you care what happens to me?" Anyone just walking in might think he is sober by his tone. His grip around my wrist tightens when I try to tug it away.

"I care what happens to you." My nose tingles with threatening tears.

He drops my hand and takes off his shirt. "I don't love her —Ainsley, I mean."

"I know who you're talking about." I fold his shirt and put it on top of my dresser. Regan is leaning in the doorway, watching our scene.

Bo presses his elbows into his knees and holds his head in his hands. His shoulders are tight, wrought with tension. Deep breaths cause the black cross to swell and deflate. He sits back up, pinching the bridge of his nose before he speaks.

"I'm sorry, November."

"Don't be sorry. I just didn't want you to drive dru -"

"No," he cuts me off, "I'm sorry for everything. Fucking everything." His speech is still slightly slurred.

I'm not having this conversation with him right now. "Just get some sleep, OK?"

The alcohol in his system forces his compliance, and he resumes his face-down position on my bed. I fetch my trashcan from the bathroom and hand it to Regan, who places it on the floor next to the bed. Walking back to the living room, I grab my cell phone, noting no missed calls or texts from Adrian. Five tries later, he's still not answering my calls, and I throw my phone onto the couch and pace to the window, pressing my head into the cool glass.

"So the rest of the party got interesting, I take it?" Regan enters the room and sinks into the couch. I tell Regan about Bo playing "Better Man" and the ensuing drunk hijinks that followed.

"Real nice of C.J. to help me out at Lost Dog, by the way," I kid as I plunk next to him.

"He's an ass. I can't believe you got Bo to the car by yourself ..." Regan trails off as he puts his arm around my shoulders.

"What?" I look up at him to finish his thought.

He stares at his knees and furrows his brow for a moment before speaking. I know that what's coming is real. "His shit with Ainsley—"

"Regan, don't." I lean forward, "I told you I didn't want to know anything."

"Just be quiet and listen. As far as I can tell, there's nothing to tell if I even wanted to. Whenever I've been at their house, he's always in the studio...alone. He doesn't ever really go anywhere."

"Why are you telling me this?"

"Honestly? Because you carried that drunk giant out of the bar, all the while not knowing where your "boyfriend" is." Air quotes and all.

"Regan?

"Yeah?"

The words elbow each other for pole position in my throat. My eyes cast downward and Regan places his finger under my chin, forcing me to look back at him.

"Ember, what is it?"

I close my eyes as a single tear slides along the outline of my nose and falls onto my lip. I feel his thumb wipe it away as he pulls me into a hug.

"I know," he whispers.

Chapter 25
Bo

My head pounds in rhythm with a bang on a door.

Shit, where am I?

I peel my eyes open and blink around in disbelief. I'm in November's bedroom. Looking to either side of me, I quickly put together that I slept here alone last night—judging by the undisturbed covers. I hear the apartment door creak open slowly and muffled greetings become louder.

"Where the hell were you all night?" She sounds exhausted.

"Pace drove down and picked me up. He just dropped me off to get my car."

Turner.

Blood races through my veins at the sound of his tone with her. I don't remember much about last night, but I don't need to remember anything to know he's been a dick.

"Is he here? Those are his shoes, aren't they?" His volume rises, and with it, the hair on the back of my neck.

"I said he could stay here." I can tell by her tone that she doesn't care for his.

"Yeah," the pompous ass interjects, "and I said he couldn't."

"Well, good thing this is my apartment then, huh? There's no way I was going to let him drive home last night with how drunk he was. If anything happened...I couldn't do that to Rae ..." I wonder if she's starting to cry based on the tightness in her voice, but their continuing argument erases those thoughts.

"Wait, he's in your fucking bedroom?" I start to sit up when I hear Adrian walk through the kitchen. She stops him.

"Look at me, Adrian, I'm in the same damn clothes I wore last night, and I haven't slept. You wouldn't return my calls, I was afraid Bo had alcohol poisoning, and I put him in my bed because he's too big for my couch. What do you think happened here?" Ember's yelling now.

"You don't think it's inappropriate for you to take your ex-boyfriend home and for me to find him in your bed the next morning?" His condescension is palpable. I'd love to punch him.

They're right outside the bedroom door. My head is spinning wildly, and I don't think I can stand, let alone engage in a confrontation with Turner. I try to calm the vortex of my brain, in case I need to intervene.

"I think it's inappropriate for you to wander down the beach after midnight and not return my calls. That's what I think is inappropriate." I can almost see her hand on her hip by her tone, and it makes me smile.

"It's him or me, Ember. When you figure it out, come find me." Adrian's voice gets softer as he walks away.

"What the fuck is *that* supposed to mean? This isn't a competition, Adrian. I'm with you."

Ouch.

"Figure it out, Em." He slams the door shut. For a moment, I can't tell if Ember's left with him, until I hear her feet pad down the hallway. I close my eyes and pretend to still be asleep.

"Bo?" she whispers as she quietly opens the door.

I don't respond. Ember walks to the side of the bed and stands still, but I can hear her breathing and smell her perfume. I hear her dresser drawer open and chance a glance with one eye in her direction. She lifts off her dress from last night and reaches for a t-shirt. She really has lost a bit of weight; her shoulder blades don't hide in her skin the way they should when she puts her arms down.

I close my eyes when she starts to turn around. She sinks slowly onto the bed. Suddenly, her hand is on my bare chest, just over my heart. I beg it to slow down, but it won't; her touch is its life. Without a word, she rests her hand there for what feels like a minute. I hate that I can't see her face. With a heavy sigh, she moves her hand to my forehead, brushing my hair aside. Her soft fingertips glide down the side of my face and her thumb traces my bottom lip, pausing long enough for me to have to suppress the urge to kiss it. I can feel her pulse pounding against the pad of her thumb.

Ember stands, balancing herself on my arm and running her fingers along the outside of the leather cuff Rae bought me for my birthday last year. She lets her fingers trail the length of mine as she pulls her arm away and walks out of the room. I hear her leave her apartment, get in her car, and drive away. I reach for my phone.

It's now or never.

"Rae? Yeah, it's me. No...I'm fine. Listen, I need your help."

Chapter 26
Ember

I drive straight to Monica's. My mind is spinning—I had to get out of there. I managed to leave Bo a note, telling him to feel free to use the shower so he doesn't smell like a frat house when he gets home.

It's me or him. Adrian's words echo through my soul. I shake my head and try to figure him out. He knows about the kiss. I didn't deny it and I don't know why. *You know why.*

Sleepy, and probably hung over, Monica answers the door.

"You look like hell," I tease as I slide in. She groans in response and wanders to the kitchen and pours coffee.

We settle onto the couch and let the caffeine work into our systems in silence. I take a breath and share my version of the night. I have to back up a bit to remind her of the parts she's hazy on, but as soon as I say "Better Man," her eyes widen as the night seems to fall back into place. Josh staggers out of the bedroom in time to hear the blow-by-blow of getting Bo into my apartment and to bed.

"Wait. C.J. didn't help you at all?" Josh rubs his eyes and gulps coffee.

Monica rolls her eyes. "*That's* what you're pulling from the story? You need help."

"Or more coffee," he grunts and walks to the kitchen.

"So what are you going to do about Adrian?" Monica sets her coffee down and crosses her arms. "I mean, clearly you're thinking about it, or you would have followed his sorry ass straight to Boston."

I snort, "Adrian Turner doesn't need me to chase after him, Monica."

"Maybe he does." She shrugs.

Maybe he does.

"I can't believe he told me he loves me."

"Yeah, right before he told you he figured out Bo kissed you.

"Good point." I arch my eyebrow.

"I know." She arches hers.

"I don't think I love him. I mean, I care a lot about him and, sexually...come on. But ..." I shake my head and look past Monica.

"Say it, November." She can see my thoughts, I swear it.

"I know I said it the night of the Coldplay concert but...I really think I might still love Bo."

Monica raises her palms to the sky. "Praise the friggen Lord!"

"What's with the revival in here?" Josh chuckles as he reenters the room. I often forget his dad is a preacher. It makes me laugh every time.

"Our girl here has finally admitted, out loud, to still having feelings for Bo."

"I said *might*." I'm ignored.

"Thank God." He sits back, seemingly relieved.

"You two are awfully spiritual this morning," I mumble into my coffee.

Monica laughs. "We're going to Josh's parents for the week, gotta practice."

We all laugh at the double life they'll have to lead before the wedding. They've agreed to keep separate apartments until the big day, but the rest of their private life is top secret around Josh's conservative parents. They nearly keeled over when he decided to move to the Cape and manage a bar. His business sense is sharp, though, and he single-handedly saved Finnegan's from going under.

"So," Josh interjects, running his hand through his sandy-brown hair, "does this mean you and Bo will stop being so shitty to each other?" The question takes me by surprise, and I furrow my brow at him.

"Oh come on, Ember ..." Monica rolls her eyes.

"I'm not with Adrian to hurt Bo, guys."

"Well, it hurts him. And after Regan told you Bo and Ainsley don't really seem to be together ..." Monica leads.

"What? Is he using her to hurt me?"

Josh senses an argument and raises his hands. "Ladies...we all know Bo wouldn't ever do anything to hurt Ember. I've seen him talk about her; it's just not possible. But, guys don't think straight—"

"Ever," I cut in.

"No, smart ass, guys don't think straight when they're heartbroken. You women chop off and dye your hair, curling up on your best friend's lap to cry for days." Monica and I stare at each other, on the brink of hysteria regarding his accuracy. "Guys," he continues, "we just want the hurt to go away. I'll reference my drunken showdown with you, Ember, as an example of not thinking straight."

I mull over Josh's words and think about Regan not having seen Ainsley and Bo together. I begin to wonder if Bo thinks I'm with Adrian to hurt him.

"Take the blackmail out of the equation completely." Monica leans forward and touches my knee. "Would you have ever second-guessed your relationship with Bo for another go 'round with Adrian Turner? I mean, Turner's fine as hell—"

"Nice, Monica," Josh chuckles.

"Seriously, is he anything more than walking sex?" Her eyebrows shoot up.

"Wow. Tell me how you really feel, Mon." I stand and bring my coffee mug to the kitchen.

"I already did," she shouts, reminding me she thinks I've royally screwed myself.

I pause at the sink, sick with the realization that a sane person doesn't take care of a drunken ex-boyfriend while their current boyfriend wanders up and down the beach.

"I've gotta get to Boston." I sigh and walk to the door.

"By the way, Asshole," Monica walks over to me and smacks my arm, "I googled your parents after the night of the Coldplay concert. You and I are going to have a serious discussion."

"Way to hold out on us, Ember." Josh fakes annoyance as I leave.

* * *

After the longest drive to Boston in my life, I'm standing at the private entrance of The W, filled with dread. Adrian's going to want answers and I don't know if I have them. Why did I carry Bo out of a bar when he was doing a perfectly fine job of drowning his sorrows? Why did I insist my ex-boyfriend stay at my house when Regan offered his? Why, for the love of God, why did I walk away from Adrian last night when he headed down the beach? I have the answers...there's only one answer.

My body has been rejecting my actions with Adrian for weeks. I've lost weight, I can't sleep, and I walk around with a solid knot in my gut most days. I've lied to my friends, my family, and myself. And for what? Because I was pissed off a few weeks ago? My spirit has become a complete disaster, a junkie tapping its veins for the release Adrian Turner provides.

"Ms. Harris." The doorman nods and I force a tight smile, mouth closed so I don't throw up all over his nice suit.

"Thank you," I whisper through my clenched teeth.

With trembling knees, I knock on Adrian's door. It swings open freely. Adrian doesn't look at me as he motions me in.

"Hi." I jump with the slam of the door behind me.

"You came." With a dead tone, he leans against the door, crossing his arms and ankles.

"You're kidding," I punch up the sarcasm. "You don't answer my calls all night, then tell me your brother drove all the way from Boston to pick you up. Then," I stand toe-to-toe with him at the door, "you barge into my apartment and demand that I choose between the two of you? What does that even mean?" I can't let Adrian know how I'm feeling until I get some answers about last night. His face doesn't change.

"I saw you watching him play. You were in your own world. Damn, Ember, you jumped three feet in a crowded bar when I came up behind you." He slides past me and paces thoughtfully toward the expansive window.

"It's music, Adrian, I'm always lost in it." I shoulder next to him with a whisper as we watch the busy city below.

"You should have seen your face when he started playing that song. It was like someone punched you right in the gut."

"It hurt my feelings."

Adrian takes my hand. "He shouldn't affect your feelings at all, Ember." Hurt saturates his eyes and seeps down his face.

As I lock into Adrian's eyes, I know Bo will always affect me. I'm miserable and it's not Adrian's fault.

"No," Adrian startles me from my thoughts, cupping my face in his hands, "You're mine, Ember, and I'm yours." His vocal cords strum panic as he scans my eyes.

"Adrian ..." My voice has never been so shaky. He tightens his grip on my face as I try to pull away.

"You're not bailing on us, Blue. We just got started." His voice is approaching a yell.

Grabbing Adrian's wrists, I pull his hands away from my face. "It's not about bailing, Adrian."

He walks over to the bar, pouring himself a shot, while I sit on the couch. I don't mention that it's barely past noon on a Sunday.

"So what's it about, then? I sat by and watched you date another guy who was lying to you. You bailed on him and came to me when shit hit the fan. What is it now, if this isn't bailing? What's it about?" The shot glass glides between his thumb and forefinger.

"Me," I state flatly.

"Goddammit, Ember, it's always fucking about you!" Adrian hurls the shot glass through the air, and it shatters against the window. Reflexively, I stand and walk into the kitchen. My heart races as he strides toward me and starts yelling. "In college you wouldn't even let me speak when you broke up with me. It was about *your* fears, and it crushed me, November. It fucking crushed me!"

His nostrils flair with each ragged breath he takes. Anger clashes with the hurt in his eyes, and I start doing the most unattractive thing possible—yelling and crying at the same time. The feral yell that comes from my throat startles both of us as tears pour down my face. I'm exhausted, angry, and confused.

"So what the hell is your problem then, huh?" I sniff back the tears that are pouring through my nose. "Why the hell would you want to be with me again if I hurt you so bad?"

In a flash, Adrian's lips are on mine, his tongue thrashes desperately through my mouth. I try to pull my head back but his fingers thread tightly through my hair. I want to give in to it; to submit to the physical intoxication that is Adrian, but I can't. I have to respect myself, and this certainly isn't the way to do it. Adrian pulls away from me and, with swollen lips, starts to speak.

"Because I'm addicted to you, Blue. Five years of withdrawal was torture without you in my life. I need you." He unwinds his hands from my hair and glides them down my shoulders before stepping back and leaning against the counter with clenched fists.

We're addicts. Co-dependent on lust. We're sick with it, and sick without it. At least without it we have the option to heal. My tears have stopped, and my breathing has returned to normal. I stare at the broken glass across the apartment before returning to Adrian's glare.

"That's not healthy, Adrian. It's not healthy that you're addicted to me, and it's not healthy that I feel the same about you. Too much will never be enough for us. You tell me you love me when you're scared, and I ignore who I am to escape with you."

"That's all I've ever been to you? A fucking escape?" Adrian slams his fist down on the island, and I wonder if granite can crack.

"I never meant to hurt you in college, Adrian. God, we were barely twenty-one! A lot has happened between then and now, but the fact remains that we're too much for each other."

His ragged breathing returns as he takes one step forward. I take one back.

"Have you been with him?" His tone drops an octave to the one called "calculating."

"No. I've told you that. Twice now."

"What do you mean *ignore who you are?*" His jaw ripples beneath the surface of his frown.

"This isn't me, Adrian. This penthouse, the doorman, the valet. It's just not me. I'm beer, beaches, and guitars. That's who I've always been."

Adrian slowly lifts his chin and studies me from head to toe. He turns around mechanically and walks down the hallway, as I stand frozen in silence. He returns with his Princeton hoodie, the one I always wear, the one I always wore back then. He tosses it in my direction but I let it fall at my feet while I wait for him to speak.

"Adrian ..." I start, but he cuts me off without looking at me. He's staring at Princeton on the floor. Faded orange sleeves and tattered blue lettering.

"I never had you, did I? I never stood a chance." He turns his back before continuing. "Get out of my apartment. I don't ever want to see you again." The finality in his voice sends chills through my body. "Go!"

Startled, I jump with my hand on the doorknob. Adrian laces his fingers together behind his neck, takes a deep breath, and looks up at the ceiling. I look between the sweatshirt and his back. With a quiet deep breath I leave the sweatshirt—and everything it represents—alone in the apartment with Adrian. I hold it together down the private elevator, through the private corridor, and past the well-dressed doorman. I manage a polite "thank you" to the valet when he hands me my keys, before pulling into the parking garage and sobbing until I have nothing left.

I'm hopelessly, helplessly in love with Bo Cavanaugh. My fears, my indecisions, and my insecurities have swirled a bitter cocktail of regret in my soul. When the tears are gone and the raw pain of my decisions sears through my nerves, I drive back to Barnstable.

I have to get my shit together.

Chapter 27

Work has provided the perfect focal point over the last week. I've had a few business calls with Rae, but everything with the community center is going smoothly. There's not much that needs to be done on my end right now. I miss it. I miss DROP's halls and Rae's smiling face everyday. I miss *him*. The constant anxiety I felt for half of every week for the last several weeks hasn't been replaced. It's just...gone. I *miss* him.

Monica was shocked to find me back at my apartment last Sunday after Adrian and I broke up. I couldn't run to Bo without making sure I was a whole person first. I've been questioning what it was, exactly, that made me bail in Concord. It was fear, many different kinds of fear. I was scared of Bill and Tristan, and confused at Bo's involvement. I was scared, wondering if there were other secrets. Mostly, I was scared of our pace. We fell in love in an instant; a split second blink and my entire world shifted. I was scared that it wasn't real...or that it was. That still scares me.

With Josh and Monica on vacation at his parents' house, I've been able to go home from work, write, play my guitar, and sleep. There have been tears. Lots of tears. But, I let them come this time. I'm looking forward to playing at Finnegan's tonight. With Josh out of town, Regan's taking over guitar and vocals. Rae smiles at Regan from the crowd as we warm up.

"She's great, isn't she?" I whisper to Regan between vocal

checks.

"She's amazing." His grin is infectious. "How are you holding up, Kid?"

"You know, Regan, I actually feel great. Seems my body knew that what I was doing with Adrian was wrong before my mind did. I can't believe how much better I feel." I settle onto the stool as C.J. taps our starting tempo between his sticks.

After a long, sweet look, Regan strums C.J.'s tempo and we get lost in our set. Regan and C.J. have played together for years, even as kids, so it's up to me to keep up with their silent understanding of our playlist. We have a page or two worth of "accepted" songs, but "The Cave" by Mumford and Sons isn't one of them. I roll my eyes and flip C.J. off behind my back as he and Regan start it as our closing number. Regan switches to the guitar for the number and sings with me. Thankfully, it's one of my favorites and I'm able to give it my best shot. Assholes.

"You pulled it off, Rapunzel. You pulled it off," C.J. teases through the applause.

"You're both dickheads." I give them a smug smile.

Regan wraps his arm around my shoulders and leans down, speaking in my ear, "You're worlds better without that Adrian guy in your head, November. That was the best I've heard you sing since I've known you." My cheeks burn at his interpretation of my performance. "You were right when you said you sing for you, that's for sure." He pulls away as Rae hugs his waist from behind. After they kiss, and C.J. rolls his eyes and heads to the bar, Rae turns to me.

"Thanks for taking care of Bo last week, Ember." I shoot Regan an accusatory stare. "No," she continues, "Bo told me ..."

"Oh. OK. It wasn't a problem. He doesn't drink much, huh?" I try to chuckle at his sloppy performance after the engagement party.

"He didn't use to." Before the awkward silence suffocates us, she perks up. "Hey, do you want to come riding with Regan and I next weekend?"

"Like horseback riding?"

"Yeah. There are some great trails a few miles outside of town. Family friends own a stable that we can use whenever we want. I thought it might be fun, me, you, Bo—"

"Rae ..." I'm not in the mood to be set up on a date. Not with Bo—we're a bit past that even if we're not together.

"Oh come on, Ember, it'll be fun!"

"You make a convincing argument," I tease, "but I just don't want to be under a microscope right now. I know you wouldn't intentionally make it feel that way, but...I mean your brother and I haven't even had a sober conversation since the community center opened." I shake my head and shoulder up to C.J. at the bar. He slides me his just-poured beer before ordering another one. "Thanks," I mumble, taking a sip.

"Ember, listen." Rae stands next to me and speaks in a near whisper, "I'm not supposed to say anything but Bo has something he's planning, and it was my job to get you to Concord next weekend." She knots her fingers and looks at me through her mile-long lashes. "I'm failing here. You've *got* to cut me some slack. If you don't want to come riding, that's fine...just meet us at Tarryn's around seven on Saturday, OK?"

"Tarryn's?" I sigh.

"Yeah, it's the restaurant where we first had dinner...when Ainsley was there, remember?"

"Oh, yeah, the time I realized I couldn't live without you!" I laugh, remembering her obvious detest of Ainsley that evening.

"That's the one. Will you remember how to get there?" Her eyes widen in excitement.

"If I decide to go I'll see you there, OK?"

"Trust me, Ember, you're not going to want to miss this. I love you!" She squeezes my neck with all the force her 110-pound frame can muster and leaves a wet kiss on my cheek.

She and Regan disappear in hand-holding bliss, and I'm left with C.J. at the bar. I study the beer he gave me.

"Thanks again for the beer, that was oddly nice of you." I don't know how to speak to C.J. with anything but sarcasm.

"No problem, Rap-"

"Seriously, dude, what's with Rapunzel?" I cut him off. "Is it the hair? It's not *that* long."

C.J. stares at me with his chocolate brown eyes and sucks in a deep breath before answering me.

"You honestly don't know?" I shake my head in response to his condescending tone. "Fine. Look, it's like...you're the hottest girl in here on any night of the year. It's a fact. I mean, seriously, Ember, look around you." C.J. gestures around the bar with his beer bottle, eyes widened. "No one comes close. You're untouchable ..." He looks down and picks at the beer label with his thumb.

"C.J...what?" Candor is not something I've come to expect from him, and I think he's joking with me.

"And the best part is you have no idea, which makes you a hundred times more gorgeous. So, *Rapunzel*, you're in a stair-less tower. No one can get to you...except for that Bo guy. Why are you locking the door on that?"

"I'm not." I shake my head in confusion.

"Then meet the poor bastard in Concord next weekend and see what he has planned, would you?" C.J. yawns while he laughs.

"Tired Ceej?" I ask.

"No, just seeing if that girl over there was staring at me. If you yawn, and someone's looking at you, they'll yawn, too. Look, she's yawning, time to make my move." With a pat on my back, he slides off his stool.

"You're a gem," I chuckle, "poor girl doesn't know what's about to hit her."

"Just go to Concord next weekend, Gorgeous. You deserve it." C.J. cocks his eyebrow and stalks toward the yawner across the bar.

I finish my beer quickly when I realize that Saturday nights are open-mic night at Tarryn's. Butterflies that my stomach thought were extinct burst to life and encircle my insides. Suddenly, I'm struck with a decision that's truly been months in the making. Bravery drives me home and holds my hand as I chase the sunrise with my notebook and guitar.

Chapter 28

I have no idea what to expect from Bo as I drive to Concord on this hot late July day. Well, I have some idea, given that it's at an open-mic night, but I'm trying to focus on my own surprise. I reassured Rae nearly every day this week that I'd be coming, but I've kept mum regarding my plan. Regan knows, since he helped me with a bit of the guitar work, but I've gotten really good in a short amount of time. Regan and Josh say it's in my blood— especially now that they know about my parents.

I pull into the parking lot at Tarryn's at 7:00 on the dot. I don't need my nerves talking me out of this if I have too much time to think. A quick scan of the room shows no sign of Bo, Regan, or Rae, though I suppose Regan and Rae never told me they would be here—they just asked that I be here. I slide my guitar case to my feet as I sit at the bar and order a drink. I'm excited to share this. I'm ready to share it. All I really need is for Bo to be here. The rest of the crowd is just a bonus.

When the MC checks the mic and announces the first act, I pull out my cell phone and check the time. It's 7:10. At 7:15, I text Rae a question mark but receive no response. I try not to check over my shoulder every few minutes, but that's a task that's proving to be impossible.

7:20 …

7:25…

7:30 …
7:35 …
Ainsley.

"Interesting seeing you here." Ainsley places a hand on her hip as she squares off next to me.

"Is it?" I mumble, turning in her direction.

"Why are you here?"

"I was invited."

"By who?"

"Bo." I grin as her cheeks redden.

"Hmm," she stammers as she tries to recover, "I guess you've been stood up, Sweetheart. He's supposed to be playing right now and he's not here." Now it's my turn for red cheeks.

I'd be lying if I said I didn't think she could be telling the truth. And the fact that Rae didn't answer my text means that she either doesn't know I'm sitting here alone, or she's fighting with Bo about it. Still, I have Ainsley to deal with.

"You'd love that, wouldn't you? For Bo to stand me up. I just have one question for you," I say as I stand and reach for my guitar. "Can you tell me where he was last Saturday night? I can, and it wasn't with you." I chuckle at Ainsley's effort to keep her face composed, while her eyes nearly bug out of her head.

I make it out of the bar and slide my guitar in the car before trying Rae again. There's no answer, so I have no choice but to call Bo and find out why I'm here alone at, now, forty minutes after we were supposed to meet. I dial his number and wait through three rings. My nervous energy has transferred to annoyance.

"Hello?" A man answers. It's not Bo. I check my phone and it says that I did, in fact, call Bo.

"Uh, hello? Bo? It's November …" I know it's not him, but I need to clarify that somehow.

"November, it's David Bryson. I have Bo's phone right now." His voice is shaky and leads my pulse into a race pace.

"David, I'm here at Tarryn's. I was supposed to meet Bo at seven—is everything OK?"

"November …" The change in his tone throws my heart to its knees in prayerful supplication.

No, no, no…Please let him be OK. Please.

Fumbling with my keys, I drop them twice before I get my door unlocked and push my guitar to the back seat.

"David, what is it? Is Bo OK?" Something awful has happened. My body knows it; I'm already crying.

"Listen, we're at the hospital," he takes a deep breath and clears his throat, "Bo's fine. Rachel had an accident on the horse today, she's in surgery right now ..." He keeps talking but I can't make out the words. I speed out of Tarryn's lot in search of the hospital.

* * *

When I arrive at the hospital, I spot David standing out front. I park as close as I can and sprint toward him. I stop dead in my tracks when I see the tears in his eyes.

"David, what happened? Where are Regan and Bo?" I'm breathless, still fighting tears.

"Rae and Regan were riding on the trail, and Regan said a swarm of bees shot up out of the ground." He pales during his pause. "Rae was in front, leading the way...her horse got spooked, and the next thing he knew, she was flying through the air." David grabs my hand and walks us toward the hospital entrance. His hand is freezing.

"She was wearing a helmet, though. Right?" I'm trying to organize the situation through my spinning thoughts.

"She was, but she hit the rocks hard when she fell. Regan said she was unconscious right away. They're concerned about internal injuries, and she's been in surgery for over an hour ..."

I think he continues the story as we enter the elevator, my hand still in his, but a million thoughts and visions are going through my head. I need to find both Bo and Regan.

She has to be OK.

When the elevator dings, I jump away from my thoughts and follow David's lead. It doesn't take more than a second for me to find Regan, sunken into the floor with his back against the wall and his forehead pressed into his knees.

"Regan!" I shout as I run toward him. The look on his face when he lifts his head sends me to my knees in front of him. I wrap my arms around his shoulders as he sobs into my chest.

"There was nothing I could do ..." he wails into my shirt.

"I know, I know ..." I try to soothe him through my shock and lack of information. I look around and see no sign of Bo.

"He's in the chapel," Regan says without looking up. "We've been taking turns going in there. I told him I'd come get him if they come out with any news."

I look up at David, who nods to me as I stand, and take my seat next to Regan on the floor. A pleasant nurse points me in the direction of the chapel and I feel like I float there, outside of time.

I've only been in a church once before, for my grandmother's funeral when I was ten. I stand outside the chapel door a few moments, unsure of proper etiquette. *Do I knock?* I decide against knocking and slowly open the door. I'm startled by Bo's voice in the small, dark space.

"Please, please, please...You can't do this to me ..." Bo's hunched in prayer position in one of the rows. I can see from here that his knuckles are white. "You can't take her, Lord, you can't. She's all I have left."

I'm struck motionless. We never talked about religion; even if we had, I don't honestly know what I could contribute to the conversation, seeing as how I wasn't raised with any sort of religious framework. However, this man before me is one with a solid faith, and he's speaking to someone he believes will help him. The creak of the door behind me whips Bo's head around.

"November?" He sniffs and drags the heel of his hand under his eyes.

I nod, and before I know it, I'm racing toward him with tears streaming down my face. Kneeling next to him, I pull his head to my shoulder while we both cry for a few minutes.

"Pray with me." He resumes his position with his forehead pressed into his clenched fists.

"I, uh," I clear my throat, "have only been to a church once ..." I make a note to ask my parents what the hell that is all about.

"Just beg for Rae to be OK, Ember. I just need you to beg with me. She hit the ground hard, it's really bad ..." A growl tries to hide his sob but fails. His shoulders shake the entire pew full of fear.

Silently, I start begging.

A few minutes of prayer feels like an eternity in the sorrowful silence of a hospital chapel. My mind wanders to all those who have come through these doors and left with prayers answered...and to those unanswered.

"We should go back down the hall." Bo stands and grabs my hand, leading me out of the chapel. I look over my shoulder and stare at the large wooden cross one more time before the door closes.

Please.

Rounding the corner, we find David and Regan have moved to some chairs that have opened up in the hallway. Sweat has formed between my palm and Bo's, but he just grips tighter each time my hand slides.

As we're about to sit, a surgeon comes through two large doors at the end of the hall. He must be on Rae's case, because Regan and Bo nearly run down the hall to meet him, while David and I sit back and observe anxiously. I can only see the doctor's face, but that's all I need.

In one blink, everything moves in slow motion like it does in the movies, and my ears shut down. Regan's hands tear through his hair as his presses his forehead into the wall. A breath later I see David race from his chair toward Bo, who falls to his knees at the doctor's feet. I feel a hand around my arm, leading me to the nearest chair as it all comes crashing down around me.

She's gone.

Chapter 29

I shake free from the nurse trying to be helpful in my state of shock and run toward Bo and Regan. David is trying to pull Bo off the floor.

"No! Let me see her!" Hoarse wailing rips through Bo's throat.

I stop behind Regan and place my hand cautiously on his back. He slaps it away and sinks to the floor with his forehead still against the wall, tears trailing his descent.

"Oh shit, they've got to be out of their mind," David mumbles, standing to address something behind me.

I turn to see a small cluster of reporters gathered where I was just sitting. David leaves Bo on the floor in a heap and yells obscenities into the crowd behind me, rubbing the tears from his anguished face. A nurse leads Bo to a private room off the end of the hallway, and a second nurse helps Regan. I'm left face-to-face with the surgeon. I wonder, briefly, how many times he's had a front-row seat to this scene, how many people have been brought to their knees by his words.

"Ma'am, are you family?" His gentle voice seems out of place. I look around and realize he's addressing me. I shake my head, unable to speak. "I'm Doctor Mashburn. I won't be able to speak to Mr. Cavanaugh until the initial shock wears off...I need to speak to a family member to discuss the next steps."

"There's no one left." With those words, a cascade of

reality streams down my face, and I'm knocked off-balance by dizziness. Dr. Mashburn steadies me; suddenly I'm weeping onto his scrubs.

There's no one left.

Looking back, I see David talking with security guards. He catches my eye, nods to the security guard, and walks toward us.

"Dr. Mashburn...he, um...needs to talk to family." That's all I can manage before sobs take over.

* * *

An hour later, I'm sitting next to Regan in the tiny grief room off the hallway—that's my name for it. If it has another title, it's wrong. David and Bo went behind the double doors to say goodbye to Rachel before facing the world. And, the world is waiting.

News of Rachel Cavanaugh's death has spread like wildfire through the streets of Concord. Reporters are snaking around, and the phones have been ringing off the hook at the nurses' desk. No one is allowed on the floor we're on, thanks to David's stern words with the security guards. Monica and Josh are on their way. David asked the security guards to meet them at the doctors' entrance and escort them to the grief room when they arrive.

"Regan," I whisper. He rubs his face with his hands and looks at the wall.

"There was nothing I could do. The bees came out of nowhere ..." His eyes clench tight, as though he's trying to wring the memory from his brain.

"I know," my voice breaks as fresh tears spill, "I'm so sorry." My shoulders shake as I bow into my hands.

"Ember!" Monica runs into the room and kneels in front of me. I cry harder, meeting her on the floor. Her arms anchor around my neck. Josh squats next to us and hugs us both before walking to Regan.

Regan tells us that despite wearing a helmet, Rae suffered extensive internal injuries when she hit the ground. She lacerated her liver and succumbed to internal bleeding. She never regained consciousness after her fall.

"I'm going to go back to Bo's house with him today if he'll let me. I can't let him go home alone—will you guys come?" I tie my hair back and rub the remainder of smudged mascara from under my eyes.

"Of course." Monica eyes Josh, who nods in response.

"Regan, come with us," I encourage, "you can't be alone either."

"I'll come." He leans back and rests his head against the wall.

"Ms. Harris?" A nurse quietly enters the room.

"Yes?" I sniff as I stand, wiping my eyes.

"Mr. Cavanaugh wants to see you, will you come with me?" I stare into the hallway, not wanting to go into whatever room Bo was just in with Rae. With her body. "It's OK, honey." Her face tells me they've already moved her body to the morgue.

I walk out of the grief room, and hear Josh confidently lead Regan and Monica in a prayer. Suddenly, his religious upbringing isn't so funny anymore. The nurse takes my hand as we head through the large double doors.

"Is David Bryson down here as well?" We walk slowly down an impossibly long hallway.

"No, he went down to address the media."

"Oh." I still can't wrap my mind around the fact that my surrogate sister, and Bo's only living family, is now gone. Forever.

Bo is sitting in an empty room that holds an end table and a couple of chairs. It's like the grief room, only smaller. His bloodshot eyes look up as the door closes behind me; the nurse has left. His skin is ashen, lifeless. I stand in front of him and take his hands. For some reason I don't want him to see me cry, so I look down, trying to blink away tears. They drop on his jeans one by one, and I collapse into his lap, failing to silence my whimpering.

"Oh my God, Bo ..." I pull his forehead to my shoulder and stroke my fingers through the back of his hair.

"What am I going to do?" he wails into my collarbone.

I slide my hands to his face and pull it away from me, staring into his eyes.

"I'm not going anywhere. I promise." Tugging him toward me, I kiss him with what little energy I have left. He kisses me back and we sit for a long time with our lips locked and noses touching. I learn in an instant that sorrow isn't the absence of passion. Sorrow is the darkest, most intense form of passion hidden in the recesses of the human spirit.

* * *

It took about an hour for me to urge Bo to leave the hospital. It wasn't until the funeral home arrived and took Rae's body that he walked in a daze to my car. Josh and Monica are just behind us with Regan in theirs. We pull up to the gated driveway, and Bo reaches for the door handle.

"No, I got it." I squeeze his hand, get out, and enter the code. Bo's phone has been ringing since before we left the hospital. It's ringing again as I get back in.

"Ainsley keeps calling." His voice is nearly gone.

"Do you want me to answer?"

He shrugs, so I answer.

"Hi Ainsley, it's November." The large white house comes into view; it looks haunted now.

"Where's Bo?" she's sobbing.

"He's home. I just brought him back to the house."

"I'll be right over."

Bo hears her through the phone and shakes his head.

"Ainsley, he's asking that people wait until tomorrow before they contact him," I lie. "He's exhausted and I'm sure it's going to be hell to try to sleep, but he's got to try." Bo squeezes my knee in thanks as Ainsley hangs up without a word.

"Thank you," he whispers.

I clear my throat. "Stay in the car for a minute, OK? Is your house unlocked?"

He nods and doesn't question me. I close the door and hold up a finger to Josh; he nods back. Turning the knob slowly, I take a deep breath before stepping into Bo's house. I glance around the entryway and adrenaline splashes over me. In a whirlwind of tears, I gather Rae's coats, shoes, bags, etc. and race them up to her room. I don't look around her room when I get there—I just hold my breath and toss the items on her bed, shutting the door behind me when I leave. Rushing through the dining room and kitchen, I rapidly collect any liquor bottles I find and place them in a box in the mudroom off the kitchen to be dealt with when Bo's asleep.

After a quick run through the house, I open the front door

and find Regan standing outside Josh's car smoking a cigarette. I don't think he usually smokes, but I'd kind of like a cigarette too, to be honest. Bo's empty eyes lead him out of the car and plod him up the front steps.

"I don't know if I can go in there, Em." He stares at the front door.

"It's OK," I take his hand, "we can go in when you're ready. If you want to go in by yourself—"

"No, please don't leave me." Bo squeezes my hand almost painfully.

"I promised I wouldn't."

Chapter 30

A pink and orange sun rises over the Eastern sky, telling us a new day has started. This is the first day since her birth that the world will be without Rachel Cavanaugh. This and every day forward. For eternity.

I splash water on my face in the downstairs bathroom and find Bo and Regan asleep on adjacent couches in the living room. Monica's brewing coffee and hands me a cup as I tiptoe into the kitchen.

"Thanks for staying all night, Mon." I feel like crying, but the well's run dry.

"Of course. I'd never leave you like this. I'll call Carrie today."

"Where's Josh?"

"He's outside talking with David about how to handle people. They'll be coming today. Thank God for a gated driveway, huh?"

I vaguely remember David coming to the house somewhere around three AM and discussing funeral arrangements with Bo. Everyone seems to be in robot-mode right now. I suppose that's the body's way of protecting us from feeling all the pain at once. I slide out of the kitchen chair and sneak to the front porch.

"Hey guys." I sit on the top step and breathe in coffee steam.

"Have you slept, Sweetheart?" David sits next to me and pats my knee.

I shake my head as his simple question beckons my tears. David draws me into his body, and I feel Josh take the mug from my hands as I give in to muscle-quaking sobs. Apart from a few errant tears, I haven't cried in front of Bo, and I've been next to him nearly non-stop since we left the hospital. It just hasn't felt right, letting my puddle of pain drip into the canyon of loss swallowing him whole. David stands in the middle of my distress, and Josh replaces him. Resting his chin on my head, I hear Josh whispering words of prayer. I lift my head and turn to find David speaking with Ainsley in the driveway. I ignore her and look to Josh.

"How do you do that?" I ask him through voice-shaking tears.

"What?" He shrugs.

"You know what prayers to say and when to say them and they fucking make me feel better." I force a frustrated laugh.

Josh chuckles. "Ah, Ember...it's just always been a part of my life. It's really important right now. I don't know what else to do." Sweet desperation flows through his eyes. Monica comes out and hands Josh coffee as he hands mine back to me.

"You're marrying a good man, Monica. A really good man."

"I know." She beams and kisses him. "Ainsley's here?"

"Shit, I forgot." As always, like she can hear my thoughts, Ainsley stalks toward the porch. I gulp a fair bit of coffee and straighten my posture.

"November." Ainsley nods at me, and I notice David narrow his eyes behind her. She's as put together as ever, with the exception of no makeup. Her puffy eyes prove she's spent some time crying, but her gorgeous ensemble prevents me from feeling bad. It annoys me. Everything about her annoys me.

"It's early, Ainsley. Bo's asleep inside. If you want, when he wakes up I can te -"

"I'll wait here," she cuts me off and shows herself to the porch swing. I shrug, uninterested in another go 'round with Ainsley Worthington.

An hour later, David's gone to the funeral home and Regan steps outside, rubbing his arms like he's cold, but it's already over seventy degrees. Ainsley prances to his side and gives him a hug as if she knows who he is and what Rae meant to him. As if she has rights inside his grief. Regan's a class act, however, and returns her condolences with some of his own. Ainsley *has* known Rae longer than any of us on the porch, after all.

"Is Bo up?" Ainsley asks Regan, her hand on the door. I roll my eyes; Josh catches me and grins.

"He's in the bathroom, I think." He shrugs and sits next to me, not giving her any more information.

Just as she turns the knob, Ainsley lets out a surprised gasp as Bo pulls the door the rest of the way open and walks barefoot onto the porch. He's showered and changed his clothes from yesterday, now wearing baggy grey sweatpants that cling to life on his jutting hips, and no shirt. Ainsley lets out a cry and throws her arms around his neck. I look over my shoulder and see him pat her back while looking painfully at me. I stand and make my way down the stairs, needing a little space between me and the blonde pixie. It's not the time for pettiness, and I need a breather.

"Ember, you're not leaving, are you?" Bo's voice takes on an exhausted panic.

"No," I turn and smile, "just taking a little walk. I'll be right back." I lock eyes with Ainsley for a second before turning back down the driveway.

I turn left and head through a wooded part of the property, until I reach a small clearing that holds a hammock next to a still pond. I collapse on the hammock and beg my body to cry it out; it swings back and forth with each released wail, and rocks me to sleep.

* * *

"Ember." Monica's whisper pulls me from a deep sleep, and I have to squint the blinding sun away.

"How long have I been asleep?" I carefully balance my elbows on the hammock's netting and swing my legs off the side.

"Like two hours, I guess. Bo was looking for you after Ainsley left. I'm so, so sorry, Ember." Monica breaks into a full cry. This is the first time we've been alone. "Did you ever meet with Bo at Tarryn's last night, or did this all happen before?"

My God, was this all just yesterday?

I fill Monica in with a timeline of my night before Bo comes through the trees.

"We're going to take Regan home to get clothes and a good night sleep before the funeral tomorrow." Monica stands up, brushing herself off. "Want me to bring you clothes?"

I look nervously to Bo, under Monica's assumption that I'll be staying here. I hope to.

"Bo, is it OK if—"

He nods and wraps his arms around me, silencing the rest of my sentence. Monica rubs my back, signaling her departure. Bo sweeps open the curtained branches of a weeping willow and rests his back against the tree; I follow and sit next to him.

"This spot is gorgeous, Bo. So peaceful." An old habit takes over and I mindlessly rest my head on his shoulder.

"It's Rae's favorite...or was ..." I slide my head to his bare chest as he kisses the top of my head. Bo runs his thumb over the hump of my shoulder and slowly drags it across my collarbone. "Are you OK?"

I look up. "What do you mean, am I OK?"

Bo squares my shoulders in his hands. "Your collarbone never stuck out like this; you've lost a lot of weight, Ember." He rolls his thumbs over my collarbone to accentuate his point.

"I'm fine, Bo." I furrow my brow at his bizarre topic of choice given the circumstances.

He gives me a concerned once-over before welcoming me back into a one-armed embrace. I replace my head on his shoulder before he starts speaking in a distant tone, still tracing my shoulders with his thumbs.

"Did you call Adrian?"

"No." I honestly haven't thought about it, though I suppose someone ought to. As tired as I am, I'm actually hoping he heard it on the news.

"Why not?" Bo sounds surprised, and suddenly, it occurs to me.

"I don't know," I shrug, "I guess when he told me he never wanted to see me again, I assumed that included phone calls." With my ear pressed against his warm skin, I feel Bo's heart rate pick up.

"He said that to you?" I nod and shrug once more. I simply don't care about Adrian Turner right now.

"What happened?" Bo asks, but we're interrupted by the sound of branches breaking beneath someone's feet.

"Here you two are." David enters our fort and squats in front of us with a light grin on his face. "Spencer, the funeral home is all set for tomorrow. Josh left some notes here for scripture suggestions."

"Whatever you think is best, David." Bo lifts his arm from my shoulders and rubs his eyes with a sigh.

Standing, I stretch my arms overhead. "David, I'll walk back to the house and take a look at Josh's notes with you. I don't think I've ever actually opened a Bible, but...Bo, why don't you just hang out here, and I'll come find you when I make lunch, OK?" Bo doesn't argue; he lets his head tilt back against the weeping willow and he closes his eyes.

Once back on the driveway facing the house, David takes my hand.

"I'm so glad you're here, November." The shaking of his hand makes me turn my head. He has tears streaming down his face.

"David, I'm so sorry." I stop and pull my hand away to give him a hug.

"I thought losing Spencer and Vivian was the absolute worst thing that could have happened to those kids," David speaks as we enter the house.

"This is so fucking unreal, excuse my language. In case anyone happens to ask, I put all of Rae's stuff in her bedroom before Bo came in last night. I can't believe the funeral's already tomorrow ..." I know I'm rambling, but David doesn't seem to mind.

"Well, the family from California's on a flight out here as we speak, and everyone else is here. Spencer doesn't want to do a wake, just the funeral service."

"Where's the cemetery? I don't even know...why didn't I ever ask him?"

"Ah," David comes up behind me and gives my shoulders a playful squeeze, "you two were busy falling in love." He says it like we never stopped.

I never did.

* * *

When the sun finally sets on the first day she's gone, the readings, the music, and all other arrangements are set for Rae's funeral. I haven't seen much of Bo since lunch by the pond. Family from California have come and gone to their respective hotels. I've just spent the evening organizing food donations in the refrigerator and freezer. When the last of the dishes are put away and the counters are wiped clean, I dry my hands and turn for the living room; Bo's figure in the doorway startles me.

"Jesus!" I scream, my fatigue causing me to be jumpier than usual.

"Sorry." He lets the fleetest of grins escape his mouth. "Thank you for taking care of all of this, Ember." Bo gestures across the kitchen.

"Of course. You should go get some sleep, if you can. I have no idea how tomorrow will be, but sleep can't hurt." I walk toward him and pick a piece of string off his shirt.

He grabs my hand and holds it to his lips. My eyes follow the length of my arm, up my fingertips, where I stare at his lips as they press against my skin.

His lips tingle against my knuckles as he talks, his eyes closed. "Thank you for staying tonight."

"You need to stop thanking me, Bo," I whisper because, without realizing it, my mouth's run dry under his touch.

Dropping my hand, Bo reaches for my face. New emotion fills his recently void eyes; intention bleeds through his gaze. With his free hand, he brushes my hair away from my shoulders before leaning down and stroking my neck with his nose, making a home for his lips just beneath my jaw. He has to feel my goosebumps beneath his lips.

"Will you come up with me? I don't want to be alone tonight."

Chapter 31

The morning of the funeral is slow chaos. I'm showered and ready for whatever I'm supposed to do before Bo wakes up. He passed out with his head on my chest last night. I was awake most of the night, listening to him breathe. David arrived at the house early to help manage the people who are using the Cavanaugh residence as a staging area. They all mean well, these people I've never seen or heard of before. It makes me feel like an outsider that they all know Bo and Rae so well. Some of the older ones call him Spencer, like David does. I chuckle a little at how pissed I was the first day he showed up at my office using that name.

David catches me alone, staring out a living room window. "How are you doing, Sweetheart?"

His warm embrace really does feel like a father's, and it makes me miss mine. My stomach sinks as I realize I haven't called my parents.

"My parents are out of town, and I totally forgot to call them." David lets go as I walk outside, my cellphone shaking between my fingers.

My dad answers my mom's phone and I'm reduced to tears. "Hey Baby Blue! Your mother and I were just talking about you. Sweetie? Are you OK?" He can hear my sobs.

"It's Rae...Bo's sister...She died—" It's the first time I've said "she died."

I stumble my way through the details when, in a salty haze of tears, I spot Monica's car crawling up the driveway.

"I've gotta go, Dad. Please tell Mom ..."

"Of course, Honey. I wish there was something I could do. I hate that you're hurting like this."

I hang up and let my phone slide out of my hands and tumble down the stairs. Monica stares at it for a second before shrugging and sitting next to me. She combs her fingers through my air-dried waves.

"Want me to straighten this for you? Here are your clothes, by the way. I picked that black seersucker you never wear, that way you don't have to wear it ever again."

"Thanks. Where's Regan?"

"He's riding with C.J. and Josh and they're going right to the church. He spent last night packing his things, says he's going back to Ireland on Wednesday." She looks to the ground.

I raise my brows. "Seriously? He's going to just take off?"

"Can you blame him? What else is holding him here? He was only planning to stay through August anyway, now that his girlfriend is ..."

I shake my head and stand. "You're right. If it had been Bo, I don't know what I would have—"

"I know." She hooks her arm around my waist and walks us into the house.

David Bryson has floated in and out for the last forty-eight hours, and we find him busying himself in the kitchen. The sound and smell of frying bacon fills the house and Monica helps herself to a plate.

"That smells delicious." She sits at the table and digs in.

"Thank you. Ember, would you like some?"

Monica snorts.

"She's a vegetarian," Bo chimes in from behind me.

David shakes his head, mumbling something about "hippies" before turning his attention back to the bacon.

"There you are. You slept heavy last night." I stick out my hand to catch an apple Bo tosses from the refrigerator. "Thanks."

"Thanks for staying." His tone is flat and, if I didn't know the situation, I'd say it sounded sarcastic.

Bo pulls away from the fridge and I watch him in silence. His grey suit matches the look on his face, and his mechanical movements catch my breath. This is what it looks like when someone is actually "going through the motions."

Pour coffee.

Pour creamer.

Stir.

Sip.

Look around.

"You know," he starts, looking at the three of us gathered around the table, "today will go a lot smoother for me if you all stop staring at me like I'm a bomb." His half-empty coffee mug crashes into the sink and he storms out of the room. Monica and I stare at each other, her fork mid-air.

"It's OK, girls," David says softly. "He's going to feel a wide range of emotions for a long time. Stick with him."

* * *

Monica finishes my hair, and when I'm finally dressed, we head downstairs. I don't trust my tears today, so I've opted for no makeup. Monica receives a text from Josh saying David and Bo are at the church. It almost bugs me they didn't tell us they were leaving, until I realize David may have wanted some one-on-one time with Bo. Maybe Bo needed to be alone.

"You slept together last night?" Monica asks as she turns onto the main road.

"Not like that. He said he didn't want to be alone …" I close my eyes and remember the feel of his hair through my fingers, as I lay awake.

As we come upon the First Congregational Church, the sheer number of people present overwhelms me. Traffic is being directed by a lone police officer in black cotton gloves. It's just like W.H. Auden wrote it, and I really wonder if anything can ever come to any good in a world that no longer holds Rachel Cavanaugh.

We park a block away and walk quickly to the church. It seems weird, having a funeral in the middle of summer on a gorgeous eighty-degree day. I picture all funerals happening in winter; grey skies, people bundled in black pea coats burying their faces in their scarves. No, today there isn't anywhere to hide our sorrows. I should have worn yellow or something, I realize too late as we file up the church steps like ants. Rae would have liked color.

I bob my head up and down and side-to-side trying to

spot Bo, as we make our way down the center aisle of the church. I see him in the front row, but the pearl necklace sitting next to him stops me in my tracks. Ainsley's perched directly between Bo and Regan. Before irritation takes over, I grin and lead my eyes upward, sharing a laugh with Rae over her choice of jewelry. Two rows behind Bo and what appears to be family, Josh flags us down. We slide into the row, acknowledging uneasy condolences from C.J. before the service begins.

The prayers and hymns are lovely, yet lonely. Although I've only been in a church once, I recognize "Amazing Grace" as "The Weeping Song" and when it's sung, I sink into the pew and bury my forehead in my hands. C.J. sits next to me and tries to suffocate the shaking of my shoulders. When it's over, the final song plays and the casket is positioned to glide out of the church with family behind it. Bo rises. David and Ainsley each try to stand and walk out of the pew with him, but he waves them off.

The congregation stands as Bo starts down the aisle. For the first time since we went to bed last night, Bo's eyes connect with mine just before he reaches my row. Time stops its sovereign march for a moment, and lets us take a breath in each other. Before his chin quivers a second time, I push past Monica and Josh and root myself at his side. Grabbing his hand, I give it a slight squeeze before he interlaces his fingers with mine. I'd be lying if I said I didn't wonder what people thought of me—a girl most of them don't know, escorting their lost son out of the church behind his dead sister.

Chapter 32

The house is empty again. After the mourners, and the hugs, and the casseroles, everyone's journeying back to their lives. Regan sat with Bo in the backyard most of the afternoon, while I continued arranging food. I plainly told Carrie that I'd be taking the week off, and she didn't argue. I've never taken care of anyone but myself before, and it's taken completely over; I don't want to be anywhere else but here. I begged Regan not to leave the country without saying goodbye, but I know he will. I would too.

When the last of the dishes are put away and I'm sure Bo has passed out from emotional exhaustion somewhere, I slide out of my heels and press my sore feet onto the cold tile floor. I sigh, wincing on my exhale, as my aching shoulders feel the weight of the last two days. It hurts.

"You're still here." Bo's relieved voice startles me, forcing me to grip the edge of the counter.

I turn tiredly and find him in the doorway wearing his suit from today—minus the coat and with a loosened tie. His messy dark hair shows how often he ran his hands through it today, and his blue eyes are tired.

"I promised you I wouldn't leave. I meant it. Not until you kick me out." I giggle. He doesn't.

My heart races with uncertainty as he walks toward me with a look of purpose in his eyes. Bo takes the dishtowel out of my hand and tosses it carelessly on the counter. I glance in its direction but am stopped by his hands grabbing my face. His lips part as he scans my face, eyes darting back and forth, trying to find words.

I shake my head in question. "Bo ..."

He kisses me. A deep, hard, anguished kiss that curls my toes. One moan from his throat instructs me to open my mouth. I do. Bo's hand runs up my neck and his fingers fumble with the elastic keeping the hair out of my face. When my hair finally cascades around my shoulders, he lifts me up onto the counter and pushes himself between my knees. Breathing hard through his nose, he grabs a fist full of my hair, pressing me deeper into his mouth. I echo his movements by setting his face in my hands. After a few minutes, he pulls away with a muted growl.

"Come with me."

Hesitating, I touch two fingers to my swollen lips, as my legs swing free from the counter. Bo holds out his hand, but it's not pleading—he's demanding my compliance. Sliding off the counter, I follow him wordlessly up the dark wooden stairs. I have no idea if this falls under any category of appropriate, but he doesn't seem to care. Bo begins unbuttoning his shirt, as his bedroom door swings open. He nods his chin toward my body and speaks barely above a whisper.

"Take off your dress."

I nod and guide the dress over my head, leaving me standing in my black bra and matching panties in front of Bo, whose raging blue eyes stalk me as he takes off his pants. He walks toward me as I back up to the bed. I can't believe we're about to do this. It's been months, but his touch has never left me. The first time we were together in my apartment flashes through my mind as my breath catches up with my body. I've craved him every second he's been gone, but he never really left.

"Bo ..." I don't know what I'm trying to say. I want this. Badly. But, like this?

He shakes his head as he repositions himself between my legs, his boxer briefs gone.

Scraping his fingers around my hips he tears off my panties a second before thrusting into me with such force that we cry out simultaneously. He fills every essence of my being, and I'm rendered senseless apart from feeling him. I reach around my legs and dig my fingers in his thighs, bringing him deeper into me as he anchors his hands on either side of my shoulders.

"My God, I've missed you." Bo presses his forehead into mine, silencing any response I might have with a forceful kiss.

I raise my arms over my head and knot them through my hair as he pushes faster. Ecstasy cries out of my throat as he gently bites my lower lip. If I'd had my eyes closed this entire time, I would still have known it's him—my body knows him. Bo slows for a moment, pulling back to look at my face. He looks absolutely broken. A tear finds its way down his face, clinging to his chin for a moment before free-falling to my neck. Reaching up, I dry his eye with my thumb. He turns his cheek into my hand as I draw my hand down his face, taking my thumb into his mouth for a second before burying his face in my neck, while he pushes harder and faster into me.

My hips and legs go numb as I try to find traction by releasing my hands and raking them through his hair. It shouldn't feel this good at this moment, on this day, but it does. Oh my God, it does. Bo sits up on his knees, still inside me, and puts one of my legs up on his shoulder, stretching every muscle in my body as he leans back into my chest. I moan into his mouth as I force myself to silence the "I love you" brewing in my brain.

"You feel so good, November." His eyes are closed and his face looks distant, as if he's pretending we're somewhere else.

He pulls out and grabs both of my hips, forcing them over wordlessly. I position myself on my hands and knees, sweeping my hair over one shoulder. Bo kneels behind me and brushes his hand slowly from my hips and up the length of my spine, before gripping my shoulder and entering me again. I grab at his bedsheets for balance as he slams into me over and over with low groans, gripping my hips with both hands now. Grief, anxiety, lust, love, and missing the absolute hell out of him brews an orgasm within me so intense that my arms give out and my shoulders press into the bed.

"Bo!" My scream is muffled into his mattress.

Bo's fingertips dig painfully into my hips as his relentless pursuit of release nears its end. His movements become ragged as he starts to pulse inside me and I know he's close. I reach between my legs and rub him as he pushes in and pulls out. It's his breaking point. Bo throws his head back as he wails through me, collapsing onto my back when it's over. He clumsily pulls out of me and rests his head on my shoulder when I roll over, his ragged breathing filling the oppressive silence of the house. Within a minute I watch the rise and fall of his chest even out, telling me he's asleep. I lay motionless as silent tears roll from my cheekbones, off my earlobes, and onto his pillow.

* * *

The sweet smell of Bo's cologne lifts from the t-shirt of his I'm wearing. I tiredly fumble my way through making coffee. The sun has risen again. At least we have that. The open windows on the first floor of the house usher in the sound of a car coming up the driveway. I grab the jeans I was wearing the night Rae died and slide them over my hips as I walk to the door. Ainsley's bleach-blonde hair glows as sunlight bounces off her empty head.

"What do you want, Ainsley?" I try to sound bored as I open the door, but my heart is galloping through my chest. I know exactly what she wants.

She flips her hair over one shoulder and pushes past me and stands in the foyer. "What the hell are you still doing here? Don't you live in Massachusetts?"

"I do. Bo asked me to stay."

Well, he didn't, but it was kind of implied.

Ainsley dips her chin as her eyebrows curl into a wicked stare. "Oh, and I'm the tramp, am I?"

"I beg your pardon?"

"You should. Why are you wearing his t-shirt? You really are no better than you make me out to be, are you?"

I calmly set my coffee on the small table reserved for keys and walk toward Ainsley. She wisely takes one step back.

"Bo asked me to stay. Unlike you, I didn't muscle my way into his grief. God, you're such an opportunist—a self-righteous one at that. I'll tell Bo you stopped by. I'm sure it'll make his day." I turn back to my coffee when Ainsley's hand snakes around my forearm, turning me to face her.

"Don't you dare order me around, you arrogant bitch."

I swallow my rage and my desire to smack her across the face. I settle for clenching my fist. My tone is cool.

"I suggest you let go of me."

"Or what? Seriously, what will you do?"

I can't swallow it anymore. I take my free hand and crack her porcelain cheek. It echoes through the house, as she drops my hand and puts hers to her face. Her wide ice-blue eyes fill with tears, and I wonder for a moment if she'll hit me back. I've never hit anyone before, and she looks as surprised as I feel.

"Get the hell out of his house, Ainsley! If Bo wants you back, he knows where to find you." I open the door and wait for her to exit.

"Oh, he wants me here. If he didn't, he would have asked me to leave the night you bailed on him after the concert." With the red cheek, her arched eyebrow makes her look maniacal.

Bo's heavy footsteps down the stairs stop both of us. "I'm asking you to leave now, Ainsley."

"But Spen -"

"Go. I'll call you." He says it so dismissively I wonder how she could possibly believe him. But, she seems to. She turns on her heels, looking back once to eye me up and down, and leaves.

"I'm sorry about that," I say as I close the door and reach for my coffee.

"Don't be. She has issues." He walks to the kitchen and pours himself a cup of coffee.

Standing in the doorway, I watch the muscles in his back flex underneath that sexy tattoo as he moves around the kitchen. I look for signs that he doesn't regret last night. His apparent unwillingness to make eye contact isn't reassuring.

"I'm sorry about last night." He finally speaks as he sits at the table.

My eyebrows pull together as I sit across from him. "I'm not."

"I meant the lack of protection. You're not on the pill, right?" He's watching the creamer swirl through his coffee.

"Oh, that. It's fine." I sigh, thankful he doesn't appear to regret having sex—just not wearing a condom.

"It was really disrespectful, and I could have gotten you-"

"Look, it's OK," my cheeks catch fire, "my cycle's normal. We're in the okay zone, it's fine." The thought of possible pregnancy was far from my mind last night.

Bo sets his mug down and stares through my eyes—through my soul.

"Ember, it's not …"

"Bo, really …" I shrug and we sit in uncomfortable silence for several minutes, drinking our coffee as darkness swirls between us.

Reaching across the table, I grab his hand. Tight. He stares at our knuckles, rubbing his thumb over mine for a while, before looking at me again.

"When did you two break up?" Bo brings up Adrian of all things.

"Um, the day after Josh and Monica's engagement party."

He pulls his hand away from mine and grips his mug with both hands. "Why?"

I watch him slide away from the table and head to the sink. I don't think I like where this conversation is headed.

"We shouldn't be together, Adrian and me. He knows you kissed me after the concert, I know I'm not myself when I'm with him…obviously." I tug at my jeans, half-blaming Adrian for their loosened state.

Bo stares at me for a while. The silence is killing me.

"I think you should go." I've heard this tone before. I used it on him in Room 323 at The Centennial.

"What? Why?" Tears sting my eyes. "If this is about what happened with Ainsley, I'm sorry."

Bo takes both of our mugs and sets them in the sink before turning around, gripping the counter as he leans his back against it.

"I love you, November. I want to be with you. But, not like this. I've got a long road ahead of me—"

I stand and walk, panicked, toward him. "I love you, too. I won't leave you. People who love each other don't leave each other …" I shake my head as he grabs my hands.

"I need to do this alone, November. It's going to be ugly and painful. The past two months have made both of us sick." He slides his hands down my ribs and grips my bony hips. "I can't pull you down any further, but I can't help you right now either. God, I wish I could." Waves of tears crash through his eyes.

"No…Bo …" I tighten my hands on his. "Please don't do this. Last night—"

"Last night shouldn't have happened, Ember. I wasn't thinking. I just needed you. I'm sorry." He shakes free from my hands and places his back on the counter. He looks away.

"I don't want to leave you here alone." I slide my hands into my back pockets.

His voice cracks. "I'll be fine, Ember. I'm going to spend some time with the therapist that helped me and Rae when our parents died. I just need space from everything right now. If we get our chance again, I want it to be when we're both healthy and ready."

If? Again?

Shit. He's absolutely right and it kills me. We're a disaster right now—apart and together—and I have no rebuttal.

"I'll get my things." I turn and make my way upstairs to collect my clothes and backpack, and head back down the stairs, where I find Bo waiting by my car.

"I'll call you when I'm ready. I don't mean to sound harsh, but…I just need …" He runs his hand over his face, sweeping away tears.

"No, I get it. You're right. Can I say one thing?" He nods as I open my door. "I'm really sorry. About absolutely everything." A sob chokes out anything else I planned on saying and he nods, pulling me into a mournful embrace.

"I'm sorry, too." Bo smoothes his hand over the back of my hair and kisses the top of my head. He takes my face in his hands one more time. The pain in his eyes is unbearable. "I love you."

I nod through tears pouring down my face. "I love you, too. I never stopped."

It's too much for both of us. Bo releases my face and walks back to his house, face in hands. I collapse into my car and sob for half an hour before I'm able to start my car and drive home.

Chapter 33

My breath floats in puffy clouds by my chin, as I anchor myself in a full headstand in the cold, damp sand at sunrise. The mid-October beach is empty as I breathe through the blood rushing to my head. My once-bony shoulders are now able to support all the physical and emotional weight I throw their way.

It's been three months.

Three months without his voice, his touch, his presence. And, I'm OK. I wasn't. But I am now. I cried for a week straight after I left Bo's house that day. Monica was at a loss for words for the first time in our friendship. I missed Bo instantly. We'd just made love for the first time in two months and, just like that, it was all gone.

Bo was right—we were a mess. The day after I got home from Concord, I took a good long look at myself in the mirror and didn't recognize the girl looking back at me. My green eyes were mossy with grief, stress, and malnutrition, and my body followed suit. Bones in my chest and hips begged warmth from a layer of fat that disappeared sometime when I wasn't paying attention. I started yoga immediately—the only form of prayer I've ever been familiar with.

The first few days I headed to the beach to practice, I ended up in a ball in the sand for an hour, my salty tears mixing with the waves. I cried because I bailed on him in May, for reasons I have yet to understand—fear is the only one I've come up with. I cried over losing Rae. I loved her like a sister, and she *was* someone's sister. Once I made it into a headstand, I cried some more. Then, I started to heal.

Three months without Rachel. It seems like much longer somehow.

I stay in the headstand a bit longer, letting Rachel wash over me. I'm so, so sad that she's gone, but it doesn't have to take me out. I can feel sadness and be OK.

Slowly bending my legs and folding into child's pose, I ready myself for flower shopping with Monica. Shortly after Rae's funeral, she tenderly asked if I was still "up" for being her maid of honor. I hugged her, and then smacked her for asking. I can't wait for their wedding; it's only three weeks away.

"You've got one hell of a headstand, Harris." Monica pleasantly disrupts the last moment of Zen I'll have for the next twelve hours.

"Thanks. Feel free to join me any time."

She ignores my invitation. "When are you going to take these sessions inside? It's cold as hell out here."

I look around and breathe in the freshest air anyone could ever breathe. "When the snow falls, I guess." I stand and we walk to the parking lot.

"Your arms are looking fierce, Ember. I haven't seen you look this good since you were twenty." Monica playfully grabs my tight upper arms. "Are you singing at Delta Blue tonight?"

"I planned on it, unless you have something else in mind."

I've been signing at a tiny jazz club on the outskirts of Boston on the weekends. I needed something new, something challenging. I wanted to flex my singing muscles just outside the shadow of my parents. Jazz and soul are the ticket for me. I can still play the guitar, but it sounds sexier somehow. Our house band took an indefinite break when, as promised, Regan headed back to Ireland two days after Rae's funeral. C.J.'s been the only one to speak to him and says he'll be back eventually, but I doubt he will. I wouldn't if I were in his shoes.

Monica smiles and shakes her head. "I'm glad you have that. You're so freaking good, like you could go on tour with ZZ Ward or something. Seriously. I can't come tonight is all. Josh's brother is coming to town so we've got dinner plans."

"It's OK. So, what is it, exactly, that we're doing at the flower shop today? I thought you had all the arrangements and whatever picked out." Poor Monica, I'm the least "in-the-know" person she could have chosen for maid of honor.

"I have to choose my flowers for the bouquet toss." She sighs as though this is something we've been over, or that I should know.

"Your what now?"

"I won't toss my super expensive bouquet, you nitwit. You pick a smaller arrangement—"

"Ah, yes, to chuck at some unsuspecting girl's forehead?" I roll my eyes and snicker.

"You laugh now, November. But my friend's cousin, Daphne, used to catch the bouquet at, like, every wedding she went to." She's dead serious as she tells this story.

"Oh did she, now? And, Ms. Pierce," I flutter my eyelashes, "did this Daphne girl ever find her happily ever after?"

Monica grabs my face and plants a dramatic kiss on my cheek. "She did."

* * *

As I sit amongst leaves and petals, my mind wanders. I try to rein it in as much as possible, but a stroll once in a while is necessary. I think about Bo. A lot, actually—I just don't make it hurt. He asked me not to call him, and I haven't. I have, however, been in semi-frequent contact with David Bryson for work purposes. Out of respect for Bo, I haven't directly asked David about him, but he has slipped unrequested information into our conversations.

"He's coming along."

"Yesterday was tough."

"I sure miss seeing you around here, Ember. You should stop up and see the center again soon."

Each time David has offered something about Bo it's been at the end of our conversation, allowing me to deliver a polite "goodbye" without addressing his information. He hasn't said anything in a while. I try not to think about why.

I wander through the flower shop as Monica talks about ribbons with the florist, inhaling hydrangeas as I think about Bo's music. I hope he's still playing.

"How about this ribbon, Ember?"

"It's great, Mon." I smile.

"OK, one more time with you actually looking at it." I hear her rolling her eyes.

"Sorry," I laugh, "let's see. I love the champagne-colored one."

"Awesome. Maybe you'll be the one to catch it." She winks and shares some sort of private laugh with the florist. I stick my tongue out at her.

"I plan on hiding in the bathroom during that whole spectacle."

After Monica finalizes her order, we drive her back to her apartment.

Monica starts to fidget. "So," she asks nervously, "still no word, huh?" Monica tries not to ask about Bo too often. She fails, beautifully.

"You say *still* as if I've been waiting around for him."

"No, that's not what I mean. It's just...you are doing so well, I—"

"Spit it out, Mon."

"I just wonder what it would be like if he...showed up."

Hope. Her words surge hope through me and it tugs a cautious smile across my lips. I take a deep breath.

"It would be ..."

Monica places her head on my leg. "Yeah. That's what I thought."

Chapter 34
Bo

I park in front of the tiny brick building and double-check the sign on the door.

Delta Blue. This is it.

I called earlier today to see when their open-mic acts go on. She won't go first—she doesn't like that—but I get here in time, just in case. I don't think I'm ready to see her face-to-face yet. Dr. Brown says I shouldn't feel shitty about the way I suspended things with us, but I do. Neither one of us *wanted* her to leave that day.

My days since then have gone back and forth between being a total mess and being functional. I still haven't gone into Rae's room. I opened the door once—the day Ember left—but I slammed it shut and haven't been back since. It was too much, seeing her stuff just...there, and knowing she wouldn't be. Anymore. Aside from the absolute fucking hole my baby sister's death has left, anger has become a dangerous ally.

I haven't been drinking away my emotions like I thought I might. I couldn't do it after I saw Ember had gone through the trouble of putting all the liquor in my house into a box on the back porch. She knew. Instead, I broke things. And punched things. A lot of things. Ember and I were both better off with her leaving that day. She didn't need to see some of the ugly shit the last few months have brought me.

Sneaking in a side door, I pull the brim of my Bruins hat down a bit as I scan the room. She's not at the bar, so I slide onto a stool, order a beer, and continue my visual hunt. I just want to see that she's good. Ember lost a lot of weight early in the summer, and then after Rae died, the life just drained from her eyes. God, "Rae died" rolls off my mind's tongue so easily some days.

There she is.

Ember's sitting at a table right in front of the stage, slowly tracing the rim of her wine glass with her middle finger. Christ, she looks amazing—better than ever. She seems to have put back on the weight she lost. I can't see her shoulder blades from across the bar like I would have been able to three months ago. Her auburn waves shine past her shoulders—her newly muscular shoulders.

I can't believe it's been three months.

Just when I think she's about to turn around and spot me, the MC steps up to the mic to introduce the first act. The lights dim, and for the first three acts I stare at no one but her. She sways to the music and claps enthusiastically for people she's clearly come to know over the last several weeks—that's how long Josh tells me she's been playing here.

I waited until I couldn't take it anymore before giving in and calling Josh, fishing for information. I know David talks to her a couple times a week, but I made it clear that I didn't want to go there with him. All Josh would tell me is that she was doing better. That I can see, as those gorgeous emeralds she calls eyes shine through everyone she speaks with. The MC approaches the mic once more.

"And now, for the last act of the night, November Blue."

My heart pounds through my chest as she takes the stage. People around me whisper their praises of her, this woman I love. Shit. I love her. I'm trying not to—someone shouldn't be in love when their whole family is dead. But, it's her. It's November. I was breathless the first time I ever saw her, but seeing her now fills me with more life than I've had in months.

"Thank you, Dex." Her voice. God, her voice..."I actually have something really personal to share with you tonight. I've worked on it for a long time. My friends were supposed to be here to support me, but, they bailed last-minute, so, here goes ..." She laughs into the mic, and I think I'm about to come apart at the seams.

I shift on my stool, contemplating my escape. I don't think I'm ready for this, to watch her sing when we haven't even spoken in three months. Then, she grabs her guitar. I choke on my beer a little when I see she's wearing the leather cuff—the one Rae got me for my birthday a few years ago—that I left at her apartment the day after she let my drunk ass sleep it off at her house.

My feet anchor into the foot rail beneath the bar as she tunes the guitar and her voice. The world around me disappears as she starts singing. Her tone is full—full of soul, full of life, full of her. She's back.

> *"Sit me down, tell me no, sweep the pieces as I go*
> *Turn up lost, that's where I was, fighting for you*
> *when I was gone ...*
> *I never left, yeah, I thought it through*
> *My heart has built a room for two ..."*

Goosebumps take over the damp skin on the back of my neck as I watch her sing through our sordid history. She's breathtaking, exuding confidence as her fingers glide effortlessly across the guitar. I'm so fucking proud of her. I want to run up on stage and sweep her off her feet, like she deserves. Instead, I jump off the stool and breeze back through the door I came in.

I'm out of breath when I reach my car, ten feet from the door. She still loves me. Thank God, she still loves me. My phone rings. It's Josh.

"Hey man, what's up?" I try to sound composed.

"You." It's Monica.

Sweet hell, can Josh not keep a secret to save his life?

"Uh, hi Mon."

"Yeah, whatever," she laughs. *Phew.* "Did you see her play yet?"

"She's on right now."

"What the hell are you doing talking to me?"

"I left."

"Men," she scoffs.

My heart's racing faster. "Listen, Monica, please don't—"

"Oh get ahold of yourself, Cavanaugh, I'm not going to say anything to her." She sounds as if she's scolding a child.

"Then why'd you call me?"

Her tone lightens dramatically. "To hear you. You sound

good—are you?"

"I will be."

She sighs. Heavy and long. "All right, Bo. Here's my thought …"

Chapter 35
Ember

Cold weather has set up its temporary residence on the East Coast. I'm contemplating a trip to see my parents in San Diego after Josh and Monica's wedding next week. I can't believe they're still there; this is officially the longest they've stayed in one place since I was in high school. Apparently, the group has decided to go by the nickname I gave them in my childhood and are affectionately calling themselves "The Six" for their next album. Lord, help me, their next album. Well, the anonymity was fun while it lasted.

It's clear that this will be my last outdoor yoga session for a while, as my shivering nearly knocks me out of my headstand. A car door slamming in the parking lot finishes the job—I crumble without grace to the ground. I sit, frozen, as I study the form walking toward me.

"Regan?" I whisper to myself. I doubt if the waves even hear me.

His copper hair hangs carelessly in front of his face. He awkwardly shoves his hands in the pockets of his skinny jeans as he crosses onto the sand.

"Regan!" I yell as I stand, startling two seagulls who squawked during my whole session. Serves them right.

"Hey." His quirky half-smile fills my heart and I race

toward him, crashing into him with all my force. "Jesus, work out much?" He teases softly, hugging me back.

"What the hell are you doing here? *Here*." I gesture to the beach around me.

"Monica told me where I could find you. My flight got in last night-"

I interrupt, "It's cold as hell out here. Come back to my place and we'll talk."

* * *

"You ditched your cell phone," I comment to Regan as I pour his coffee.

"Yeah, I just needed to disappear for a while."

I join him on the couch and pass him his cup. "Mission accomplished. I was worried about you, you know."

"I'm sorry ..." he trails off as he shakes his head. I wasn't looking for an apology, and there's really nothing more he can say.

"How've you been, anyway?"

Regan settles back into the couch and tells me about the last almost four months of his life. After returning to Ireland, he picked up some summer courses to fill his time and his mind. He's kept minimal contact with C.J. but had RSVP'd that he'd go to Josh and Monica's wedding. He misses everyone, he says.

Regan sets his coffee down and looks me square in the eye. "I'm taking a drive up to Concord tomorrow. Do you want to ride with me?"

I spit some of my coffee out. "Uh, no thanks."

He furrows his brow as I speed into the kitchen to refresh my coffee.

"Why not?" he asks in all heartbreaking honesty.

"I haven't spoken to Bo ..." I say from the kitchen.

"Since when?"

"Have you talked with him?" I deflect the question.

"About once a week. When's the last time you talked to him?"

"If I haven't come up, that should be some indication."

"Ember ..."

Deep breath.

"The day after Rae's funeral."

"Are you fucking kidding me?" Regan sounds angry as he enters the kitchen.

"Listen, *Ireland,* you have no idea what the hell happened between the two of us. I tried calling you that day but you didn't answer anyone's calls. Then, poof, just like that you're gone the day after that with a cancelled cell phone account. Don't 'are you fucking kidding me' me, Regan. Are *you* fucking kidding *me?*"

Tears sting my eyes as I replay the desperation I felt on my drive back to Barnstable the day after Rae's funeral. I called Regan that whole day without any answer. I was hoping he could just...I don't know. Whatever it was, he didn't do it. He wasn't there. He disappeared.

"I wanted to talk to you," I continue as he stares at me doe-eyed. "Bo and I had sex the night of the funeral, and he fucking kicked me out the next day after Ainsley tramped around his front porch, and ...and I was so goddamned sad about Rae ..." Seeing Regan's face for the first time since the funeral shatters me into a million pieces. A million disastrous pieces. My voice shakes as I try to keep the meltdown at bay.

"Ember, I'm—"

"No way, don't tell me you're sorry. You lost someone, too. We both lost her—we all lost her—and nobody wanted to fucking talk to me about it! My best friends were planning their wedding, the happiest day of their lives, and I was just looking for someone to talk through my shit with. Bo kicked me out and you disappeared."

Regan grabs my hands and it's all over. He's crying, I'm crying, and we sink to the floor in a puddle of grief. Sobbing into each other's shoulders, we cling to each other on my kitchen floor.

* * *

"Wow, you sure know how to show a guy a good time," Regan laughs as we pass the only bottle of beer in my fridge back and forth between us.

Our backs are against the cabinets as we sit on the cold floor. We cried for about an hour; neither one of us realized it until we were thirsty.

"See, had you answered your phone that day, we could have gotten this out of the way a hell of a lot sooner. Now, if you'll excuse me, I've gotta go get ready." I stand and stretch my arms overhead.

"Look," his tone is serious once again, "I'm sorry. I screwed up by bailing like that. I was so—"

"Messed up? Yeah. Been there. Listen, it's all right. Just ...don't disappear again, OK? I like you and I want you in my life." I help him to his feet, and he gives me a small hug.

"What do you have to get ready for?" he asks.

"My gig at Delta Blue."

"Oh yeah, Josh told me about that. He said you're really nailing it."

"No thanks to you," I tease. "Josh had to take over my guitar lessons. Maybe you can come sometime, when you don't look like total trans-Atlantic flight shit."

I laugh. He does too. It feels good.

Regan walks to the door, pausing for a moment before opening it. "OK, smartass, hint taken. I'm a mess. Are you sure you don't want to come to Concord with me tomorrow?"

I nod and attempt a reassuring smile. "I'm sure."

Chapter 36

Slowly sipping my wine, I'm only half paying attention to the acts on stage tonight. My mind is with Rae. And Bo. It was such a relief—and release—seeing Regan today, but I wish he'd come sooner. I remind myself that examining old wounds doesn't have to make me take two steps back, but it's hard. As my name is called, I tighten Bo's cuff on my wrist one notch tighter. I feel like I really need him with me tonight, and this is all I have left.

I'm surprised I went a week without spotting it in my apartment, but it'd been kicked under my bed. He must have taken it off before he showered. By the time I found it, Rae was dead, Regan was gone, and so was I. It's been my talisman, reminding me of what we once had and what I hope to have again. I dash on stage amidst a huge applause.

I use up the full three-song allotment tonight and ask the MC if I can sing a fourth. The full bar hoots their encouragement and he complies. I need just one more song. I've sung my love song to Bo every time I've come here for the last month. One more time can't hurt.

"November Harris." A slender young woman grabs my attention as I leave the stage with my guitar in hand.

"Yes, that's me."

"Elizabeth Cantwell, nice to meet you." She sticks out her hand, and I accept. "I handle concert bookings for several large venues on the East Coast, mainly the Southern East Coast. I'd like to talk to you about booking a show."

Huh?

I shake my head in confusion. "I'm sorry, what?"

She smiles warmly. "I'd like you to come play at one of my venues, Ms. Harris. You've got the talent."

"I don't...like...do this." I gesture around the bar. "It's just a hobby, really."

A sandy-haired guy with a cute-as-hell lopsided grin laughs as he comes up beside her.

"It seems like it should be a bit more than a hobby." The way he casts his eyes over Elizabeth tells me she's his.

I miss being someone's.

Sensing my speechlessness, Elizabeth continues. "We're just here on vacation, so here's my card. It says "Bradshaw," but just ask for Elizabeth Cantwell. We just got married—this is my husband, Ryan." I shake his hand. When he pulls away, he hooks his arm around her waist.

I smile wide at the thought of next weekend's nuptials. "Congratulations! My best friends are getting married next weekend."

Ryan plants a soft kiss on Elizabeth's head. "I hope they're as happy as we are," he says through a charming grin.

"It was nice to meet you, November. I hope to hear from you soon." Elizabeth and I shake hands one more time before she and Ryan leave.

Still in shock, I wander to the bar.

The regular bartender, Dane, senses my daze. "What's up, Ember? You OK?"

"Yeah, just talked with a woman named Elizabeth Cantwell. She wants me to do a concert or something. Anyway," I shake my head, "you've got my money from tonight, right?"

He nods and waves an envelope. "I sure do. You want it all to go to DROP again?"

I nod. Delta Blue insisted on paying me when, two months ago, they got feedback that people were coming in "droves" to see me. I put up a fight, saying this was all just for fun, but relented when they agreed to send my money directly to DROP, in Rae's name.

"Why don't you just give it to Bo Cavanaugh yourself?" Dane says as he puts the envelope in the register.

Keep your poker face.

"You know Bo Cavanaugh?"

He chuckles. "Sweetheart, everyone knows Bo Cavanaugh. I meant, you could just give it to him here."

I feel my face flush. "Here?"

"Yeah," Dane drags a rag across the wet bar, "he's been coming in here for like three or four weeks—"

"What?" Suddenly, I'm extremely lightheaded. Thankfully, an empty stool is nearby.

He stops mid-swipe. "Relax, Ember, it's not like he's a celebrity or something. Just a good-doer socialite."

"No...no...that's not it." I lean over the bar, grab a bottle of tequila, and pour myself a shot.

"What's this all about, Ember?"

The tequila sets fire to my insides. "Was he here tonight?"

"Of course he was, he comes in—oh. Shit." Dane seems to be calculating something.

"What, Dane?" I stand and grip the bar.

"He's the ex-boyfriend, isn't he?"

"How'd you put that together?" I mindlessly twist the cuff around my wrist. "Never mind that, what were you saying before? He comes in and what?"

"He comes in just before your set and leaves right after. Every time. The first time I thought he was just late."

My cheeks burn. "Was he here tonight?" Dane swallows hard. "Dane, was he here tonight?"

He nods.

"Shit." I race away from the bar, knocking over the stool.

My heart is beating mercilessly against my chest as I run outside. Without thinking, I yell.

"Bo?" I look around, a few people turn in my direction, but most ignore me.

I circle the small parking lot, looking for signs of his car, or him. There aren't any. He's gone. As I stand in the middle of the lot with my hands on my hips, breathless from frustration, Dane comes outside.

I launch in, "What the hell? He's been coming here for three or four weeks and he can't come up and say *hello?* I would've liked to—"

"Whoa, what are you talking about? What happened with you two?" He grips my shoulders.

"Psh," I huff, "you got four months?"

And, for no good reason whatsoever, I give Dane a rather horrible Cliff's Notes version of our story. For the love of God, we have a story.

When I finish, we're still standing in the parking lot and Dane has a stupid grin on his face.

"So?" I ask, bugging my eyes for effect.

"So," he shrugs before squeezing my shoulders, "what the Christ are you doing here talking to me about this? Go get him."

Forty-five minutes.

That's all that separates me from Bo—if I decide to turn left. Home lies an hour and a half to my right. It's a drive I've done every week for the last two months.

Left it is.

Chapter 37

Buzz. Buzzzzz.

The sound from the call button on the gate barely drowns out the buzzing of my nerves. It's 1:00 AM, so I determine—after pressing the buzzer two more times—that Bo is either not home, or he's ignoring me. The latter is certainly not acceptable after finding out he's been sneaking around and watching me perform for the last month. I smile, biting my lip. He's been watching me. I should have known. The last few weeks I've felt so good, so alive, on stage. I realize it's not just because I feel at home on stage—it's because I feel at home with him.

When he doesn't answer, I tentatively punch in the code he gave me months ago. It works. With nervous energy, I jump back into my car and head down the long driveway. My heart races when I find the lower driveway empty. *He's not here?* He left Delta Blue long before I did. It didn't occur to me he'd make other plans for the night since it's already so late.

Wait for him.

I sit on the front steps for ten minutes; hope sinking with each changing number on my cell phone clock. I screwed up. Not recently, but five months ago, when I flipped my hormonal shit and kicked him out of my life. I rejected Bo's advances, dove into an ill-fated relationship with Adrian—a decent guy who didn't deserve my mess any more than I deserved his expectations of me—and I, worst of all, left Bo after Rae's funeral. Shit, I *left* him. Yeah, he asked me to, but what would have become of us if I had held onto him?

I panic, wondering briefly if it was some test—some grief-soaked test of my faithfulness to ask me to go. When he needed me most. *Shit.* I jump to my feet and head for the front door—I know it's not locked.

"Bo?" I try, even though I know he's not home. You can't enter a house and say nothing.

On a whim, I decide to call Regan. I know he was meeting up with Bo earlier today—maybe they're drinking together somewhere now.

Regan answers, sounding exhausted. "November? What the hell? It's...Jesus, one AM."

"Shit, Regan, I'm sorry, were you sleeping?"

"Trans-Atlantic shit, remember?" He laughs.

"Sorry. I was just wondering, do you know if Bo had plans tonight?"

Awkward silence.

"Regan?"

"Uhh ..." He sounds conflicted, making me laugh.

"Well, besides hiding in the back of a bar while I performed?"

Regan suddenly sounds more awake. "Did you see him?"

I explain the night's events to Regan, ending with me standing in the empty foyer of the Cavanaugh house.

"No," Regan answers, "we met for lunch today, but he didn't mention anything about his plans for the rest of the night. Sorry, Em."

"It's OK, just thought I'd give it a shot. Go back to bed. This was all a dream." I laugh and hang up.

I quickly decide that I'll stay here all night if I have to, but I'm not leaving until I talk to Bo. I can't walk away again without telling him how I really feel. Not again. I decide to wander down to the studio, where I find evidence of Bo scattered everywhere. His guitar. Sheet music with his handwriting. God, even his smell circulates through the eerily silent studio. Sandalwood and sex. I chuckle thinking about the first time I really smelled him, out on the beach behind Finnegan's five months ago. I glide my fingers across the tops of the piano keys, letting the sounds of a broken scale fill the anxious space around me.

"November?" I jump at Bo's voice as his heavy footsteps race through the first floor. "Ember?" He calls me again from the top of the stairs. Bo doesn't wait for my reply as he runs down the stairs. I'm afraid he'll fall going at that pace.

Only the hall light is on as I wait in the darkness of the studio. I straighten my back and pray that he'll hear me out when he walks in here. In a second, his broad shoulders fill the doorframe. He flicks a switch that illuminates dim track lighting just above the piano. A second flick turns on a light above his head. I'm breathing through my mouth as he walks slowly toward me.

"You're here," he whispers.

I nod. "You watched me sing tonight."

He nods back.

"And the last few weeks?" I question, knowing the answer.

"Yes." He shifts side to side and puts his hands in his pockets. With his chin lowered, he looks at me through his thick, gorgeous lashes. "You're smiling?"

"You make me happy," I whisper.

I step forward, reaching for his chin with my hand. When my skin connects with his, his lips part with a gasp. His eyes meet mine, and he slightly furrows his brow when he speaks again.

"You're not mad?"

I smile. "No. I spent months trying to be mad at you for something so stupid, Bo, and I was miserable. Irreparably miserable." I swallow hard and put my hand down, remembering why I'm here. "I'm sorry, Bo." My chin quivers as I struggle to maintain composure.

"Oh, my God...Ember...no." Bo grabs my face with both hands.

I stare into his eyes and it's there. Everything's there. Kissing him first in the parking lot of Finnegan's all those months ago, waking up in his arms, and singing "Heaven When We're Home" when we were just strangers. Though I suppose we were never really strangers—a thousand lifetimes is a powerful thing. And it's there.

His thumbs trace my cheeks. "I was never mad at you, ever."

"I left you after Rae's funeral ..."

"I told you to go. I needed you to go, Ember." Bo moves one thumb to my chin and presses down on it to stop the quivering.

"But I love you, Bo. I shouldn't have left."

His eyes fill with tears as he smiles. "You loved me enough to leave that day, Ember. I needed to grieve and to be angry. I didn't want to hurt you, and I would have if you'd stayed." His hands scoop down my neck and grip my shoulders.

I reach up and pull his hands away from my shoulders and interlace my fingers with his. "Why the hell did you hide from me at Delta Blue?"

He bites his lip. It's the first time I've ever seen him bite his lip and it's driving me crazy.

"The first time I went, I just wanted to see if you were OK. Josh said you were doing well."

"Ha. I should have learned after the 'thousand lifetimes' debacle, that Josh Dixon can't keep a secret."

"Good point." His face relaxes for a moment. "Seriously though, when I saw you, it took my breath away all over again." He lifts his head and chuckles a little. "You sounded perfect. I just thought...I don't know...I didn't want to ruin you."

"Ruin me?"

"You just looked so happy. I guess I was kind of afraid that if I barged back in ..." He puts his hands back in his pockets and takes a step back.

"Bo Cavanaugh, you don't get to decide what's good for me and what's not." I keep my tone light. "You. You're what's good for me. I spent the last few months getting healthy for me, but I wanted to make sure that if—like you said—you and I ever got our chance again, that I was perfect for you. For us."

"I'm sorry about the night of Rae's funeral." His voice breaks slightly over the word *funeral*.

"You needed me. What's there to be sorry about? I spent five agonizing months trying to be mad at you, but all I did was end up falling deeper in love with you than I even thought I was before. I needed you that night, too."

He's standing there, shaking his head with a sexy, crooked grin on his face. I can't stand it anymore.

Chapter 38

"I needed you that night, too." Ember lowers her eyes for a fraction of a second, and I grin in disbelief.

We were madly in love with each other this whole time, and both did just enough to screw it up without blowing it into total disrepair. When she looks up, her eyes are ignited with a look I've waited months to see cast back in my direction. She arches her eyebrow—always the left one—and steps forward so we're standing hip to hip. She's got these crazy-hot knee-high boots on over her jeans that have a heel on them, putting us about eye level with each other. My mind calculates how I could get away with taking those jeans off while leaving the boots on.

Before I can plot any further, she hooks her thumbs through my belt loops—God, I love it when she does that—and tugs so our hips grind into one another as she leans up and kisses me. Hallelujah, Ember is kissing me. She immediately releases her thumbs and weaves her fingers across the back of my neck and through my hair. I've never felt anything like her kiss before. If I could feel one thing forever it would be this.

I let her take the lead on this as I slide my hands down her sides and grab her ass with both hands. A hungry sigh leaves her mouth and finds its way into mine. She steps back slowly, begging me to follow as her hands move to my belt, then down the outside of my jeans where she grabs me. I can't hide how hot she makes me, and I don't want to.

She backs into the piano, causing my knuckles to pound against a few high keys. Neither one of us pays them any attention. I turn slightly and sit on the bench behind me, pulling her onto my lap. I need the pressure of her body on me. Pulling away from my mouth for the first time, she doesn't break eye contact with me as she takes off her shirt and lets it fall to the floor. Her breasts are perfect. Everything about her is, but damn, those breasts ...

"Kiss me," she pleads in a breathy tone when I'm struck stupid by her perfect nipples in that lace bra. She holds my head in her hands with her thumbs just behind her ears. I grab her hips and force her down on me as my tongue licks her from her collarbone to her ear. She groans again, and I can't hold back any longer.

"We gotta go upstairs." I hate to pause this moment, but who keeps condoms in a studio?

Ember nods and slides off my lap, leaving her shirt on the floor as she makes a break for the stairs. I chuckle as she runs up the stairs, slapping her ass as we pass through my living room. I take the stairs two at a time as I pass her, heading to the second floor. She snickers just low enough that I know I wasn't meant to hear it.

We crash into my room, and I lift her into my arms as she instinctively wraps her legs around my waist. I want to be inside her so bad I feel like I'm going to burst through my jeans. I set her on the bed and start to undo my belt. She slaps my hand away and does it herself. When my jeans slide to the floor, I kick off my shoes and step out of my pants all at once. That left goddamn eyebrow of hers shoots sky-high as she toys with the waistband of my boxer briefs.

I place my hands over hers, guiding them down. "Ember ..."

She bites her lip as she pulls my boxer briefs down, sighing through her teeth. Just as I lean forward to push her on the bed, her hands dig into my hips, stopping me. Ember's tongue dances across her lips for a second, and before I know it, her mouth is on my dick. I nearly lose my balance and have to grip her shoulders for balance.

"Holy shit," I half-growl through clenched teeth. Her tongue swirls greedily around me, while she slowly moves her head forward and back.

"Mmm," she hums as her hand holds me in place. I'm

going to lose it standing right here if she keeps that up.

I force myself to say the word, "Stop." I push on her shoulders slightly. "This isn't going to last very long if you keep doing that, and I want to be inside you. Get up on the bed."

She grins a wicked grin, cheeks flushed under my command. I take no time unzipping and pulling off each one of her boots while she unbuttons and unzips her jeans. As I toss her second boot to the floor, she has her jeans halfway down her thighs. I want to crack a joke at her eagerness, but it's not funny. I want it just as bad. I help her pull her jeans and panties—Jesus, her panties match her bra—down her legs, and throw them to the floor.

"Bo ..." she calls out after I've rolled on the condom.

I hover over her, staring into her gorgeous green eyes. "I love you," I say as I slide into her. She moans low and long in response.

She. Feels. Amazing.

I pull out just as slowly as I went in. I grin as she squirms beneath me. Ember roots her feet onto the mattress and lifts her hips, forcing me back into her. She digs her fingertips into my biceps.

"Don't stop," she begs.

My tongue finds the silky skin beneath her breast. I lick it feverishly, feeling her pulse quicken beneath my lips. I could stay inside her forever; she drives me numb and makes me feel absolutely everything all at once.

"More," she moans into my ear.

Before laying her head back down, Ember's lips capture my earlobe, sending shivers down my neck and arm.

"Damn," I groan.

"Roll over," she suddenly commands.

Reluctantly, I pull out of her and quickly flip to my back. She grabs the base of my dick as she straddles me, her eyes teasing. I think she's going to start slow, but she slides down on me hard. Her insides shock me like a million lightning bolts.

"November...ah ..."

"God, I love it when you say my name." She leans back and rests her hands on my thighs as she finds her rhythm.

I grab her hips, admiring her perfectly shaped landing strip. She sits up, takes my wrists, and leans forward, planting my hands on the pillow behind me. Ember's breathless mouth lands on mine, her lips swollen with desire.

"Don't move," she instructs as she pulls away.

She shifts a little, so she's squatting with me still inside her. Her feet are on either side of my hips, and she starts riding the hell out of me.

Her eyes squeeze shut as she throws her head back. "Ahh."

I'm under her control, and I have the best view in the house as I watch her breasts heave against her heavy breathing. Need takes over and I reach down, pushing her knees out so her feet give way and I'm as deep in her as I can go.

"You don't move," I say with as much authority as I can manage.

Her chest collapses onto mine as I grab her tight ass and anchor my feet into the mattress. I thrust into her as hard and fast as I can, making her moan loudly into my neck. I catch a whiff of her perfume from the back of her neck and it drives me near insane. I lift her off me and roll her onto her back. Her hair falls carelessly over her breasts. She's a goddamn dream.

Pushing faster, I lower my mouth to hers. Her sweet tongue takes over my mouth as I take over her body. She lets go of my arms and claws at the sheets as she arches her back. She's so damn close, I can feel it. Pulling my mouth away, I suck on one of her nipples.

"Oh my God ..." she wails, her voice growing hoarse.

I suck hard, pushing deeper and faster inside of her until her entire body clenches around me like a fist and she screams my name. I can't hold it in. I bury my face between her breasts to keep from biting her nipple too hard as I come harder than I ever have in my life. I stay inside her as we make out deep and hard, holding onto each other as tight as we can.

"I love you," she whispers between shortened breaths. I kiss her breasts once more before pulling out of her. "That was amazing, Bo."

"You're amazing."

Ember props herself up on her elbows and rolls her neck side to side. I watch goosebumps pop up along her skin. I tug her into me and shimmy under the sheets.

"So," she asks, propping her chin on my pecs, "what now?" I smile and kiss the top of her head.

"Everything."

* * *

Dawn breaks, as I lay awake, watching Ember sleep. I've been sitting here playing with her gorgeous hair for hours, listening to her breathe as her soft cheek presses against my chest.

"Mmm." She shifts slightly, nuzzling her chin closer to mine. Her lips seek mine before she opens her eyes, and I happily kiss her back.

"Morning, Beautiful," I speak onto her lips.

She opens her eyes. "I love you," she whispers.

"I love you, too."

"Don't go anywhere." She tightens her grip around my waist.

"This is my house," I chuckle, "where would I go?"

Ember yawns before snuggling back down on my chest. "I mean ever."

She falls back asleep and I'm left in the most perfect silence in existence.

Chapter 39
Ember

"I wish you didn't have to go today," Bo says, nuzzling into my neck while I pour coffee.

"Mmm, I know, but, I only have two days of work this week before taking the rest of the week to help Monica's mom prepare for the wedding on Saturday. Man, I can't believe it's already here." I turn and give him a quick kiss before sitting at the table with my coffee.

Bo sits across from me with a suddenly serious look on his face.

"Adrian called me."

I clear my throat. "Yeah? When?"

"A few days after Rae's funeral. He expressed his condolences, and then made a sizable donation to DROP."

"That was nice of him. I haven't heard from him since we broke up."

"Seriously?" Bo's eyebrows shoot up.

"Seriously."

"He asked how you were doing when he called. He said he knew you and Rae were close—" Bo struggles through the sentence. This is the most we've talked about Rae since she died.

"Mmhmm." I drink down some of the warm coffee.

"Do you want to talk about what happened between the two of you?" He sits back and crosses his arms with a cautious grin on his face.

"Eh, I happened. He happened. He's not a bad guy, we were just all wrong for each other." I don't need to force my indifferent tone. Adrian made it clear he didn't want me in his life in any capacity when I left his apartment three months ago. My heart made it clear long before that. Out I've stayed. "And," I add, "you know...you."

A full smile takes over his face. "Fair enough."

"Can I ask what happened with you and Ainsley? Apart from the night of the concert...I still don't want to know about that."

Bo rolls his eyes and gives me a heavy sigh. "Nothing of consequence happened with Ainsley, November. She was there ..." He shrugs.

"Fair enough." I mock with a smile.

"And," he teases, "you."

"You're good, Cavanaugh."

"Also, your parents sent me a really nice card." He smiles.

I smile. "They didn't tell me that."

Bo leans forward and places his elbows on the table. "When's the last time you talked to them?"

I shrug. "A couple weeks, I guess? They're writing songs for their album, recording, you know ..."

"Call your parents, November." His eyes are sad. I nod.

"I will."

I stand and walk over to Bo, who suddenly looks grey. Cautiously placing one hand on his shoulder, I breathe a sigh of relief when he leans into it.

"You OK?" I ask softly.

"Yeah," he sighs, "I just...sometimes I get these moments where I feel it all at once, you know? My parents...Rae...everything. Sorry—"

"Don't apologize, Bo. Rae just died," I choke up as I continue, "it's going to take a lot of time."

"She loved the shit out of you, November."

"I know," I smile, "I loved the shit out of her, too."

"Nice cuff, by the way," he teases, rubbing the leather around my wrist.

"Hey, your drunk ass left it at my place, finder's keepers. Do you want it back?"

"No. Rae got it for me for my birthday a few years ago. She'd love that you're wearing it."

Jesus.

"Are you sure?" I ask, suddenly uncomfortable.

Bo turns, kisses my wrist, and looks up at me with his absurdly beautiful blues.

"I'm sure."

A few minutes later I'm standing at my car, delaying leaving. Last night and this morning were wonderful—everything I always wanted for Bo and me. Now, I have to slip back into real life and hope this wasn't a fluke.

"Hey, dream girl." He snaps his fingers to pull me away from my daydream. I smile, thinking about him calling me that when we'd only known each other for a few days. I was lost in a daydream then, too.

"Sorry, just a busy week ahead. Hey," I bite my lower lip and smile, "do you wanna be my plus one for Josh and Mon's wedding?"

Bo reaches for my waist and pulls me roughly to his body, laughing.

"I'll be your plus one for a hell of a lot more than Josh and Monica's wedding, November."

* * *

The phone rings six times while I twist the cuff around my wrist.

Damn landlines without answering machines ...

"Blue Seed Studios, this is Willow."

Of course it is.

"Hi, this is November Harris, I'm wondering if you've seen my—"

"November Blue?"

"Um, yes?" Isn't it funny, when someone sounds overly enthusiastic you start to question yourself?

"Willow. Willow Shaw!"

"Hi Willow. Oh my gosh, how are you?"

Willow Shaw is the daughter of two of my parents' bandmates, Solstice and Michael. Yeah. Michael Shaw. Bet his parents didn't see Solstice coming from a mile away. Anyway, even though the band was largely apart when we came along, our parents still traveled a lot together. Willow and I spent a good part of our childhood as the only constant for each other. I haven't heard from her since my freshman year of high school.

"Excellent. Holy shit, yeah, your parents are in the studio, I'll go get them. Hey, when are you coming out here? Your parents have gone on and on about your voice, you've got to jam with us."

As irritated as I would have been a few months ago by her voice and her general enthusiasm, she invigorates me somehow.

"Soon, I hope. That's what I'm actually calling to talk to them about." I can't keep the smile off my face.

"Sweet, I'll go get your parents."

After a few seconds, my mom picks up. "Hey you!"

"Hey Mom." My lip quivers instantly.

"What's the matter, Ember?"

Breathe.

"I was hoping to come out and see you guys soon."

"You want to come to San Diego?" Her cautious optimism makes me giggle.

"Yes. And, I'm calling you Mom from now on. It's just something I need to do. Pass the message along to Dad, would you?"

Pause.

"Mom?"

"It's good." Her voice sounds tight with tears.

"Thanks for sending a card to Bo, by the way. He said it was really nice."

"Oh? You've spoken with Bo?"

"I have."

"I can hear the smile in your voice."

"Good. Monica and Josh's wedding is tomorrow and then they go on their honeymoon, so I shouldn't ask for next week off, but maybe the week after?"

She tries to rein in her enthusiasm, but fails spectacularly. "Sounds great, just keep us posted."

"I love you, Mom. Tell Dad I love him, too."

"I love you too, Baby Blue."

Chapter 40

"You are absolutely stunning, Monica," I whisper with tears in my eyes.

Monica spins once, crisp sunlight highlighting the lace overlaying her princess-cut dress.

"Really? Thank you. Also, thank you for helping my mom so much this week."

"Of course. My duties, you know." I wink and hand her a glass of champagne.

"Look at you. God, Ember, yoga and Bo Cavanaugh do a body good, huh?"

Last week, when I got home from Concord, Monica was waiting—in true Monica fashion—at my apartment. She wanted details. She got them. She asked lots of "what now" kinds of questions, questions that I don't yet have the answers to. I hope in the next few weeks Bo and I can sort out the nuts and bolts. But, today is about my two best friends getting married.

As the music cues the opening of the chapel doors, I walk down the aisle, tearing up at Josh's expectant smile. Out of the corner of my eye, I spot Bo, sitting in the front row next to Monica's mom, beaming at me the way Josh is looking past my shoulder to Monica. I give him a wink and blush the rest of the walk toward the altar.

This is the good stuff.

* * *

Bo

"I now pronounce you husband and wife. Joshua, you may kiss your bride." Josh's father concludes the ceremony amongst the hoots and hollers of the small beachside chapel. I'm sure it's freezing outside, but the atmosphere in here is absolutely perfect.

The procession begins, and after Josh and Monica breeze by in a flurry of applause, Ember steps down the aisle. The champagne-colored dress sets her auburn hair on fire. And her smile? I'll take complete credit for that full smile cast in my direction. She's responsible for mine, too.

A half-hour later, I'm waiting anxiously inside the Inn for the wedding party to arrive. Thank God they didn't request a zillion pictures from the photographer—I want to dance with the love of my life. When the wedding party and Mr. and Mrs. Dixon are announced, and they have their dance, Ember joins me at my table for dinner.

"You are drop-dead gorgeous in that dress, November," I whisper into her ear as she sips her wine. Her ear turns pink as she blushes.

"Thank you." She tries to be polite at a table that holds her boss and some co-workers, including David Bryson. David just looks at me and winks. "I've got to get up there for my toast. Be back in a few."

Always the picture of grace under pressure, she looks unflappable as she heads to the mic. Tiny white twinkle lights illuminate her flawless face. She licks her lips before she starts speaking, and I think back to the first time we sang together. She licked her lips then, too, and it drove me mad.

As she toasts her best friends, I remember the first ten beautiful days we spent together. We did everything backwards —fell in love first, and learned about each other after. But, it allowed us to fall in love all over again. Who am I kidding? I never fell out of love with her. Those several weeks when she was working at my office were the worst in my life. She didn't want me. Worst of all, she wanted someone else. Every single day, my love for her grew stronger, until it exploded in anger and frustration after the Coldplay concert. That whole night was a fucking disaster—by all accounts neither one of us should have spoken to the other after that. But we did. Because we have each other. Deep in our souls, we have each other.

"So, Josh and Mon, Mr. and Mrs. Dixon, my toast to you is that you spend a thousand lifetimes in your perfect love song. To Josh and Monica." She raises her glass and looks between me and Josh and Monica as we all toast the newlyweds.

Finally, we get to dance. The first song is upbeat, designed to get everyone on the dance floor. Josh, Monica, Ember, and I all dance and laugh together, bumping hips and jumping around like idiots. Happy idiots.

"So, Bo," Josh says as we hit up the bar, "what do you have planned for Ember's birthday?"

"When is it?" I ask, taking my beer from the bartender.

He raises his eyebrows. "She didn't tell you?"

"Uh, no. When is it? I don't want to screw it up."

"Tomorrow, you rat's ass. Her birthday is November fourteenth."

Shit.

"Thanks for the heads up, Bro."

"Ha," he chuckles, "it's the least I can do."

A few minutes later, a slow song comes on, and Josh and I find our ladies on the dance floor.

"Dance with me?" I ask, extending my hand.

"Always." She smiles.

Her lavender scent radiates off her skin. I bury my nose in her hair and take a deep breath. "You always smell amazing, you know that?"

"Stop making me blush. I don't blush," she teases. "I want to talk to you about something."

"OK, shoot."

"The week after the happy couple gets back from their honeymoon, I'm taking two weeks to go visit my parents in San Diego. Would it be crazy of me to ask you to come? I want you to come. I haven't seen my parents in a few months, but I haven't really seen you in a few months either, if you think about it. Come with me to San Diego." She laughs at herself for rambling. I love when she rambles.

"Of course I'll go with you to San Diego." It's a no-brainer. I don't want to leave this woman for a second. This past week was brutal.

"Really?" Her face lights up. I love when I'm responsible for that.

"Really. It'll be my birthday present to you."

Her jaw drops. "How do you know when my birthday is?"

I look over my shoulder to Josh and Mon, who are grinning at us. Ember and I say, "Josh" at the same time and fall into a fit of laughter.

Deep in our souls, we have each other.

* * *

Ember

"Crap, she's doing the bouquet toss, come with me." I take Bo's hand and lead him out of the reception room, Monica shaking her head sarcastically as I run by her.

"What was that about?" Bo laughs as we run into the cold November air.

"Long story. So, you're sure you can come to San Diego with me? Or, that you want to?" I rub my hands over my arms for warmth. In a chivalrous moment, Bo takes off his black suit coat and wraps it around my shoulders.

"Of course I want to. I want to get to know your parents." He hugs me close and I breathe in his scent.

"I want you to know them. And I want them to know you."

Bo's voice sounds a little further away. "My parents would have loved you."

"Yeah?" I untuck my head from beneath his chin and meet his glistening eyes. "What were they like, Bo?"

Bo drapes his hand over the back of my head and nudges it back to his chest before continuing.

"My dad was...stern with me. He loved me a lot, and I loved him. He wanted the best for me and wanted me to be the best at everything. Rae was the one who melted his heart." A smile overcomes his voice. "I really hope to be like him someday."

"And your mom?"

Bo takes a deep breath, and for a second I think he won't say anything. "Man, did my dad love her. Fiercely. She was quiet, but strong. She would come in my room at night in high school, after she knew I should have been asleep, and tell me to put the books down. She would turn off my light and pull the covers over me after I climbed into bed. She smelled like vanilla ..." Bo trails off and looks into the distance.

"I think I would have really loved them, too." I say into his shoulder.

I don't know the moment it happened, but here we are, out in the cold holding onto each other, swaying to music decades in the making between us. Music no one else can hear.

Chapter 41

"Here it is. Blue Seed Studios. Are you ready for this?" I say with a deep breath as Bo wraps his arm around my shoulders.

We've been in San Diego for a little more than a week, and have spent a lot of time with my parents and plenty of time alone. Despite their offer to have us stay with them and Willow's family, we opted for our own oceanfront condo. Waking up on the warm ocean everyday is something a girl could get used to. The constant sun's not bad, either.

"Let's go, Chicken." He holds the door open.

The smell of incense sends us back about forty years as we wander down the long hall toward the single studio. A larger stage and bar-looking area sits in the center of the building, with small practice rooms along either side of the hallway. In the back, we reach the studio, where all six original band members are jamming.

"November Blue! Good Lord, Raven and Ashby, you didn't tell me you grew a super model!" Solstice, Willow's mom, races to me and hugs me with might. "And, this must be Bo Cavanaugh. Nice to meet you, I'm Solstice Shaw."

"It's a pleasure to meet you. This is a great studio you've got here." Bo smiles as he looks around.

"Oh please," my dad interjects teasingly, "we know you've got a state-of-the-art set up in Concord. We're just waiting for the invite."

"Dad!" I shout, mortified.

"It's OK, Ember, your dad and I talked about it last night. I'd love to fly them out to record in the studio." Oh, so he and my dad were chatting when I wasn't around...special.

Michael, Willow's dad, pipes up. "Raven and Ashby tell us you two came up with a piano version of "San Diego." Care to share it with us?"

"Oh, did they? I didn't ..." My ears burn in embarrassment. Bo. Bo told them. I chuckle, wondering which parts of that night he included in the story. "Oh, what the hell." San Diego is breathing fresh life into me, a life with less inhibition.

Bo walks over to the piano and pats the bench next to him. All seven sets of eyes, Willow's included, are on us as he starts playing and I sing:

*"The San Diego sun setting in your eyes
The taste of salt and sweet summertime ..."*

Bo joins in at the right spot and I watch, from the corner of my eye, my parents and their best friends wiping tears from their eyes as we sing their song at the top of our lungs. When it's over, the shocked-silence lasts a nanosecond before deafening applause takes over. A second later, we're accosted by a pile of hippie hugs.

"November Blue! That was amazing!" My mom squeezes both Bo and I at the same time.

"Will you two consider recording some tracks with us?" Natalie, the third female in The Six, casts a sudden silence over the room.

I swallow hard. "What? Are you serious?"

"Of course they're serious, Ember," Willow squeals. "You two are friggen gold! What do you say?"

"Just let them think about it for a while, would you?" Michael elbows Willow, who shrugs. She winks a hazel eye at me before she drops the subject.

I look at Bo, who's grinning like a schoolboy, biting his lip as he stares at the piano keys. He loves this as much as I do.

After sitting back on the couches for a while, listening to The Six play and record, I walk outside for some fresh air and sunshine. My mom follows closely behind me.

She rests her hand between my shoulder blades. "You're happy, Ember."

"Of course I am, Mom. I was just in a room with my favorite people on the planet." I rest my head on her shoulder.

"You look amazing, too. You've been doing yoga again?"

"Yeah, for the last few months...since Rae died, actually."

My mom pulls me into a hug. "Bo is absolutely wonderful. Watching him look at you reminds me of when I first met your father. He had that same look on his face."

"He still does, Mom. Dad loves you so much it's not even embarrassing to watch."

"You have that, too, Honey. Hold on to it. For dear life."

* * *

"You were quiet during dinner," Bo grabs my hand as we walk down the beach at sunset.

"Just thinking," I sigh.

"Anything you want to talk about?"

I find a quiet spot and sit in the sand facing the horizon.

"I think I want to leave The Hope Foundation."

"Really?" He sounds mildly surprised.

"Yeah. I mean, I can do freelance grant writing. I could still help where Hope needed me, but I'd like to work with DROP again. To be honest, David's been hounding me about it since I left." I chuckle.

"He is relentless, if nothing else." Bo shifts so his knees are bent and he's leaning back on his hands.

"It would also free up some time to do...other things, I guess ..." My heart races as I prepare what I'm about to say.

Bo sits back up. "What's going on, Ember?" He takes my hand, which is incredibly hot under my nerves. He kisses it regardless.

"I want to do it."

"Do what?"

"Record. With my parents, me, you...whoever. I want to call Elizabeth Cantwell and perform in front of however many people she can get to come. I want to live with you and never stop kissing you. I just want to go." As I talk, Bo's smile widens with his eyes. He squeezes my hand.

"November Harris, are you asking me to run away and play the guitar with you?"

"Maybe." I shrug.

"What happened to Ms. "I'm-not-that-kind-of-girl" and "I don't fly by the seat of my pants," he teases me about the first in-depth conversation we ever had in my apartment months ago.

"You happened. You reminded me that I've been that kind of girl all along."

Bo leans forward, sweeping my hair aside, and resting his hand on the back of my neck. His soft lips brush against mine, teasing me for a second before I lean in to meet him. He grants my tongue access to his hot mouth, and we sit, kissing, for several minutes as the sun sets in front of us.

"It would be a big move," I tell the Pacific.

Bo pulls me into his embrace. "It would."

"Do you like yurts?" I chuckle, nervous that I've dumped too much on him at once.

His finger lifts my chin. "I'd follow you to the beginning of time, to the end of time, and back, November. Just say when."

I grab his face and kiss him softly before pulling away. "When."

Coming April 2013... In the Stillness

A new work of contemporary fiction by Andrea Randall

Chapter 1

I exist. Right?
  The blood rolling haphazardly down my left forearm says I do. The blade in my right hand agrees. *Sheryl Crow is so full of shit.* The first cut most certainly is not the deepest. If you started with the deepest, where would you go from there?
  I never thought I'd cut again, until I found myself thinking about it. I mean, I've thought about it a lot in the time that's gone by since the last time I did it—the time I thought, *damn this is dumb.* Yeah, I often thought a lot about how crazy that all was. Until I no longer had a choice. Until I found myself rifling through my bathroom cabinets trying to find a clean, sharp blade.
  Eric's been in the lab so much these days, that I feel trapped in a hell decorated with playdates and PBS. The release is euphoric. It's just like the first time; only a little scarier since I know where this road can lead. I don't think too far down that road as I deliberately carve three lines into my soft, shiny skin. It hurts at first. Like hell. But a second later it's gone—just gone—and I'm left with a visual reminder for the rest of the day that I'm in control of my pain, anxiety, and fear.
  Do I even fucking exist?
  Ryker doesn't exist anymore. I mean, he didn't come home in a body bag like Lucas did, but he may as well have. They took his soul over there, *fuckers,* and left me with the breathing carcass. Then I left him. He's married now, supposedly happy.
  So am I. Married, that is.
  I don't think about him much anymore—that's not what this is about. He's just the first person I ever saw not exist while they were still walking the Earth.
  Bang! Bang! Bang! The bathroom door rattles under the force of four-year-old fists.
  "Mommy! Ollie pulled my hair!"

They're always around.

I sigh, turn on the sink, and address the situation from behind the closed door. "Max, don't tattle. Oliver, leave your brother *alone!*"

God, is it too much to ask for it to be Kindergarten already?

My blood forms a candy cane pattern in the white porcelain sink. I stare at the cat as I wash my arm.

I never wanted to be a mother. My twenty-three-year-old graduate student self happily reminds me of that whenever I'm cleaning yogurt from the boys' backs. Seriously, their backs. She had enough of my shit and left. Just packed right up and vacated the part of my spirit that mattered—that made me...me. That's when my twenty-year old self started whispering that I could buy twelve razors for something like three dollars at Wal Mart. She's a crazy bitch, but she's right.

You buy them, bring them home, and break off the little line of safety plastic that prevents you from cutting the hell out of your legs. It really was no different than the last time I bought a bag of generic razors—except this time I had four-year-old twins in the cart.

I still can't decide if that made the purchase easier or harder, seeing their faces, but here we are anyway, washing blood down the sink.

A few hours later I'm washing dinner dishes in our dishwasher-less kitchen, when Eric comes home.

"Hey, Baby, where are the boys?" His eyes scan our Amity Street apartment as he tosses his messenger bag carelessly on the couch.

I sigh, "Sleeping, Eric. It's after seven. How was your day?"

"It was great, actually . . ." Eric launches into a series of events I should care about.

I don't.

He's a doctoral student in chemical engineering at UMass Amherst. His research is in biofuels and sustainable energy. I know that sounds all "hip" and "responsible" of him, but all that means is he's nearing thirty with no job and hours upon hours in a lab. Sure, we get a decent stipend to live on, and full financial aid; but it still leaves me with a twenty-nine year old husband who has no job. I slap my former grad student self for bragging his major up to my parents. They loved it. So did I. Then, everything changed.

"Nat, you okay? Natalie?" Eric walks over and shuts off the faucet I left running while I stare out the window. I hate when he calls me "Nat", it sounds like a bug whenever he says it.

"Huh? Shit, sorry, I spaced."

I reach for a towel to dry my hands when Eric's tanned hand wraps around my much paler arm.

"What happened to your arm? That's a huge scratch." Those honey-brown eyes, one thing left that I don't resent, tell me they can't handle the truth. He'd never get it.

"Stupid cat." I shrug and tug my arm away.

"Maybe we should get rid of her, that's the second time this month she's torn your arm up." He kisses my cheek, right by my ear. For a second I remember what it felt like the first time he did that. Then I remember everything that happened after that kiss.

"It's fine." I shake my head and pull away. "I tried to give a her a bath, serves me right."

Eric laughs just under his breath. "Want some wine?"

"Badly," I sigh.

Well, that was easy.

Eric slides me a glass of white. I hate white. "What were the boys up to today?"

That doesn't stop me from drinking it. "What happens after graduation?" I ignore his request for information on our children.

"What do you mean?" He sits back against the couch.

"I mean a *job*, Eric. It's been a long time—"

"Oh Jesus, Nat, not this again." He rolls his eyes and walks back into the kitchen. "How many times do we have to go over this? I would have been done two years ago—"

"Yeah, I *know*. Trust me, I know. You would have been done two years ago if we hadn't had twins in the middle of everything. You graciously demoted yourself to a part-time student while I became a *full-time* mom." I swallow the rest of my wine and walk to the kitchen to pour another glass. "Do you want my list about how the last two years would have gone? Screw that, do you want to know how the last *four* years would have gone?"

"Enlighten me, *please*." Eric holds out his hands, as if to give me the floor. We're speaking in whisper-yells to avoid waking the identical monsters down the hall.

"You're the one who wanted them, Eric. *You're* the one who begged me to keep them, to pull out of that parking lot and come home." He winces under my tone, but I continue, "Yet, somehow, I leave my degree program to raise them while you play mad scientist in Goessmann. I point out the window in the general direction of campus.

Eric bows his head; placing his hands on his hips while he takes a careful breath. When he looks up, his face is a mess of exhaustion. We've had this argument almost every single day for the last two years. For every single minute of the last two years since he returned as a full-time student, I've hated him. I've said it, too, *I hate you*. But he just thinks I'm crazy or stressed when I say it. I am. And it's because of him.

It's because of him and his assertion of "the right thing to do" that I find myself staring past his jet black hair that needs to be cut, past the athletic physique that makes him stand out amongst his colleagues like he's just there to pretty up the department, and find myself fantasizing about those little blades twenty-five feet away in the bathroom. Hidden in an empty tampon box.

* * *

I didn't always hate him. In fact, the first time we met it was something else entirely. In April 2005 I was preparing to graduate from Mount Holyoke College. South Hadley, Massachusetts had provided a picturesque existence for me over the previous four years. I'd only applied to UMass Amherst for graduate programs; I was more than academically qualified, and their anthropology program is great, but I really just wanted to call this place "home" for a while longer.

"Yo, Natalie, over here." Tosha waved me down at the front of the Odyssey Bookstore, where she was cashing out. I was glad that UMass was only a short drive from here because I loved that bookstore.

I approached Tosha's petite frame as she tried to sell some of her text books. "Did they take anything back?"

"Just the novels," she shrugged, "it's something." Tosha threw her curly blonde hair into a ponytail while she waited for the cashier.

"You want to go to Antonio's for lunch?"

Tosha shrugged. "All the way in Amherst?"

"All the way?" I laughed. "It's just a few miles. You act like 116 is a fortress." I joked about the stretch of road that separates our campus from those of Amherst College, UMass, and Hampshire College.

"It ought to be." She rolled her eyes. Tosha was a snob, but I loved her anyway. She was irritated that Mount Holyoke wasn't exclusively women, as it had been in the past, and really wished that it could be an island all its own. "Let's go, though, their pizza is too good to turn down—even if we have to slum it with ZooMass."

I laughed and kicked her as we left the bookstore.

Twenty minutes later we were sitting at the bar in the window of Antonio's. The place is tiny, and usually standing-room only, but damn they make good pizza.

"Fluid Mechanics?" Tosha scoffed as she drank her soda.

I looked around. "What the hell?"

"That pretty face down there with the UMass t-shirt." She nodded to the benches just across the sidewalk and down a bit. "He's reading a fluid mechanics book . . . outside in the sun . . ."

I looked up, and there he was. He was pretty. Too pretty, almost. His skin was bronzed, but it looked natural, like he'd be dark even in the winter time. His black hair was longer than I cared for, but it was tucked just behind his ears and hidden under a Redskins hat.

"What's your point, Tosh?" I chuckled, trying not to stare as he thumbed through the book with concentration searing across his face.

"He's totally checking you out, Nat." Tosha slid off her stool and threw her paper plate away. I followed.

I whispered as we walked out of Antonio's "He was *not* checking me out. Now, shut up so he doesn't hear us."

"Whatever, I'm going to grab a coffee, want one?"

"No, caffeine-a-holic, I'll get some vitamin D while you fund Starbucks," I laughed and took a seat on the bench next to the boy she'd been staring at. The line was long and I knew

Tosha would wait, no mater the length. I needed to get comfortable.

People passed by like they were on a conveyor belt as I checked out what would be my new surroundings come fall. North Pleasant Street in Amherst was not foreign to me; it held some of the best bars and restaurants in the area. I breathed in the smells of fresh-baked popovers from Judie's restaurant right across from me as I turned my head to the right—where I found "fluid mechanics boy" watching me.

You know that split second? The one where you decide if you're going to just smile and continue looking around, or chance an encounter with a stranger? It's a dangerous moment. It changes absolutely everything.

* * *

"Come on, Natalie. Let's not do this again." Eric pulls me back to the present.

I roll my eyes and walk to the bathroom. He doesn't try to follow me; he learned early on I lock doors behind me. Plus, the boys are sleeping and he won't want to wake them . . . being that he's "Father of the Year" and all.

Reaching under the bathroom sink, I locate the peroxide and alcohol and run them over the razor I used earlier. There's no need to risk infection; I've been there, and it's just a sure-fire way to get caught. I can't cut somewhere new this time because the "cat scratches" are already on Eric's radar. I stare at the marks from earlier and decide that reopening them is the easiest route to go; the easiest way to be mad at him without screaming and starting a blow-out. I'm sick of yelling. Sick of fighting. Sick of crying.

Just a little. Just one more time

Acknowledgments

Scott- Thank you for taking over extra household duties, including our monster children, so I could write this. Your support means a lot.

Michelle Pace- Thank you for spying my original outline and being on board with me even when the story looked a lot different than it does now. Hours-long phone calls about motivations, "are they going to hate me?" and "no, really, are they going to hate me?" helped me get through this in one piece. You're more than a beta reader; you're my person.

Maggi Myers and Melissa Brown- Pretty Little Writers. I love navigating this crazy new world and am thrilled to have you ladies on either side of me. Geography means nothing as far as our friendship is concerned. Thank you for the Skype sessions, responding to panicked text messages, and making me smile. I love you both.

Charles Sheehan-Miles- While I'm honored that you came on as a last-minute beta reader, I'm even more honored to call you a friend. Thank you for taking the time to hash things out with me and always pushing me to be better. I look forward to working with you for a long time.

Lori Sabin- Glorious editor, fabulous friend. Thank you for your time and care with this novel.

Sarah Hansen- This cover is more than I dreamed it could be. Thank you for being a rockstar.

Erica Ritchie- I'm so grateful you took the time and care to produce the amazing photo shoot that lead to this cover. It's breathtaking.

Valerie Laramee- Thank you for the impromptu New Year's Day photo shoot so my author picture could be from something other than a cell phone. Even if it was nine degrees outside.

The Indie Bookshelf- You're a supportive and intelligent group of women, of which I'm proud to be a part.

Janna Mashburn- Thank you for your beautiful work on the trailer for this book and for Ten Days of Perfect. They capture the true spirit of each book.

My beta readers- We shared laughs, tears, and dozens of

posts about specific words *wink*. Thank you for your dedication to help make this book the best it can be: Melissa Brown, Maggi Myers, Janna Mashburn, Charles Sheehan-Miles, Erin Roth, Lindsay Sparkes, Angela Cook McLaurin, Jennifer Roberts-Hall, Michelle Pace, Nina Gomez, Lisa Oliver Bryant, Kacie Walker, Darcie Sherrick

Finally, to all of you- Thank you for reading this book and sharing it with your friends. Your support is the only thing that keeps Indie authors going.

About the Author

I write every single day. I simply can't help it. While some people might look at it as "being lost in my own world," I'm simply lost in the world of my characters. For whatever reason, they chose *me* to tell their story, and I do my best to do right by them. Remember, indie authors live by word-of-mouth. If you like this book, tell a friend. Better yet, write a review so others can see your thoughts. Thank you for all of your support!

Connect with me:

Blog: www.andrearandall.com
Facebook: www.facebook.com/authorandrearandall
Twitter: ARandallAuthor

CPSIA information can be obtained at www.ICGtesting.com
Printed in the USA
LVOW06s2130041113

360026LV00002B/65/P

9 781481 866866